What We Sacrifice for Magic

What We Sacrifice for Magic

《 *A Novel* 》

Andrea Jo DeWerd

alcove
press

Copyright © 2024 by Andrea Jo DeWerd

All rights reserved.

Published in the United States by Alcove Press, an imprint of The Quick Brown Fox & Company LLC.

Alcove Press and its logo are trademarks of The Quick Brown Fox & Company LLC.

Library of Congress Catalog-in-Publication data available upon request.

ISBN (paperback): 978-1-63910-875-6
ISBN (ebook): 978-1-63910-876-3

Cover design by Amanda Shaffer

Printed in the United States.

www.alcovepress.com

Alcove Press
34 West 27th St., 10th Floor
New York, NY 10001

First Edition: September 2024

10 9 8 7 6 5 4 3 2 1

For my Grampy,
who gave me the most beautiful place in the world

One

I first defied my family the summer after I turned eighteen. By eighteen, I knew I didn't need to be pretty. As the older Watry-Ridder girl, my power was in my name. Unlike the other girls in town, I didn't need to catch a man with passing beauty trends or by mastering chicken a la king. But that didn't stop me from wearing my hair the color of rain-logged corn silk long and wild past my waist, a small defiance of the pins and plaits of my mother and grandmother. Even a promise from John Weseloh—a farmer's son, one of the good ones—didn't stop me from tossing my hair that summer in a practiced casual way to see who might be looking.

That hair toss was the very thing that caught John's eye, or so he said, at the Solstice bonfire after our sophomore year. Two years later at a different party in the same park with the same people, I watched John break away from a knot of yelling boys, some stripped to undershirts in the surprisingly warm air of the early western Minnesota summer. It felt like a normal night, thankfully, after the highs of finishing school and our high school graduation followed by the sudden shock of Robert Kennedy's assassination in the same week, yet another tragedy deeply felt in our very Catholic town.

There were a few somber conversations around the park, but overall, it felt like any other glorious start to summer as Annie, my best girlfriend since kindergarten, and I sipped warm beers perched on a picnic table. We liked to stay on the edge of the fray, where we could survey the high jinks and mating rituals of the midwestern teen without having to participate. A Doors song floated up to us from someone's tinny old radio as dusk descended into night and the early-summer lake flies were drawn out toward headlights and lanterns borrowed from our fathers.

Other boys sometimes looked our way, but they emphatically looked away when John made his way toward me. They knew better than to pick a fight. That particular jaunt had run its course many times over. I sighed, bored and a little disappointed. Annie and I secretly loved watching John calmly stare down the other boys who so much as glanced my way—anything to ward off the monotony of small-town life and the looming threat of adult responsibilities.

We didn't get together until we were sixteen, but John and I had known each other our entire lives, as it goes in a small town. He followed me in class or in line for assembly, John Weseloh behind Elisabeth Watry-Ridder by sheer alphabetical luck. John's family had a respectable farm outside of town, growing green beans and corn and shipping them off to God knows where. John worked on the farm all summer and fall, but winter was his, when he was a guard on the high school basketball team.

Where John shone, though, was in the town snowmobile races. He tinkered all winter in the workshop at the back of his family's livestock barn with his homemade snow machine for the races on the frozen lake in January, showing off his latest developments on Sunday afternoons to his basketball teammates. When we were thirteen, John Weseloh had become somewhat of a local celebrity when he came in a close second in his first race on an abandoned sled he had commandeered from his older brothers.

Even after growing up in such close proximity, I was still tickled each time John ditched his meathead teammates and their shoptalk to entertain me.

Annie poked me in the ribs as John threaded his way toward us.

"Tonight must be the night," she said with a knowing nod in his direction and a flutter of her jet-black shellacked lashes.

"Maybe." I rolled my eyes, refusing to take the bait.

Annie rolled her eyes back at me. "Don't you think it's time you let John get lucky? He's waited for you long enough."

Annie'd had sex twice already, and for a small-town girl with nothing better to do, that made her an expert. I loved Annie like a sister—sometimes more than my own sister, Mary—but drugstore lipstick and lemon juice highlights didn't mean she knew better than me. Still, sometimes she made me feel like I'd better catch up.

"Besides," Annie continued, "how are you gonna do better than John Weseloh anyway?"

I nodded noncommittally as John approached, but Annie's words held the sting of truth.

"Hey," John said, suddenly in front of me, mere centimeters from where my bare thighs—tight and muscular, I noted with pride—beneath white cotton eyelet shorts dangled over the end of the picnic table. John rested the flat of his palm against my thigh like the way you'd soothe a flighty goat kid, not the way you'd caress the thigh of a lover.

"Hey," I said.

Annie's gaze shifted pointedly from me to John. She cleared her throat and said, "I'll leave you two lovebirds to it."

She turned and sprang off the picnic table confidently, her full prairie skirt swirling around her in a pastel blur. I loved that about Annie Holbrooke: whatever stupid thing I did, she would be right there to outdo me, especially when it drew the attention of boys in the vicinity.

I was feeling brave after watching Annie strut off toward a pack of boys, and slid off the edge of the picnic table into John's orbit. I took him by surprise, something I did all too often, and he jerked back, throwing me off-balance. Despite his booze-dulled reaction time, he managed to keep me upright, gaining purchase with one arm around my waist.

John's eyes widened, another surprise, when I said, "Let's go park."

Parking with John seemed like exactly what I wasn't supposed to be doing, the elder, responsible Watry-Ridder girl—which made it all the more appealing.

"Really?" he half slurred, and let me lead him to his older brother's El Camino. He stopped to open the passenger door for me, handing me into the cab clumsily.

John was exactly the kind of boy I should marry, my grandmother Magda said all too often. We had walked in our commencement just days before; I had finished in the top twenty of the class of 1968, John somewhere toward the middle, slipping by with Cs and athletic prowess. I'd worked as little as possible to earn the As and Bs—and the respect of my teachers, classmates, and community—expected of me as the granddaughter and heiress of Magda Watry.

"See how hard your father works," Magda would say. "He's always out and around town for us."

She meant that Dad wasn't at home to be in the way of the family business. Someone who'd be a supportive partner—a quiet partner—to sit beside me in the front pew of church every Sunday, keep his hands busy and his opinions to himself while the women ran the business, and give me a daughter to teach: that was the perfect match for me in Magda's mind. Someone like my father. A good man. A quiet one.

* * *

I was raised by my grandmother, surrounded by women. Neighbors and classmates were always crowding around the kitchen table in our white farmhouse on the edge of town. Magda presided over us all, and I had worked beside her since I insolently called my grandmother by her first name as a toddler—everyone else called her that, why shouldn't I!—and it stuck. I was beside her for all of it. Mary, my younger sister by two years, was underfoot too. My mother was there and not there at the same time. She was a shell of a woman, even in my earliest memories.

My father would occasionally poke his head into the kitchen for a can of pop or a Thüringer sandwich or to forage for fresh silver-dollar rolls from Magda's cousin Mildred. But the minute a neighbor opened the kitchen's side door, never knocking first, my father skedaddled to his shed or into town and made himself scarce.

The kitchen was my grandmother's domain.

∗   ∗   ∗

John strangled the steering wheel, focusing hard to avoid swerving from nerves or the six-pack of Schell's he'd handily consumed at the park. As the houses thinned on the road west of town, he eased the truck onto a dirt road that cut through one of the innumerable cornfields around Friedrich. Impulse took over, and I did something that generally went against everything my grandmother had ever taught me.

∗   ∗   ∗

They called us many words over the centuries—seers, energy healers, alchemists, shamans, magicians, heretics. Magda preferred to call us practitioners, or when muttering in her inherited mix of Alemannic German and English, *Doggderin*. She hated that one word that persisted, chasing us through the generations—witch. That word made us outsiders, instead of the pillars of the community we had become over the years.

My family had lived and worked in the farm country around Friedrich for over a century, since my relatives from the Black Forest made their way across the ocean, through the Port of New Orleans, and up the Mississippi River to the jeweled sky and lake-dotted prairie lands of Minnesota territory before the North Star State was a state. The men of the family had various jobs over the generations—hardscrabble farmers, cavalrymen, merchants, and later, lawyers and millers.

My father, Jacob, grew up in Friedrich to become a sort of mover and shaker about town in his own right. He ran a handful of flour mills and grain elevators with his brothers and his father, a first-generation Dutch immigrant, and somehow found time to sit on the town's chamber of commerce. As I grew older, I learned it was actually Magda's influence that put him there, and I wondered how that made my father feel.

There, in the southern-facing kitchen of the Watry house, was where the real family business happened: spells, charms, and energy healing—whatever the people of Friedrich might need to protect their homes and families from the everyday dangers of bad fortune or weather, or petty hexing wars among neighbors.

*   *   *

I took John's hand in the dim light of the cab, closing my eyes as I silently cast out to connect to the powerful energy field my grandmother had taught me to call the ice floe. As I burst through the barrier between the spirit world and ours, a frozen river of light opened before me in my mind's eye, a pure energy river separating life and death and encompassing all of the past, present, and future at once. It was the source of my power, the source of the ancient magic Magda had passed down to me, and visible only to those with our capabilities.

An explosion of light, energy, life force exploded forth from my and John's clasped hands, visible only to me through eyes capable of seeing the other side. I followed our entwined lights forward, not to see the future exactly, but for some hint of how things would turn out with John. Truthfully, I wanted anything to tell me how far I should go with him, since my gut didn't seem to have the answer.

My own emerald-green energy burned brightly and jogged ahead; John's soft lavender energy, as unique to him as a fingerprint, floated behind. I felt myself leaning forward at the edge of my mind's eye and glimpsed a shadow of a fork, our energies splitting away from each other. But the river of invisible energy bucked wildly and threw me back into the present moment, a reminder of the dangers of soothsaying Magda warned against.

I plunged back into the darkness of the El Camino, gasping as if emerging from an actual frozen river. John nodded slowly, lips pursed, turning toward the window, and pulled his hand away from me.

"I wish you wouldn't read me without asking," he said, gazing out into the pitch-black cornfield.

"I didn't mean to—" I started, then sighed. "Sorry. I let my guard down for a second, and you know how it pulls me in sometimes," I said, not entirely a lie. After all, John had heard me say for two years how thin the veil was between the worlds, how the spirit world tugged at me every time I closed my eyes at night.

It was a grave offense but worth it, I figured. I cracked a small smile and looked at him through the hair that fell across my face, knowing I looked every bit as nervous and shy as he did every time we were alone together, every time he thought he might get some. I slid across the bench, and he softened. He pulled me onto his lap, and I kissed him deeply, all the while anxious that my unwelcome reading would be the final straw that broke John's patience for me and my family's strange ways. But then he hooked his thumbs in my waistband, surprisingly suave for the big-handed farm boy, and I was relieved to feel his annoyance fall away as male biology took over.

John explored my mouth and neck, working his way down toward my breasts beneath the open V of my blouse. He tentatively rested one hand on my breast but didn't dare venture further. I let my hair fall forward to graze his face and tried to tune out all the voices that told me I shouldn't be doing what I was doing. I desperately wanted to be outside myself, to enjoy what was happening, but the steering wheel digging into my back, and John's obvious maleness pressing against his fly and my thighs, brought me crashing back into myself.

As John's attention slid lower, I guided his mouth back up to my lips, a firm hand on either side of his face. His cheeks were flushed warm with sweat and excitement.

"We shouldn't," I whispered.

John groaned and buried his face into the exposed skin of my shoulder. I worried that he would be disappointed, that he'd think I was a tease. I felt pressure—from my family, and Magda in particular—to keep him happy, to keep him interested. I knew John was as good as they came in Friedrich, but the further we went, the more serious our relationship became, it felt less like falling in love and more like a foregone conclusion.

"You sure?" he asked, his lips brushing against my bare clavicle.

Still, a primal longing rose deep in my belly, an emptiness I didn't recognize, straining toward release, but the unfamiliar and my inexperience took me out of the moment. *Is this normal? Is this what everyone feels? Am I doing it right?*

"I can't," I said louder, untangling myself from his limbs and the steering wheel.

John shrugged but couldn't suppress a sigh. He recovered quickly, flashing me his easy smile across the sudden distance between us.

"It's okay," John said. "We have all the time in the world now."

I flinched involuntarily when he said it.

We were quiet on the drive home. John smiled to himself, dumbly satisfied—he had gotten to second base, after all—as I prayed my father, or worse, Magda, wouldn't be waiting up for me.

Two

Magda barely gave me the weekend to savor the first few days of summer, enjoying the end of mundane worries and schoolwork. I rode my bike to the public beach and swam for hours, or read magazines with Annie. At night, John picked me up, and we went to the movies in St. Agnes, or got Cokes at Sharp's Soda Shop on Main Street, or drove around the cornfields listening to the radio and making out. I was too spooked to go any further. That truck, shared with an older brother who was in Vietnam, was John's freedom, and for a few days that summer, it was mine too.

But Sunday evening after graduation, Magda summoned me to her room. She said it was time for me to attend to the family business. The next day, Mary and I rose early together and went our separate ways: Mary to the beach, where she was a lifeguard, and I to the lake to ground myself in water.

*　　*　　*

From a young age, I innately understood that I belonged to my grandmother and Mary belonged to our mother, Helene. As I watched from behind Magda's flowy silk skirts and saw Mom's pale hands silently braiding Mary's long, dark hair or rocking her to sleep, jealousy like hot bile rose in the back of my throat. Fire obscured my senses. Magda taught me early on to cleanse my energy field with water, and eventually, I learned I wouldn't make it long without the salve of water.

Our house—where my mother grew up, and Magda before her— was on the east side of Friedrich, where the houses on Lake Street began to thin and the shore dropped off sharply to the water below. Every day I rose early and descended the wooden staircase from the road to our family dock. The lake was like glass at that hour. By the time I heaved myself, dripping, onto the sturdy wooden dock, I had only pristine, radiant energy left. All jealousy, impatience, and unvoiced anger had drained into the water, and I returned with the calm confidence of the lake.

*   *   *

I returned the morning that Magda named as my first official day with my mind clear except for a persistent sort of first-day nerves. I fumbled with the antique Watry family coffeepot as lake water trailed across the rust-colored linoleum floor. I softened my gaze, holding the water particles with intention, urging them to vibrate. I made the requisite gesture, a subtle side-to-side motion and sweep of the hand, and mouthed the words to myself: *Fiir und Wasser, Wasser und Fiir.* As the last drops evaporated into the air, my mother came down the back stairs with Sam, the gray tabby cat that was her constant shadow, on her shoulder like a fourteen-pound parrot.

Mom looked pointedly at my cup of coffee.

"I know, I know. *Always let water be the first thing to pass your lips,*" I said, imitating Magda.

She nodded, and I rolled my eyes skyward. I sipped my coffee just the same.

My mother rolled her eyes right back at me in practiced exasperation. She opened the refrigerator for the water pitcher, then sat at the round oak kitchen table, all the while expertly balancing Sam across her thin shoulders. Sam stepped down gingerly and made himself comfortable on my father's discarded newspaper.

"You'd better change," Mom said. She pressed her lips together tightly, looking for all the world like her mother when she did, and I knew our conversation was over.

That was how it was with my mother. Sometimes she went weeks without saying two words to me. She rarely spoke to anyone, for that matter, except my father. I'd hear the low rumble of his voice from behind their bedroom door sometimes, and the unfamiliar alto of my mother's voice. It made me so jealous, but that was my father's privilege in the house. My mother would otherwise drift through the house, or shop for groceries and cook supper, but mostly she cared for the animals of the county, often with Sam on her shoulder. She understood animals in a way that neither Magda nor I had patience for, and I secretly thought she preferred them to us.

The cruelty of it all was that, except for a three-inch height difference and her painfully slim shoulders, I was the spitting image of my mother. Whereas Mary had the same long, elegant neck as Magda and the tall, lean build of our Dutch father, my mother and I shared a compactness, a tightly wound energy in every fiber. In my mother, this manifested as a skittish energy like a cat's, while I was a coiled spring ready to explode at a moment's notice. At least I had my father's eyes, a sparkling Dutch blue. Mary had the same eyes, and we shared our father's heart-shaped face. My mother was cursed with Magda's eyes, a cool watery blue that appeared enormous in her thin face. But Magda's eyes, that same shifting watercolor blue, were smaller, quicker, noticing everything.

I watched as Mom's gaze drifted, seeing something beyond the kitchen walls, and she was out of reach again. Whatever she saw coming, I couldn't sense it myself.

*　＊　＊

When I returned in blue jeans and a clean blue cotton blouse, the iron smell of lake water clinging to my blonde hair tumbling loose over my shoulders, Mom was nowhere to be seen. Magda was busy taking inventory of the rows of tiny glass bottles and jars of herbs, lake water, and God knows what that littered the shelves of the large oak armoire on the kitchen wall opposite the stove.

Without looking up, Magda handed me a ledger and pencil— just when I had thought I was done with the woody smell that instantly reminded me of long division.

"Update the numbers as we go," she said without further explanation.

The book was opened to a page with a long list of ingredients in my grandmother's tiny, neat cursive. She started to rattle off items as I frantically scribbled.

"Only seven water charms. Mugwort, half a jar. Need to dry more apple blossoms. Mustard seed, full jar. Good on rosemary, need sage from the garden today. Out of wolfsbane. Almost out of milk thistle. Three jars of valerian root. Good on lavender, need watercress."

My hand flew across the page.

Despite being raised in that kitchen, Mary and I hadn't seen the real work, the actual day-to-day that happened when we were at school or running around town in the summers. That summer was to be my initiation into all the things that made what we did in the kitchen a real business to sustain our family, which apparently included lots of inventory.

"Milkweed, twelve dried stalks. Catalpa sap, half a jar."

Magda was holding a dark jar to her nose when she suddenly froze in place. Her head tilted to the side, flipping her thick silver braid over her shoulder. As I picked up what she sensed, I heard shuffling feet at the kitchen's side door.

I was ready for this part of the day, ready to show off my skills for our good neighbors of Friedrich.

The supplicant didn't wait to be bade to enter before swinging open the door, as was standard practice. *A returning client*, I thought. Mr. Leroy Lindsey, a rumpled, sun-weathered man with a large red nose and a broad, hunched back, stood in the doorway.

Magda pushed me forward with one hand, her attention fixed on the armoire.

"Elisabeth's seeing clients today," she said without looking at him.

I shook off the monotony of inventory and found a friendly smile. I took a step toward Mr. Lindsey, rolling my shoulders back to stand at my full five foot six before the hulking farmer, who seemed to take up half the kitchen.

"What can we do for you today, Mr. Lindsey?" I asked.

Mr. Lindsey removed his sweat-ringed hat and held it in both hands.

"Elisabeth," he said, nodding to me. "Glad to see you."

He glanced at Magda over my shoulder but seemed happy enough to be seen by me.

"Please, sit down. What can we do for you?" I repeated.

Mr. Lindsey lowered his frame into one of the kitchen chairs next to me. In close quarters, the sweet scent of grass from his skin and clothes was overwhelming, with a subtler note of earth and, underneath, animals. Cows. Chickens.

"Well, you see, I haven't been feeling like myself since I lost my Emily last fall."

As Mr. Lindsey began to speak, I took one of his hands in my own. In my peripheral vision, I noticed Magda reaching to replace a jar on the top shelf of the armoire, a challenge from where she stood at just over five feet. She gave up and, with a flick of the wrist, levitated the jar back into place. The armoire doors closed behind her as she turned away, locking neatly back into place with a quiet click, and Magda receded from the room.

I cast out the ice floe, the spirit world opening before me like a ghost map. All the energies in the vicinity appeared to me as small bursts of light, glowing auras with their own stories to tell. By tapping into the ice floe energy like an operator's switchboard, we could manipulate it for the benefit of our clients. I reached for Mr. Lindsey's hand as I swept my emerald-green energy through his energy, poring over every ounce of him. I sent my concentration into our joined hands and stared into him, eyes open but not seeing the man sitting before me. The kitchen faded away, and I truly saw.

Mr. Lindsey's energy was a sort of dusky cornflower blue. It was one of the stillest energies I had ever seen, a pure wall of stagnant blue. I forced my emerald energy through his, leaving a trail of concentric rings, like a rock skipping on the lake's surface, urging him to wake up. The words to a common incantation, a routine treatment for our clients, formed on my tongue. After years of shadowing Magda, I knew the words to say silently and sent them into Mr. Lindsey with all my focus. *Wachst auf, wachst auf,* I urged. *Bisch do, bisch unter Lebenden, bisch do.* I felt Magda's regal amethyst energy at the edges of my vision. I took a deep breath and tried not to mind her checking my work.

Back in the kitchen, I nodded and rubbed Mr. Lindsey's hand as he told me of the hardship of his first spring without Emily in sixty years. His children and grandchildren were hours away in Eau Claire, Wisconsin, and he spent his days drinking at the VFW.

In the invisible ice floe, I swirled my energy through a cornflower-blue energy field, urging it to move with me, exploding a cluster in a firework ring of dark blue, buoyed up by my brilliant emerald energy. I said the words silently to myself: *Bisch do, bisch unter Lebenden, bisch do.* I patted Mr. Lindsey's dusty-blue energy back into place, feeling the particles vibrating at a higher frequency than before, and smiled to myself.

In the kitchen, I was nodding as Mr. Lindsey talked, holding his large, callused hand in my own. I had started a final sweep over his body, energy all tucked back into place where it belonged, when I saw it. His liver was failing. *Damn*, I thought to myself, and instantly felt Magda chide me, her amethyst energy like a slap to the back of my head. I heard her clear as day in my ear: "Only positive energy when you're reading a client, Lisbett."

I took another deep breath and refocused. All the possibilities flashed through my mind, and I tried to hold on to the positive branches rushing into the future, the possible good outcomes for Mr. Lindsey, but I didn't know what to do for a bum liver. So I sent all of my living, thriving energy into Mr. Lindsey's liver, sealed it with the words of protection, and hoped for the best.

Bisch wiff. Bisch wusle. Bisch starch.

Coming back into myself in the kitchen, I squeezed Mr. Lindsey's hand and said, "That's tough," as he ended his story.

He blinked and sat up straighter at the table, testing out the new vibrations in his body. "I feel a lot better already," he said cautiously, as if waiting to see if it was true.

"Good," I said, squeezing his hand again.

I glanced up at the clock above the sink and realized that half an hour had passed. I crossed the room to the armoire and unlocked it with a quick gesture.

"It sounds like you need a beacon, something to light you up again. That should do the trick," I said. I started opening drawers and rolling twigs and herbs into a bundle.

"Yeah, that sounds like just the thing," he said.

I could feel the change in him: his voice brighter, his energy quietly thrumming again. But it was easier to accept something tangible outside the spirit world. The men in particular had a difficult time believing in what they couldn't hold and press and tear apart with their own two hands. The real work had already been done, but sending him home with a beacon, something to burn, would be easier for him to understand than me telling him he needed his energy rearranged.

I wrapped the bundle of sticks and herbs with twine three times, holding the elements, the building blocks of life, in my mind. I whispered on each pass of the twine: *Fiir und Wasser, Äther und Ëërde. Äther und Ëërde, Fiir und Wasser.* I tied it off with a square knot and presented it to Mr. Lindsey.

"I want you to burn this in every room of your house, then hold it up to each of the four cardinal directions around the foundation outside. It won't flame, but it will smoke for some time. It will be most powerful at tonight's full moon. And while it's smoking, think about Emily, and think about how much life you have left." I cringed internally, knowing it might not be much. "And think about how she would want you to live your life. When the beacon smolders down to ashes, you'll be ready to face a new dawn and move forward."

Mr. Lindsey held the beacon firmly in both hands. He wanted it to work so badly, hope radiating in his face and the square of his shoulders. *Damn*, I thought again.

He stood to go, delicately holding the beacon in one hand, as if it might come alive and bite him.

"Thanks. This looks like just the thing."

Magda appeared in the doorway between the kitchen and living room, arms folded over her chest like a witchy garden gnome, to appraise my customer service.

"Feel better, Leroy," she said.

"Thanks, Magda." He nodded toward me. "She did great today. You should be proud."

Magda raised a thin eyebrow and nodded knowingly, as if this wasn't news to her. It took immense self-control to not roll my eyes.

"Thank you, Mr. Lindsey," I said, guiding him toward the door. "Come on back and see us in a few weeks. Let us know how you're doing."

"And lay off the bottle, Leroy," Magda said to his turned back. She couldn't help herself.

He paused but didn't turn around. "Come on, then," Mr. Lindsey said to me over his shoulder. "Your payment is in the truck."

I followed him outside, walking barefoot out of habit, as uncomfortable as it was on the crushed-rock driveway. He handed me a squawking wooden crate with three black-and-white speckled hens inside. I stood there holding the crate as he drove away.

More chickens, I thought, suddenly tired.

We rarely accepted cash; too much prosperity would draw the wrong kind of attention. Magda typically haggled for handmade clothes or linens, fresh dairy, produce, baked goods, live animals, what have you—enough proper payment to run the business, purchase the necessities, feed the family, and supply Magda's evening whiskey.

I prayed to the Virgin Mary and our grandmothers before us as Magda had taught me for Mr. Lindsey's protection, more out of habit than belief, while I introduced the speckled beauties to the backyard coop. Dad would be happy to see them, at least. When I came in the side door, Magda sat at the kitchen table with the heavy leather-bound volume of client records open for my evaluation.

I slumped into a chair, drained from the effort of the reading. I had often seen Magda lie on the davenport in the living room for a half hour after a reading to recalibrate her own energy. Sometimes she took another approach, taking a nip of whiskey in the black coffee she drank all day.

Magda slid the book toward me. Each client had a line or two next to their name. It took a week, sometimes two, to fill a single page with notes. I wrote the date—*June 10th, 1968*—and Mr. Lindsey's name, followed by a short description. *Farmer, 70s, large man.*

"Stop," she said, before I could write the next line. *Diagnosis.* "Start at the beginning," Magda instructed. "Tell me everything you saw."

I know, I thought, but didn't dare sass my grandmother out loud. As if I hadn't done this with her hundreds of times before.

I closed my eyes to call up the exact pathways of the session. Although barely forty-five minutes had passed since Mr. Lindsey first walked through the kitchen door, it had begun to blur in my mind.

"His energy is blue," I started. "Pale, dusty blue. Very still. It's like he's barely there. He's just waiting to follow Mrs. Lindsey to the other side. I tried to wake him up. Give him my energy. Set a little fire in his vibrations."

"And?" Magda asked.

I paused, and my tongue slipped between my teeth in concentration.

"He's heartbroken," I said, as if it were the most obvious thing in the world.

Magda gave me a pointed look under a raised eyebrow, like I was being purposefully obtuse. "And what else?" she asked in a singsong that made me cringe.

"Well . . . his liver . . ." I trailed off, unsure of the right words.

Magda nodded once. *Right.* "He was vibrating beautifully. That will bring him some peace in these last few months."

I blinked hard. *Months.* "All that was for nothing?"

"There's nothing any of us can do about that liver. I would've done the exact same as you," Magda said firmly.

She softened when she saw the dismay on my face. "You'll get used to it," Magda said, gently. "We do what we can, but there are things out of our control. Your Grandpa Earl, rest in peace, would've lived forever if I had anything to do with it."

Magda said this last part quietly, as she always did. It had been eighteen years, but mentioning the name of her late husband remained painful.

I nodded slowly and sighed, unconvinced.

"You have given Leroy more life in these coming months than he would've had otherwise. That will make his time easier when it comes. That is all we can do sometimes," Magda said.

When I didn't react, she tapped the tabletop with both palms and said, "Well, then." My signal to get on with it.

I picked up the pencil and wrote in my round print, so different from Magda's even cursive on the previous lines. *Heartbreak, loneliness, liver disease. Treated with energy reading, rearrangement, recalibration. Fire beacon for home.*

Magda squinted across the table at my work and nodded. "That about does it."

*   *   *

The rest of the day flew by. Farmers from surrounding Kandiyohi County came by for water charms to bring the rains to their fields in what had been a dry year. Two giggling girls from Mary's class stopped by for love charms, their summer plans clearly in sight. In the late-afternoon lull, I peeled potatoes at the kitchen table. My mother was silent as she set about roasting a chicken for supper, then she left to take a house call for Mr. Pedersen's horses outside town, the only kind of clients she ever took.

Magda didn't cook anymore, saying she had done her time in the kitchen after putting a hot meal on the table for Grandpa Earl for decades. When my mother was a newlywed and freshly installed with my father in the renovated attic bedroom, she had assumed all household duties—a baptism by literal fire, as she burned her first Thanksgiving turkey to a crisp without Magda's supervision or the aid of magic. There were some things we liked to do the old-fashioned way, and cooking was one of them, a domestic magic in its own right. There was something soothing about peeling vegetables or kneading dough by hand after a day of moving invisible hands through the frozen energy river.

As I peeled potatoes, I pictured what my mother might have been like as a newlywed, filling the kitchen with thick black smoke as Magda, Grandpa Earl, my handsome young father, and Magda's mother, my great-grandma Dorothy, all watched TV in the other room. My father never spoke about those early years or how they'd gotten together, but I guessed it was a familiar story. My parents had grown up together in Friedrich, and like John was for me, my father had always been there, except when he was serving in Europe. He didn't talk about the war, but I knew my parents had gotten married as soon as my father came home. Try as I might, I couldn't imagine my mother introducing herself to him, or laughing at his jokes, or telling stories to his brothers. She must've done all those things at one time, but any shadow of that girl flirting with the handsome soldier was long gone.

I thought of Magda, fixing the broken hearts and making the rain come in our small town, day in and day out for decades on end, the queen of her realm—which felt smaller to me every time I heard my classmates talk about their plans for college and trade school and getting out of Dodge. I thought of my mother's far-off gaze, as if she were seeing everything at once beyond our four walls. I was destined to end up like one of them, if I was to believe Magda's version of my future, in which the women moved heaven and earth to help the people of Friedrich and managed to prepare hearty meals for the men of the household, who would return from their daily tinkering just in time for supper.

I was starting to see Magda's point about having John by my side—a good man, a helpful man. I hoped I was strong enough to carry the responsibility like Magda, lest I crumple like my mother under the weight.

I felt that familiar fire rising in me as I put the potatoes to boil on the stovetop.

Don't think about that, I said to myself. *What choice do you have anyway?*

Three

I was sitting at the table replenishing water charms when Mary strolled into the kitchen, already a little tan and freckly from her first week of lifeguard duty.

"Where's Mom?" Mary asked, dropping noisily into a kitchen chair. She closed her eyes, and I knew she was calling Mickey, her own feline familiar, a distant cousin to Mom's cat Sam. Mickey appeared a moment later and made himself comfortable in Mary's lap.

"Pedersen's," I said as I held up a water charm for inspection.

Mama's girl flashed through my mind involuntarily, even though I'd told myself I had given up caring about their bond that excluded me long ago. But I was concentrating too hard to be more than mildly annoyed.

Mary nodded and reached for a charm bottle, working beside me seamlessly as we had for years, two parts of a whole. Light and dark, fire and earth, intuition and tactile sense. Water charms were one of the first things Magda had drilled into me. I could make water charms in my sleep, and as if by osmosis, Mary had gotten pretty good at them too.

Mary matched my movements as I filled each three-ounce glass bottle with lake water from a large steel kettle and held it to my lips. *Chunsch im Wasser. Wasser, chunsch. Wasser wiff. Wasser, chunsch.*

With both hands cupping the bottle, I set the molecules humming with the positive power of attraction, sending my life force through the glass into the water. Satisfied with the water rippling with energy, glowing a faint green in my hands, a reflection of my own energy, I stoppered the bottle to trap the kinetic energy and powerful summoning inside. It wasn't unusual for a rain cloud to gather over our house on those afternoons when we created water charms, the summoning charm hanging in the air as we captured it bit by bit in each bottle.

*   *   *

I knew I belonged to Magda, but I had never fully understood why. From the beginning of my memory, my mother was a husk of a woman. She had some magical abilities but reserved them for the animals of the county. So Magda carried the family business alone and trained me to be her sole heir from the first appearance of my abilities. Magda taught Mary too, but it wasn't the same. She was stricter with me, more exacting. The bar was higher for me as Magda's successor. Mary was a two-for-one deal.

Even at age four, I felt chosen in my own household, important enough to do something I had never seen even my mother do, only me and Magda. It hurt my childish pride to have Mary tag along. But even as I was honing more challenging skills, reading energies, making charms, Magda gave Mary only the fun stuff.

"Do it too?" I remembered Mary asking in her still-baby voice as Magda taught me the painstakingly nuanced steps of water charms and beacons at the kitchen table.

"Sure," Magda said with a shrug, handing her a glass bottle and stopper.

But Magda never bothered to check Mary's work, her eyes on me and me alone. The more Magda's attention shone on me, the more I felt a growing sense of pride in what only I could do.

*   *   *

The thing about growing up in such a small town is that everyone knows everyone's business. And as much as a town could hush up about what services they sought from our kitchen, they sure liked to talk about us Watry-Ridder girls. When I was about five and Mary three, old biddies would eye us at Juba's Grocery and ask our mother if there were any "signs" yet, raising their eyebrows dramatically as they scanned from Mary to me. Mom said nothing, as was her way in public, just shrugged and pushed her cart down the canned-goods aisle with her mechanical, straight-backed walk. Little did they know I had been levitating since before I could walk.

When a classmate stole my favorite pencil in kindergarten, the whole town knew I tried to curse her. They also knew it sort of worked. A stubborn, persistent rain cloud hung over her family's house for two days. It wasn't quite what I was going for—raining toads—but it was a pretty good first attempt.

The next time, when a boy dared to throw mud at me during recess, I got closer. A large box turtle stalked that boy for a week and a half. I was particularly satisfied to see how disconcerting it was for the boy to look up from a math lesson and see that snub-beaked box turtle staring at him from the second-floor grade school window, or know that he'd wake up in the middle of the night with its little turtle feet standing on his chest.

That became a favorite of mine over the years. Magda hated it, and she let me know.

"You have more important things to do," she'd snap when Mary inevitably tattled.

But there was nothing Magda could do. She needed me as her apprentice, and I learned early on how far I could push the limits, although usually not in my grandmother's presence to avoid the scolding.

Around the same time, Mary started playing Snow White by summoning all the neighborhood cats and dogs and deer and gophers to our yard to watch her one-woman shows. It was a good party trick but hardly a valuable addition to the family business.

*   *   *

Like our near-silent mother—or maybe because of her—Mary had a way of hearing what was unsaid. She could often taste snow in the air days before the clouds formed. Mom's and Mary's tactile senses worked on another level, while Magda and I were all gut, all intuition. Also like Mom, Mary excelled at working with animals. Some extrasensory input allowed them both to hear what a horse or cat or chicken couldn't say out loud.

With a dozen water charms shimmering green and gold between us, Mary ventured to ask, "So, how was it?"

I paused, considering. *How was it?* Mary's expression was eager. She was genuinely dying to hear about it, and her enthusiasm annoyed me.

Mary widened her eyes at me, an expression she had picked up from our mother. Even though she easily could have read me without permission, Mary knew better. That was an ultimate boundary in our household. Precisely because we had the skills to read each other's thoughts and secrets, there had to be a firm line that could be crossed only with invitation—which we had learned, as sisters often do, the hard way.

"It's strange, you know," I started slowly. "We've been doing this our whole lives. I've been preparing for this since forever. But today still surprised me. Sink or swim, you know? I guess I didn't really believe it until I was reading Mr. Lindsey."

"I'm sure you were great today," Mary said, covering my hand in a way that made me feel like the younger sister.

I pressed my lips together. "I mean, sure. I did fine. My readings have been precise lately," I told her, which was true. But I told her about Mr. Lindsey, his broken heart, his liver like Swiss cheese. She was quiet as I spoke, studying the table beneath her splayed fingers.

"Today was the first day I doubted that what we do here is really helpful. What if we're giving people false hope?" I asked her.

"We can't fix everything," Mary said after a long pause, oblivious that she was echoing Magda. "But you know that what we do is real. Our water charms have saved nearly every farm in town at some point or another. That's real. That makes a difference."

We sat in comfortable silence as the potatoes burbled on the stovetop. I shook my head finally and stood.

"I don't know, Mare. You don't know what it's like," I said, more harshly than I intended.

Mary shot me a lopsided smile from under the curtain of her long, raven curls, a dimple appearing under unsmiling Dutch blue eyes. "Focus on the good," she said. "I'm sure it was tough, but you must have brought some peace to Mr. Lindsey today."

Annoyed at being lectured by my little sister, I turned my back to strain the potatoes over the sink. *Who does she think she is, Jiminy Cricket?* As I added fresh cream and butter and started to mash, Mary spoke again.

"I know, Lisbett," she said quietly. "But look who I was raised by."

Mom, I thought. *You got Mom, and I got stuck with Magda.* But I didn't say that.

"Sure," I said, to avoid a fight.

I glanced back to see my long-legged, dark-haired beauty of a little sister disappearing up the back stairs to change her clothes for supper. I stood dumbfounded as I realized she had read me outright without asking.

What ever happened to privacy in this house? I wondered as I overmashed the potatoes to a gummy oblivion.

*   *   *

As the heat of the day burned off, Mom crept back into the kitchen, washed her hands, and took the chicken from the warm oven. Dad arrived home from the mill and announced to anyone within earshot, "I'm starving. What's for supper?"

I set the round table with five settings—all equals, no head—then retrieved warm dishes of mashed potatoes and green beans from the oven and delivered them to Mom's pewter trivets. Dad took his place nearest the fridge, and I sat opposite him, nearest the side door. Mary, long legs bared in pleated shorts, charged back into the kitchen to sit between me and Dad. Magda wandered into the kitchen, likely having felt the presence of a Ridder man upsetting the feminine energy in the house.

"Ooh, look at that," Dad marveled as my mother served him first, an empty honorarium reserved for the men tied to Watry women. Mom plated a thigh and drummy, golden-brown skin perfectly intact, and smothered the plate in piping-hot gravy.

When everyone was served, we folded our hands in our laps, and Dad led us in a perfunctory grace. Once the Lord was thanked and our chests crossed, the room fell silent.

"Mm, what a treat." Dad eventually broke the silence.

Mary and I made eyes at each other, and my earlier annoyance with her instantly fell away. Dad's love of food, any food, even a plain old chicken dinner, was one of the constants in the Watry-Ridder household, and it delighted us to no end.

"Look at that," I said, admiring a green bean.

"Simply divine," Mary crooned to a forkful of potatoes.

We giggled into our napkins.

"All right, all right," Dad said. "That's enough." But he was smiling, blue eyes crinkling with mischief as he looked from me to Mary and back again.

I caught my mother's eye over a bite of chicken, and she rolled her eyes, making fun of my father and his love of gravy in her own way.

"So you saw Mr. Sayre yesterday, Helene?" Dad asked Mom after swallowing a large bite.

Mom nodded.

"And you saw Mr. Sayre after Helene did, apparently?" Magda asked loudly, knowing full well that Mr. Sayre, the owner of a decent-sized egg production operation, must have stopped by the mill and talked up Mom's services.

Dad watched my mother patiently for a response.

"Coyotes," Mom said quietly.

"How was output today?" Magda asked my father, guiding the conversation toward the other family business, the Ridder Family Company mills and grain elevators.

My mother closed her mouth with a small sigh and studied her plate.

You interrupted her, I had the sudden impulse to scream at Magda, sympathizing with my mother as she wilted under Magda's gaze. I knew all too well how domineering my grandmother could be. But as always, I said nothing against her.

"Oh, fine," Dad said with a smile. He rarely said more, unless it was to complain about one of his "pigheaded" brothers. "Big production day, for June anyway."

No matter how much the men in town talked or what gossip Dad heard, Magda would say as little as possible in front of my father, the outlier Ridder man, to avoid confirming who we had seen that day, just enough to corroborate rumors from the mill. Even though Dad knew as well as anyone who came to our side door, he played along.

We chewed in silence for a few minutes, lost in our own thoughts and the pleasant, filling meal.

"Pop called the office today. He and Mother would like to come by for Sunday supper," Dad said after a few minutes.

Mom winced, then rearranged her face into a neutral expression and set down her fork.

*   *   *

When the Watrys arrived in Minnesota territory, my grandmothers made quick work of blending in with the locals. The town had been there since the Friedrich family first put down roots in the 1850s. The first Friedrichs were farmers and merchants, and a small

community started to form around the Friedrich General Store—
including the mill, which had a wheel turned by the inlet on the
east side of Clear Lake and was eventually bought by my grandpa
Ridder. As in many frontier towns, German and Dutch relatives followed soon after to fill the surrounding farmlands tucked between
the lakes that dotted the flat western Minnesota landscape.

My great-grandmother many times over helped to start the
Catholic church on a hill on the west side of town. Magic tends to
be looked down upon in polite society, so church became our way
of disappearing into the crowd. History had proved it was the solo
hags on the edge of town thumbing their noses at the church who
were hauled away to burn first in the witch hunts over the years,
and we learned from those Puritan escapades. The Watrys and
all of our grandmothers before us had slipped by unscathed, the
innocent lambs in the front pew among the faithful in Minnesota
territory.

That first good deed by my forward-thinking *Urgroßmuedere*
gave our family the goodwill of the small community clinging to
life alongside Clear Lake, and my grandmothers started to see clients quietly in the old barn that once stood on the edge of our
property or by the light of the original kitchen's wood-burning
stove. When they saved the town during the flu outbreak in 1890,
including both of the grandsons of William Friedrich, the Watrys
forever earned their place in the fabric of the community. Generations of children of Friedrich grew up respecting the Watry women
and our abilities.

But there were those in town who feared us, who didn't understand our work. And my Grandma Ridder was one such skeptic.
She had grown up in neighboring St. Agnes, and after moving to
town to marry Grandpa Ridder, she was suspicious of Magda and
Great-Grandma Dorothy. I wondered how much Grandma Ridder
had known about my mother and Magda before my parents were
married, or if Great-Grandma Dorothy might even have charmed
Grandma Ridder for convenience in the beginning. But years after

Jacob Ridder fell for and married Helene, Grandma Ridder still questioned our business and "all that nonsense."

*   *   *

I watched Mom intently, but I knew she would never object. Part of her duty to her husband, who so carefully kept up appearances in town so we could continue practicing with scarcely a glance from the people of Friedrich, was to entertain his unbelieving parents from time to time. It was never a fun visit for my mother or Magda, but thankfully, Grandpa and Grandma Ridder had retired to a small hobby farm outside Olivia, several counties away, and didn't visit often.

Mom nodded twice, signaling her acquiescence, some private language having passed between my parents.

"Thank you, Helene," Dad said.

At this display of practiced Dutch and German stoicism, Mary and I rolled our eyes in unison. *Typical*, I thought. *Yep*, her eyes blinked back at me. Magda caught my eye over this exchange and winked at me, never one to miss the rare opportunity to make fun of my mother's in-laws. Mary and I thought she secretly enjoyed making Grandma Ridder uncomfortable during those visits.

I glanced at the clock above the kitchen sink and shoveled the last bites of supper into my mouth. The Watry-Ridders were a Clean Plate Club family.

"John's picking me up soon. May I be excused?"

"Go on, then," Dad said. "Have fun and give our best to the Weselohs."

As I dashed off up the kitchen stairs to tame my hair, I heard Dad musing behind me, "Just wait, Mare. Soon enough you'll be running off on dates too, and I won't have any of my girls left."

Four

John pulled up in front of the house at seven on the dot. I was watching out the front windows and ran out to greet him as he got out of the El Camino. He caught me around the waist and kissed me chastely on the cheek, assuming that at least one of my family members was watching. Somebody surely was.

"You didn't want me to say hi to your family tonight?" he asked.

I shrugged and made my way around to the passenger side before John could open the door for me. I was feeling antsy. "I've had enough of them for one day."

"Mm," John said slowly, sounding like my father in a way that was both comforting and off-putting. "I know what you mean." He shook his head to wipe the serious look off his face. "Anyway, I think we have time to make the next movie in St. Agnes," he said as he climbed in on the driver's side and turned the key in the ignition.

"Sure," I said. I had assumed we would do exactly that. There were only so many options for date night around town.

"What's good at the farm?" I asked, trying too hard to be interested in John's father and his experimental tomato seeds.

"The corn is gonna be small this year with the drought, but it's coming up nicely," he said with a yawn.

"Knee high by the Fourth of July," I replied instinctively, like all good Minnesotans.

"Hopefully," he said, shooting me a sideways look. "But there's something off with Lucy. She keeps running off, and that's not like her at all. Or she's sleeping all day under the porch." Lucy, John's beloved pointer, was never far from John's side, having followed him in the fields around the farm since she was a puppy. "Maybe your mom can come by this week?" he said quietly, as if he were afraid to ask for her services directly.

"Of course," I said. "Poor girl. Mom will take care of her."

I didn't like to admit that my mother's skills with animals far outstripped my own. I had the impulse to offer to take care of Lucy myself, but the worry in John's voice pushed my ego aside. The idea of watching Lucy dog around for hours while listening for some sign of what she might be trying to say made my heart race. Mom would know in minutes. Mary said animal auras were similar to humans', but I didn't have the patience to practice through my inexperience and refused to let someone like John see me flail through a reading.

"Are you sure?" he protested weakly. "If you think that's best . . ."

I squeezed his hand. "We'll be there. Don't worry about it."

Rolling farmlands whizzed by the windows, sloping away from the highway. A few houses dotted the fields. Beyond the horizon, a shockingly blue sky blazed above the living green earth. The sun showed no sign of setting, stretching on into the Minnesota summer evening.

"Any word from Gene or Frank?" I asked gently. The Khe Sanh incident had wormed its way into my consciousness that spring, and I found myself often wondering where John's brothers were.

John trained his eyes on the road, a steely set to his jaw. "No," he said.

It unnerved me when John, usually so happy-go-lucky, turned moody, even momentarily. He sucked on his bottom lip so hard I thought he might break skin.

Shit, I thought, searching for anything to say to snap him out of it. "At least you're around to help your dad out," I said too quickly, too brightly.

"Yep," John muttered.

End of subject. Okay then, I thought.

The constant stream of images from Vietnam flashed through my mind, the crew-cutted young men still pimply faced or with a shadow of baby fat. Some weren't even older than me—manlings fighting the perils of communism half a world away. John's brothers, Gene, who had left the El Camino to John's keeping, and Frank, the quiet middle brother, were among them. We never talked about it. Rather, John never talked about it, except when they received the rare letter.

I thought sometimes, since John had turned eighteen in March, *They won't take him too. Two Weseloh boys must be enough.* But a few boys from town had been drafted in the spring. I thought of Charlie Abrahams and Mike Hale and Joey Sayre and wondered if they looked like the empty boys on TV now, if they were over there yet or training somewhere in the States. *Annie would know*, I thought. She would write letters to all of them, sealed with a rub of perfume from her wrist or a pass of her lips if it was for Charlie with his dark, sad eyes and beautiful, thick hair.

Once or twice I had tried to send out the ice floe to check on those boys on the other side of the world. I'd focus on a face on TV or think of Gene, handsome with sandy blond hair and light-gray eyes, taller than John, with hulking forearms like all of the Weseloh men from years of farm chores. I reached for them, trying to see past the immense masses of energy. But they were too far away. There were too many lives in between. All the energy ran together, the frozen river in my mind stretching into an impenetrable canvas of light that extended in every direction, all of humanity an indistinguishable blur. I said a prayer for them silently as I watched John so focused on the road, shoving down my overwhelming sadness for those boys and locking it away for another time.

I reached over to switch on the radio, and John softened, taking his eyes off the road for far too long to watch me. His brow uncreased and a smile crept into the corners of his mouth. I was a creature of habit: John knew I could sit in silence for about three minutes tops.

"I love you, Elisabeth," John said suddenly, flicking his eyes to the road and back to me. A light blush crept up his neck toward his ears.

That was new. In our two years together, we had never said it. I resisted the urge to check that my jaw wasn't hanging open.

John watched me expectantly, and as the seconds ticked by, I realized I hadn't said anything. Some song whined in the background, so quiet I could barely make out the words. *Johnny Cash*, I thought absently.

John retrained his eyes on the road, but a miniscule quiver, a downturn at the corners of his eyes, betrayed his worry.

"I love you too," I said, unsure of myself but knowing it was expected of me. The words were out of my mouth before I could question myself. "But I'm a one-way ticket to you getting stuck here." The first days of working with Magda had made that more apparent than ever.

"What's wrong with being here?" John asked. "What else am I going to do?"

I could tell he meant it as a joke, but it came out sad. There had been a time when we thought mechanical engineering or even basketball would be John's ticket out of Friedrich. But that ship had sailed. He didn't have the money for college without enlisting, and John was good at basketball for a county full of white farmers but not scholarship good, so he hadn't bothered to apply to college or trade school or anything else. John's future was the family farm—until his brothers came home, God willing. Over the two years we'd been together, John's future had become increasingly, inextricably linked to my own. There was only the farm and his hunting dog and me.

John's nervous eyes flashed to me, and I felt an enormous weight settle on my shoulders.

I held out my hand, a peace offering, and John covered my hand in his. I was filled with a deep anxiety that I didn't love him enough, that he could feel my boredom, my claustrophobia. I'd scramble to do one more thing, one more kiss, one more drive through the cornfields, to keep him interested. I pushed him away for reasons I didn't understand, and at the same time I was terrified of losing him when Magda so clearly intended for him to be the one to support me like my father supported my mother. Besides—he was kind, and maybe that was the best I was going to get.

"I know. I'm sorry. I do love you, John." I said it to smooth things over, not knowing if I meant it, worried John would question my hesitation.

"I know," he said, and that was that.

Industrial sheds and businesses announced the edge of St. Agnes. We made our way around Lake Lorna as the highway ended suddenly and the town sprawled before us, four times the size of Friedrich. We made it into the dark of the theater as the previews ended and Charlton Heston appeared.

Five

Magda was reading the paper under the glow of a single lamp in the living room when John dropped me off just before midnight. He widened his eyes at me, afraid of being in trouble with my family. I gave a shake of my head and kissed his cheek. Magda could never be mad at John Weseloh.

As I came in the front door, Magda gave her newspaper a shake and carefully recreased the pages, even though it would be chicken bedding in the morning.

"It's late, Elisabeth," she said, biting the *t* in my name, the way my father and his Dutch immigrant family did: *Eh-leeSS-a-beTT*. She used my full name to signal a Matter of Great Importance.

"So sorry, Magda," I said, my voice dripping with honey.

I turned to run upstairs, but her voice stopped me.

"It's time you grew up and stopped running around town, even with the Weseloh boy," she said, her face severe in the yellow circle of light. "You don't need to give people a reason to talk, or worse, give the Weselohs any reason to worry concerning you and John. You're going to need him."

Magda's hints had gotten less subtle over the years.

* * *

When I was thirteen, my breasts had seemed to materialize over-
night: unfamiliar, foreign things that belonged on an adult woman,
too much for my five-foot-six frame. When a male classmate com-
mented on the "free show" that summer at the beach, another boy
shut him up.

"Uh-uh," I heard as I swam past the aluminum raft that separated the swim lanes from the free-swim area. "That's Elisabeth
Watry-Ridder. I wouldn't if I were you."

After the box turtle incident, the boys in town had learned to
hold me at a respectful distance, but many had overcorrected and
would only mumble polite greetings or avoid me altogether. John
was one of the brave ones who would actually talk to me about
school or music or books, normal things, ignoring the awe that
came with my name. Sometimes I wondered if Mom had dealt with
the same things in school. Was Dad the only brave one back then?
Was that how they had ended up together?

But the summer I was sixteen, John Weseloh caught my attention. I didn't know what it was at first, but something finally nudged
me toward the quiet, serious boy I had known since kindergarten,
making me see him in a new light. Like many things in my life, that
nudge turned out to be Magda.

That was the summer Annie went boy crazy, and I followed,
mostly out of boredom. In the afternoons when I wasn't shadowing my grandmother, Annie and I would walk up and down Lake
Street, endlessly looping on the same six-block stretch downtown:
Lake Street, Rose, Main Street, Hill. We waited for boys to pass
by—on their bikes or better yet in borrowed cars—and notice us.

Annie had a different boy every week. I didn't know where they
all came from. We'd be sitting on the curb outside Sharp's or on a
bench at the park, and boys would magically gravitate toward us.
They'd lean out of a car and yell, "Hey," and Annie would smile and
toss her head, and they were done for. She'd be with that one for a
week, until she inevitably got ahead of herself and asked them to go
steady, and they'd stop calling her.

I mostly observed. The friends of the boys Annie liked would say hi to me, then clam up.

Shortly before the summer solstice, Magda noticed.

"Come talk with me," she said one afternoon as she sat sipping black coffee between clients.

The house was comfortably quiet, one of those blazing-hot summer days when everyone had something to do and was off in their separate corners of the house. Obediently, I sat across from her, ready for one of our chats that I treasured as a child.

"You've been spending a lot of time in town with Annie," Magda said with a subtle raise of an eyebrow. "Any special friends caught your eye, then?"

I shook my head earnestly as Magda scrutinized me. If she was reading me uninvited, she gave no sign. And even then, there wouldn't have been much to read. The boys were all scared of me, and I didn't want to deal with that.

"You're sixteen now. Two years and you'll be taking your place here, and then you won't have much time for suitors."

I smiled at her old-fashioned way but said nothing, waiting. Magda always had a point; better to let her come to it naturally, or I'd be listening to a lecture all afternoon.

"You'll need a good man by your side then," she said.

I frowned. *A man? I can barely stand any of the boys around here*, I thought.

"I suppose," I said.

Magda smiled over her coffee. "Look at your father. I know you didn't know your Grandpa Earl, rest in peace, but he was much the same. A good man. A thoughtful man. Someone who understands our values and the value of the work that we do."

She gave me a knowing look at that. She meant someone who didn't get in the way.

"I don't think I know any boys like that. All they think about is cars and sports and boats, and they're too scared to talk to me anyhow," I said.

Magda was quiet for a long time, and I thought our chat was over. She looked as if she were distracted by something on the other side of the kitchen. I sighed and was about to find Mary to practice levitating things across our room.

"I've heard good things about the youngest Weseloh," Magda said with a shrug, so quietly I later wondered if she had said it at all.

In the light of the Solstice bonfire that year, I found myself turning over what Magda had said. If she had even said anything. I watched John Weseloh in the crowd. I was surprised when he caught me looking, but I held his gaze and smiled as sweetly as I could manage. That was all the encouragement John needed.

*   *   *

"Sure, Magda, sorry," I mumbled in the doorway to the living room, one hand on the doorframe to steady myself, although I knew every inch of that house even in the dead of night.

I fought the urge to say, *What does it matter? John said he loves me. He's not going anywhere. Who cares what anyone else thinks?* Still, I blushed furiously in the dark foyer, as Magda surely assumed I had gone all the way with John. *You don't even know how good I've been. I'm a virgin, Magda. Still your perfect Watry-Ridder girl.*

"Mm," Magda murmured. She hauled herself out of her armchair and extinguished the lamp. "Go to bed, Lisbett," she said.

Six

I quickly fell into a rhythm working alongside Magda those first few days. We didn't get daily readings, but when we did, she made me take as many as possible. Mom wandered into the kitchen sometimes, but mostly she kept to herself or left us for hours to attend to the county animals.

Between visits, I pored over the client records with Magda, or she'd quiz me on charms. Sometimes we'd sit in her first-floor bedroom at the back of the house and go through the old cedar chest at the foot of her bed, a huge thing that had been passed down through the women of my family since it was first carved and painted by hand in the shadows of the Black Forest. It held the artifacts of ancient magic: the words of life imprinted in Alemannic on tanned hide; another grandmother's notes scribbled in English on scraps of paper; a family tree back to the 1500s; the wheel of life carved into a small animal's skull. That one I always understood: the continuous flow of life, the river of time looping on itself so each moment is simultaneously past, present, and future, the snake eats its tail and keeps on going.

A voice would call out, "Hello? Magda? Elisabeth?" and Magda would shoot me a look that said, *Get to work*, while she kept right on doing what she was doing. I had no choice but to treat our clients in the kitchen alone.

But Mrs. Mildred King was a different kind of regular. Whenever she stopped by, Magda would emerge from her bedroom or turn off the radio that was always in the background in the days since Dr. King had been killed. Magda was always on hand to serve—and gossip with—her old friend and cousin.

Magda and Cousin Mildred clasped hands in greeting; never a hug or kiss on the cheek, not from these stoic German matrons. They were actually second cousins—Mildred was the daughter of Great-Grandma Dorothy's cousin, from the line whose skills had faded over the generations and who'd been phased out of the family business—but only Great-Grandma Dorothy had ever been able to keep the family tree straight, with all of the once- and twice-removeds in the right places, so *cousin* was a close-enough term for Magda's primary source of gossip from town.

"Lisbett," Magda said as I turned to give them privacy during Cousin Mildred's visit my first week working. "You'll do this one today." It wasn't a request.

Cousin Mildred was in a decade-old feud with Mrs. Andersen, her neighbor and one of those fulsome Swedish Lutherans in town. Magda supplied Mildred with a steady flow of hexes, which I suspected were weakened versions of the real thing.

"You'll never believe what that busybody did yesterday," Cousin Mildred said as I settled hesitantly at the table with the clucking septuagenarians.

Magda sipped her coffee and said, straight-faced, "No. Tell me."

First came the airing of grievances. I was impatient to learn the secrets of the hexes Magda provided Mildred, but the ceremonial wagging of tongues must come first.

"She marched right into my house when I was coming home from Juba's, my arms full of groceries and things. I couldn't shoo her away, and she marched right into the kitchen," Cousin Mildred said.

"Oh no," Magda clucked with little urgency. "She didn't. That busybody."

Mildred shook her head and turned her eyes to the heavens. Magda winked at me over her raised coffee cup.

Picking up the thread, I asked, "How did you ever get rid of her?"

Cousin Mildred huffed. "You won't believe it. She nosed around in my kitchen for nearly an hour—an hour!—before I said I needed to lie down. She stood there in my kitchen getting into everything as I put the groceries away. Can you believe it?"

Magda and I shook our heads sympathetically.

The old bat won't let someone help carry her groceries, I thought.

The "trouble" had started when Mrs. Andersen—tall, blonde, in her knee-length wool skirts and sensible clog shoes—moved in next door, an annoyingly bubbly, young, inexperienced housewife, and—the nerve!—tried to befriend the older Mrs. Mildred King to exchange recipes.

Years had passed, but I could still hear Cousin Mildred, already crochety in her sixties when the Andersens came to town, say, "Now, what would I want a recipe for lutefisk for? Can you imagine me serving that sour old fish at Home Ec Club? Lutefisk! Can you believe it?"

In a small town like Friedrich, sometimes you needed a feud for something to do.

"The nerve," I tutted, and raised my own coffee cup to cover my insuppressible smile.

"So what'll it be today, then, Mildred? Another frog infestation? Lake flies? Something to keep her mouth closed for a week?" Magda asked, as serious as she'd be with any other client.

Cousin Mildred looked grave, taking a moment to consider all the possibilities, which she knew better than most.

"Actually," Cousin Mildred said, "I was thinking of a little protection. Can you keep her in her own yard and out of my business for a while? Zap her if she tries to cross over?" Her face fell. "I tried to do it myself but couldn't quite figure it out."

Magda patted her hand sympathetically. "Now, Mildred. You know what happened last time you tried your hand at a hex. You leave it to us."

Magda pushed her chair back from the table and unfolded her petite frame. She looked witchy as ever in a floor-length black caftan, her silver hair swept up under a turban.

"Hop to it," Magda said to me over her shoulder, moving at a surprising speed for her age.

I flashed a smile at Mildred and hustled behind Magda to her bedroom.

Behind closed doors, I raised my eyebrows at Magda. "That is what Cousin Mildred requests each week? What can you possibly give her that won't knock Mrs. Andersen clear off her feet?"

"We're not here to judge our clients," Magda snapped as she started digging in the cedar chest at the foot of her bed. Bracelets tinkled up and down her wrists as she dug through the powerful objects there. She turned and shot me a devilish grin. "I make it half or quarter strength for Mildred—and slip a little memory charm in her coffee so she doesn't know the difference."

My mouth hung open in surprise. "You do what?"

"Oh, just a little something to help her remember how *well the hexes are working*, you know," Magda said as she continued digging. "I whisper the words in her coffee when she's not looking."

She pulled something from the depths of the cedar chest, clutching it in her hand suddenly, and held it out to me. A cluster of long feathers shone in her hand, so black they were nearly purple.

"Raven's feathers," she announced.

"But I've never used them before," I said slowly.

*   *   *

I had been reading energies, playing with minor weather patterns, and helping Magda hex the other biddies in town since age ten.

Water charms were my specialty—for the farms that struggled in the hottest summers on record, the new houses accidentally built on soggy, shifting ground in neighborhoods springing up on either end of town. Mom hated it when I did what Mary called "reverse Jesus," turning wine into water, calling the molecules to relinquish their structure and reform as H_2O. Magda would smile her closed-lipped smile and change it back, allowing me these small rebellions, as Mom sighed and turned away.

"Very good, Lisbett," Magda would say without smiling or so much as a glance when I finished with the early clients I helped. "You were born for this," she told me all too often. I anxiously craved her approval, every sentence setting me apart, making me feel superior.

By age fifteen, I just nodded. I knew better than to expect real praise from my grandmother. By then, my perfect performance was expected, a given.

In high school, girls started to whisper to me in class, asking for a hex or, too often, a love charm. I haggled with them for gum or magazines or a ride in their older brothers' cars. But for gum, I never provided a full charm, just enough so they knew it worked. They'd smile and invite me to the country club pool with them on Saturdays, but if they wanted the full shebang, they'd have to tell their mothers what was ailing them and bring a chicken to the side door after school.

"Please," they would say. "I don't want to tell my mom . . . Your charms are the best anyway. You're a Watry. You're so good at this."

It was hard to say no when they invoked our family name, and I would sometimes flout Magda's rules and give them charms anyway. But it felt dangerous to practice outside Magda's purview, and when the girls pushed or asked for too much, I shook my head and quietly persuaded them to come to the house under the pretense of needing a beacon or herb or some ingredient that could be found only in our kitchen.

Truthfully, I was terrified that I would mess something up, leave a girl blind when she asked me to change her eye color from brown to hazel. There was real power emerging in my hands, and I didn't trust myself yet to fully wield it. Every time someone told me how good I was, I stretched myself as tall as I could go and tried to live up to their expectations, all the while feeling like a fraud.

*   *   *

Magda let the heavy lid of the trunk close with a thump and motioned for me to help her up. Her creaky joints shouldn't have been kneeling on the floor in the first place. She watched my face.

I wrinkled my nose, searching the limits of my knowledge. Somewhere in the back of my mind, a foggy idea took shape.

"Ravens are smart," I said slowly as the words formed, the knowledge coming from God knows where. "They remember faces. If you're kind to them, they'll remember you and visit you looking for treats or bring you presents. If you wrong a raven though, they'll never forget. They'll remember where you live . . ."

"And haunt your doorstep *für hundert Tage hintereinander,*" Magda finished, as if delivering a bit of a broken incantation. "Exactly, good girl. You get it. It's like a reverse summoning spell."

I wasn't completely sure I did get it, but I didn't say that. I couldn't voice a shred of hesitation in front of Magda, especially not for an important client like her cousin. I would bumble my way through it. I took the feathers from Magda and turned toward the door.

Magda followed behind and whispered to me, "Remember—a raven's curse may last a hundred days, but Mrs. Andersen can only take three or four. Got it?"

While Mildred and Magda continued their kaffeeklatsch, I worked steadily at the armoire in the kitchen. I bundled the raven's feathers with birch twigs and fresh green grass, squeezed blueberries over the whole bunch, and wrapped the beacon three times around with a thin strip of tin. While working, I cast out the ice floe. The town's energy field unfurled before me, a grid of entangled life forces. I picked my way through the town's rainbow tapestry of energies to find Mrs. Andersen's perfect blonde bob and beaming smile. I found her shiny cerulean energy in her kitchen in the center of town, a few streets over.

Concentrating fully, I drew a mental fence around Mrs. Andersen's yard. The brightness of freshly cut grass filled my senses. My hands imbued the beacon with purpose: *It's time to bake. It's time to make. You must get the baking done. It's time for pies.* The sweetness of ripe blueberries rose up to me.

Watch the front door, I whispered to a nearby raven, summoning her to Mrs. Andersen's yard. *You are on guard duty until the next new moon.* Mary or my mother might've skipped the beacon entirely and gone straight to a raven for help, but I needed the extra insurance from the beacon and its charm.

Satisfied, I opened my eyes and presented the beacon to Mildred.

"This should do the trick," I said. "Burn it around the four corners of Mrs. Andersen's house tonight at midnight. But be careful to not light it until you are on her side of the yard; otherwise you might fence yourself in with her." *And bake pies with her for a week,* I thought.

Cousin Mildred smiled and held the beacon delicately with both hands. I beamed down at her, picturing the impish blue-haired Mildred running around like a sprite in the middle of the night.

"Excellent," she said. "This one will do you proud, Magda."

Mildred winked at me and presented our payment, a treasured staple in our house: two plump loaves of her famous bread, with a crisp, golden-brown exterior that gave way to a perfectly soft, chewy interior. I turned to straighten up the armoire while Magda and Cousin Mildred finished their coffee and clucked about the horrible dress Mrs. Grundahl had worn to mass on Sunday.

"Just awful."

"That thing should be burnt."

"She must've made it herself."

"But no idea where she got that God-awful fabric."

"Who would make such a thing?"

"What would you call that color anyway? Dog rolling in mud?"

The septuagenarians laughed until they wheezed, schoolgirls again reigning over the playground. I smiled into the armoire, glad that Magda had such a close friendship with her cousin after all these years—even if Cousin Mildred was a demanding old dinosaur and Magda was charming her cousin to keep her away from the strongest magic. I was happy that Magda was happy and confident that my performance was up to snuff, any anxiety over the unfamiliar raven feathers quickly forgotten.

Mildred gathered her things to go and clasped Magda's hands again.

"Thank you, Cousin," she said.

She glanced at me once more, letting her eyes wash over me for a moment too long, squinting as if she were trying to remember something from long ago, far away—*memory charm fog*, I realized.

Mildred turned back to meet Magda's gaze with clear eyes. "You were right to choose this one. You chose right."

I froze with my back pressed against the armoire, the smile plastered across my face. *What does that mean?* I watched Magda intently for any indication that what Cousin Mildred had said was anything more than the nothing murmurings of an old coot, but Magda just nodded and knit her fingers together in front of her.

Mildred smiled at me, like she had given me the highest compliment or maybe even dropped that particular grenade on purpose to watch me squirm. After watching her dealings with Mrs. Andersen, I shouldn't have been surprised.

I tried to respond normally, after a beat that felt like an eternity. "Thank you, Cousin Mildred. Happy to help. We'll see you soon."

Magda put a hand on Cousin Mildred's shoulder to steer her to the door, but her eyes flitted my way involuntarily. And then Mildred was off, doddering out the door with her enormous velour handbag over her elbow, the beacon waving in her spindly old claw.

What the hell was that all about? Magda chose me?

Before I had a chance to ask Magda, she disappeared behind closed doors. It would have to wait.

Seven

Later, I watched as Mom scooped a mountain of knudeln, streaming with rivers of melted butter, into a serving bowl. She opened the oven to retrieve a loaf of Cousin Mildred's bread, wrapping it in a clean white tea towel, and a cast-iron crock of slow-roasted beef. It was a heavy meal for a warm summer evening, but my mother's repertoire was limited: if she felt like making knudeln and goulash on a hot June night, that was what she would do.

My father, for one, didn't mind.

Mom lifted the lid off the goulash, and we were all hit with the aromas of savory beef and sweet cream, the tang of summer tomatoes, and the essence of earthy sage. She heaped my father's plate high and topped it off with a thick slice of bread to soak up the sauce. We met one another's eyes around the table in shared contentment.

"Helene! You've outdone yourself," Dad exclaimed between mouthfuls—even though he had eaten this exact same meal in the wake of countless visits from Cousin Mildred.

Mom smiled and flushed, the color creeping easily into her peaches-and-cream skin.

I was unsettled after the strange interaction with Cousin Mildred, but the comforting meal temporarily put that aside. With my mouth full, I met Mary's gaze and flicked my eyes to the ceiling.

So good, I telegraphed to her openly.

Mary met my eyes with a smile. *The best.*

"So Mrs. King must've been by." Dad stated the obvious to no one in particular.

The rich goulash turned to acid in my throat at the mention of Mildred. I looked to Magda for some acknowledgment. *What aren't you telling me? What did that old bat mean, you chose me?*

Magda chewed slowly, deliberately, before answering. "Yep, Cousin Mildred was here today," she said, betraying nothing.

Dad nodded, oblivious or in too good a mood to care, and swiped another knudeln across his plate, loading his fork with the perfect bite of dumpling, sauce, and beef. He knew better than to ask for more detail than Magda cared to offer.

I hung my head low over my plate, dazed as the unspoken mystery between me and Magda sucked up all the air in the room.

What does it mean that she chose me? I thought Mom wasn't capable of taking over the business because of how she is. Was there ever another option?

My head was spinning. My path had been set for me, a fact I'd been resigned to from early on. I was thoroughly shaken to think there may have been another way. Everything I did was built on the knowledge that I would be Magda's sole heir—something I had thought I wanted. If there could've been another way, it would change everything. But only Magda could confirm that.

"May I be excused?" I asked abruptly. "I'm pretty tired after today."

Dad frowned at my very-much-not-clean plate but didn't argue.

"Fine, then," he said, eyeing me. "But before you run off without talking to us all night, tell us something interesting that happened today."

I froze, half hovering over the table as I stood. Sometimes I thought our abilities were rubbing off on my father.

You were right to choose this one . . . Mildred's cryptic words rang in my ears. I stared at Magda.

Magda's gaze was steady, daring me, *Go on, ask.* I looked away.

"I saw four loons this morning, all in a row, out on the water. Strange to see so many together. Maybe two pairs of mates?" I offered to Dad in a rush, surprising myself with how easily the lie fell out of my mouth.

"Good," Dad said. "Must be a good omen."

He glanced for confirmation at my mother, who only gave a noncommittal "Mm."

Mary cut her eyes at me. She knew immediately that it was a lie but said nothing.

* * *

I pretended to be asleep when Mary came up later, getting ready in the dark so as to not disturb me in the small room we shared. I wasn't ready for the inquisition from my little sister yet, even as I was sure she knew I was awake.

Just when I thought I was off the hook, Mary's voice, small and thoughtful, cut through the dark. "What was all that about? Did something happen today?"

I knew she knew. Mary always knew. Even when she didn't know for sure, she knew. It was the most annoying thing about her.

I sighed, unsure of what to say. I rolled on my side to face Mary in her twin bed, identical to mine, an arm's length away. Mary didn't understand the pressure I was under, the monotony of every day with Magda. But it was Mary, the only one who could remotely understand, and she was the only one I had to talk to about these things. Annie and John weren't family.

"Cousin Mildred said something strange as she was leaving today. She said Magda was right to choose me. What the hell do you think that means?"

"Don't swear," Mary said reflexively. I could practically hear her nose crinkle. "Hmm," she said, after a beat.

For all she knew, she said very little sometimes. *Say it*, I thought.

Mary spoke slowly, considering her words. "You have two choices."

What does she know anyway? I groaned, turning my head to smother the sound in my pillow.

Mary continued calmly. "You can ask Magda . . . I think she'll have to tell you something, either way. Or you can be mad and not do anything."

Like it's so easy? I didn't say.

"Do you think she'd tell me the truth?" I asked after a long pause.

"Maybe not," Mary said. "But think about it: she would tell you the truth if she thinks it will help your *precious work*." Sarcasm didn't suit her. "And if she doesn't," she continued, "maybe it doesn't mean anything."

"Then why hide it?"

"Sometimes people need their secrets."

What does Mary know about secrets anyhow? I thought.

As if to answer that, Mary whispered, "How's John?" I could hear the smirk in her voice.

"Fine," I whispered, annoyed. I rolled away from her to face the wall.

"What did you guys do last night?"

"Nothing," I said. *And then . . .* I closed my eyes and felt the ghost of John's clumsy hands on my body. If Magda was so determined for us to end up together anyway, we might as well have some fun along the way.

"Mm-hmm," Mary said, injecting so much doubt into those two syllables.

I only sighed in response.

I tossed fitfully for hours, turning Mildred's words over in my head, and fell asleep wondering who I would have been if I hadn't been born with my name. Who would I be if Magda hadn't claimed me for her own, if the girls in town didn't tell me they needed me, all the while whispering about me behind my back?

Eight

After a dreamless night, I found Mom making pancakes early the next morning. Fridays were for pancakes, and Mom dutifully made sure Mary got her Friday pancakes before she was off to the beach. My mother offered me the platter heaped with blueberry pancakes as big as a dinner plate.

I shook my head. "Later," I said impatiently.

I slid into a seat at the table, watching as my mother turned back to the kitchen counter with the tiniest sigh. She slipped two cakes onto a plate, every vertebra in her back visible as she bent over to pop the plate into the oven.

You were right to choose this one. Mildred's words echoed in my head.

I fumed silently, thinking, *What other choice did Magda have? Magda chose me, because Mom is . . . how she is . . . What other choice was there?* I asked the spirits silently, bewildered.

Mary crashed into the room at full speed, interrupting my thoughts as Mom replaced the platter of pancakes on the table. The kitchen had a certain gravity like that: add food and hot coffee, and it acquired a summoning power all its own. My father shuffled in suppressing a yawn, the newspaper tucked under one arm. My mother hated when he retrieved the newspaper in his robe, and she frowned her displeasure.

As Dad and Mary served themselves and Mom sat down at the table with a cup of coffee, I addressed my mother. "Mom, the other night John said Lucy has been acting strange. Can we go out there today?"

Magda swooped into the kitchen in an equally well-worn housecoat. It was the color of dried-up mint toothpaste, and I wondered if it had ever been green.

"What's this, then?" Magda asked, as Mary scooched her chair over to make room.

"Apparently there's something wrong with John Weseloh's dog," my father said from behind his paper with a practiced indifference.

My mother's eyes shifted from me to Magda. "I—" Mom started.

"I thought we could go together?" I offered gently, when Mom closed her mouth again. I secretly hoped for the time alone with my mother. I needed to ask her things about Magda and Mildred, even if she might not answer me.

"What's this, Helene?" Magda repeated, staring down my mother.

Mary stopped chewing, a wad of pancake lodged in her cheek. Her eyes were wide as she watched the proceedings.

Mom lifted her downturned face to meet Magda's. An entire conversation took place in the steady gaze between them. I knew better than to interfere. My mother broke first, dropping her gaze to the floor again.

"That's what I thought," Magda said smugly. "That silly animal stuff is all fine and good for you, darling, but I need Lisbett today."

Mary chewed quietly across the table from me, studying her plate intently. She snuck a peek at me, and I gave the slightest hint of a shrug. We had seen how this played out before.

"For heaven's sake, Magda. Elisabeth wants to go," my father said suddenly, dropping the paper again.

In my eighteen years, I had only witnessed my father disagreeing with Magda over the landscaping, the chickens, and other things of my father's domain. This was new.

"You stay out of this, Jacob Ridder," Magda snapped in a low voice, biting every syllable. She pointed a thin, elegant finger across the table at him.

Dad shrank immediately. "No, I—well. No," he stammered, raising his hands to show he didn't mean anything by it.

Dad looked from Mom to me to Magda and sighed. He stuffed nearly half a pancake in his mouth, picked up the paper, and scurried up the back stairs, his robe flapping behind him. I found myself trapped between my grandmother and everyone else, a position that was as familiar to me as breathing.

"Sorry, Mom," I said with a sigh.

As much as I resented how much time Mom spent with Mary and their secret understanding, I felt bad for my mother as she withered under Magda's thumb. I pleaded to Mom with my eyes. *Forgive me. Love me.*

"Do you mind going to Weselohs' alone for Lucy?" I asked. I was forced yet again to side with my grandmother.

My mother nodded once, her blue eyes watery, and that was that.

"I like the silly animal stuff," Mary mumbled through a mouthful of pancakes.

*   *   *

When I came in from the lake, Magda was dressed and waiting at the kitchen table for me. Everyone else had peeled off to their days: Mary to the beach, Mom to the Weseloh farm, Dad to the mill.

"Don't make me wait all day, Lisbett. I've got things to do too," Magda said without looking up from the newspaper.

It's barely nine AM, I thought, rolling my eyes. I turned my back to Magda and grabbed my warm plate of pancakes from the oven.

I ate them dry, rolled up like how the Norwegians in town ate lefse, hovering over the sink to catch the falling crumbs.

"You were up early anyway," Magda said to my back.

Everyone was up early, I thought. *It's pancake day.*

"Don't talk back," she said.

While Mary usually gave me the courtesy of not reading me, I could never count on that privacy from Magda. Too bad I couldn't reciprocate. It would have cleared so many things up for me. I had barely slept since Magda had caught me sneaking in, bursting with a million questions. I could no longer contain myself, and I was sure Magda knew it too.

"What did Cousin Mildred mean yesterday, that you chose me?" I asked, feeling suddenly brave.

Magda sighed. "Get dressed. We need to talk," she said.

Surprised at the candor, I rushed to rinse my plate in the sink and slunk off up the stairs to change and wrangle my hair into a braid for the day.

* * *

"Don't let your mother and sister distract you with their animal things," Magda said when I rejoined her in her bedroom.

I said nothing. I sat with my knees splayed on the floor at Magda's feet, ready for a lecture.

She sat in a tapestry chair, its legs carved with the whorls of the wheel of life like so many other things in Magda's room. She had ditched her housecoat for her preferred summer style of long black chiffon dress, the skirts draped around her thin legs making her look like the Queen of Sheba, or that dreaded W-word: *witch.* Bare feet to match my own—better for feeling the earth's vibrations—peeked out from under the folds of fabric. Her silver hair was swept up into an elaborate knot, a sign that she'd had plenty of time to get ready.

I waited.

"Elisabeth," Magda said. "You are meant for greater things than soothing spooked horses and cursing coyotes."

I fought the urge to roll my eyes, nodding solemnly. I had heard this speech a hundred times since I had started levitating. *You are special. You are meant for greater things. Und so weiter, und so fort.*

"You know I love your mother very much. But she could never do what we need you to do. Now, Cousin Mildred was right the other day." I sat up straighter at this part. "Your mother didn't choose this path. She . . . couldn't. So yes, I was forced to choose it for you."

I swallowed hard and raised an eyebrow at Magda, an approximation of the look she gave me all too often. "What do you mean, she didn't choose this path? What choice did Mom have?"

I didn't voice the real question that had picked at me: *What other choice could I have had?*

Since I could remember, Magda had told me I was made for greater things, that I was born to carry responsibility for our family, that I would take my place with her after I turned eighteen. That it was only me, no one else, who would succeed her. That I was born to inherit our family's greatest treasures.

"Why not Mom?" I asked when I was old enough to understand.

"You were born with an even greater gift," Magda had said.

I stopped asking questions when I realized the extent of my mother's limitations, how Magda only gave Mom animal cases. I had never seen my mother work with people. Even as a child, I knew I was special, different, that there were things I could do that my mother couldn't. *But what if I was wrong? What if she just didn't want to?*

Magda leaned in, almost whispering. "Helene wasn't always like this." She paused. "I can't begin to tell you how it hurts me to say anything against my only daughter. The truth is, Helene is as talented as you or me, but she chose long ago that she wouldn't accept the responsibilities of this family. She saw the long days, the heartbreaks, the constant threat of the town turning against our kind, and she chose to hone her practice on things with lesser stakes. Chickens. Horses."

My world threatened to come apart at the seams. "Mom just didn't want to do it," I said slowly.

Magda winced. "You could say that," she said with an exaggerated shrug.

So I'm not special. She didn't want it. And you're stuck with me, special or not, I thought. I could've sworn I saw Magda's eyes flash dark for a fraction of a second, so briefly I thought I had imagined it.

"Why didn't you try to . . ." I asked.

She cut me off with a shake of the head.

"You know as well as I do that I couldn't change your mother. Look at her. She made her choice, and this is what we have left of her," she said, her face falling. Her delicate manner surprised me.

"Best to leave her be," Magda continued. "And I will teach you, darling girl, like I always have. Don't I always teach you?" she asked in a singsong voice that made me feel like an oblivious child again.

I nodded. "Yes."

And look where it got me.

"Then that's how we'll be, you and me. I will teach you, and all of this will be yours, forever, darling."

Later, Magda drove to St. Agnes to see the "good" tailor—Mrs. Gerhardt, the wife of the Lutheran minister, was the only option in Friedrich and one of those women who staunchly refused to do business with us. As I cleaned the kitchen absently, I realized Magda hadn't actually answered my question. *Why didn't Mom want this? And why should I?*

*   *   *

I was taking inventory when Mom returned home and began to pull things from the fridge for supper. She browned hamburger in a pan on the stovetop and added onion and celery.

"Tater Tot hot dish?" I asked when she pulled a bag of Ore-Ida from the freezer.

She shot me a smile over her shoulder.

As the meat sizzled, I asked her casually, "What happened with Lucy?"

Mom turned and watched me, holding her spatula aloft, finding the words.

"She'll be fine," Mom said after a while.

A wave of relief washed over me—at least John would be happy about Lucy.

But relief was quickly replaced by so many questions. Why had my mother been given a choice when I was not afforded that freedom? I had grown up thinking I had no choice in the matter, even that I was special, chosen. I loved serving our town and neighbors. It made me feel helpful, proud. I had never stopped to think if I wanted it for myself—Magda had always told me what to want.

It was mind-boggling to think that might've been different if only my mother had been different. My curiosity was piqued: Who had my mother been before? I remembered that shadow flashing across Magda's face, and I had the feeling she hadn't told me the full story. What did my mother know that she couldn't say?

As Mom watched me, I felt she must know a lot more than she let on.

I sighed and tucked a jar back into the armoire. My mother crossed the room suddenly and took me into her arms, spatula still gripped in one hand. I couldn't remember the last time my mother had hugged me.

It was too much. I pulled away and retreated up the back stairs.

Nine

I was relieved when Annie called the next morning and offered a reason to escape the strange energy in the house. I looked around for someone to ask permission of, but alone in the kitchen, I shrugged to myself. Magda wouldn't miss me on a Saturday.

As I biked Lake Street to meet Annie at the beach in town, the sun promised to make it a perfect June day. The sky was a stunning blue, unblemished by clouds, the lake motionless. It was the kind of summer day that could stretch into eternity.

The public beach occupied six hundred yards of lakefront real estate sandwiched between the city park on one side and Harry's Supper Club on the other, one of the few real restaurants in town. There was a steady stream of weddings at Harry's on summer weekends, and it was already packed with cars that morning.

I threw my bike down on the grassy mound next to the public parking lot. No one bothered to lock their bikes in Friedrich.

Annie was late. I strolled up to the whitewashed wooden lifeguard station and glanced in the open door, where a freckly faced redhead I vaguely recognized from Mary's year—*Kathy? Connie?*—looked up from the engrossing pages of a magazine touting "New Pictures of the Heir and the Spare." On the cover, a long-faced Prince Charles stood uncomfortably far from his kid brother Prince Andrew.

Same, I thought.

I smiled, but before I could say a word, the girl's eyes widened at the sight of me. She jumped up from her chair, and words gushed too quickly from her chapped lips.

"Elisabeth! Hi! I hope you're having a good summer! It's so nice working with Mary. She's so nice, and it's fun working together . . ."

Calm down, child, I thought.

She shut her mouth with a small pop. *Did I do that?* I thought, surprised at the efficacy of a single thought in making the girl shut up.

Aware of the formidable look on my face, I forced myself to smile and blinked slowly, waiting, enjoying making her sweat.

"What's your name again?" I asked.

"Oh. Karen. I'm Karen Cooper," she said, deflating.

"Right, Karen. I knew your sister Paulina a little."

Paulina was a few grades ahead of me. Magda and I had made a love charm for Paulina Cooper nearly every month before she married some boy she met at the movies in St. Agnes and moved to the Cities. Karen was one of the few girls in town who had never asked for a love charm, having learned from her sister's mixed success. She was one of the few I didn't know.

Karen nodded like she had exceeded her word limit for the day.

"So where's Mary now, then?" I asked, exhausted by the interaction.

"Oh." She opened and closed her mouth like a freckled walleye bass. "In the stand. With Tim."

I raised my eyebrows at that. *Tim who?*

"Oh! I didn't mean like that. You know, on duty together. But not like *together* together."

I turned away as she babbled on.

"Thanks," I said over my shoulder as I marched across the sand toward the lifeguard stand, where Mary was hidden from view.

That was a common occurrence. The girls knew who we were—in a small town, everyone knew everyone—but they also knew what we were capable of. If they didn't, their mothers and grandmothers did. They also knew what we had done for the town, whom we had helped, whose aunts and children and distant cousins we had served. They were nervous and stammering around us, or overenthusiastic and awed like Karen. And some, like many of the boys at school, felt threatened and reacted with fear, taunting, shooting subversive looks behind our backs at Juba's or Sharp's. Never fully trusting but tolerating us, allowing us to work for them and among them and share bread at their tables, for they knew our strength and dared not test us outright.

I found Mary and the aforementioned Tim side by side in the lifeguard stand, which was meant for one person. But two slim teenagers could fit when so determined. The length of Mary's long, lean thigh under the high cut of her red lifeguard suit pressed against Tim's thigh under his red trunks in a way that suggested they were accustomed to fitting themselves together.

I recognized Tim from Mary's class. His father was the superintendent of schools for Friedrich and the next town to the west, Crichton, so his son was free to work as he pleased in the summer, not tied to a farm like most of the county boys. The golden brown of his skin was nearly identical to Mary's, which made me irrationally jealous. Mary, who had applied to be a junior lifeguard the minute she was allowed at fourteen, perpetually had a better tan than me. It wasn't fair that Tim did too.

They weren't talking as I approached but wordlessly gazing at the swimming area, one unit with four legs. Mary jumped up when she saw me. I rolled my eyes at her and smiled. She visibly relaxed at that, then turned to climb down the ladder. Tim's ears turned a noticeable shade of pink above his summer tan.

"I didn't know you were coming today," Mary said.

I shrugged. It felt like Mary didn't know a lot about me anymore.

"I didn't know they were putting two guards in the chair these days." I flicked my eyes up toward Tim, who kept his eyes studiously on the water. I flashed a smile at Mary to soften any sting.

Mary didn't respond right away, her expression clouded as she studied me. *Damn Watry women and their secrets.*

"What's wrong?" she asked, catching me off guard.

Is she still reading me? I thought, anxious that privacy in our house had gone by the wayside. Or Mary was more intuitive than I gave her credit for.

"Nothing," I said automatically, a lie. *Everything.* "Don't worry. I'll leave you alone. Annie's on her way." I glanced up at Tim, who was well within earshot. "Have fun," I said with an exaggerated lift of my eyebrows.

It was Mary's turn to roll her eyes at me. "It's not like that," she said quietly.

How was I supposed to know if my little sister was driving around the cornfields at night with this pink-eared boy?

"Okay," I said. "Big-sister duty, you know. See you later."

"Sure," she said.

Mary didn't climb back up into the stand right away. I felt her watching me as I walked toward the water.

In mid-June, the water was barely sixty degrees on the clearest, sunniest days. I stood ankle deep in the cold water, my backpack hooked over both shoulders, as the waves tossed the glint of sun back at me. When I closed my eyes, I imagined myself a world away.

Annie's voice jolted me back to earth. "You gonna stand there all day?"

I turned and threw her a grin. Nothing, not even my family's nonsense, could ruin a day of *Cosmo* and Coke in the sand with Annie.

"What's happening there?" she asked with a nod toward Mary.

Mary stood at the base of the lifeguard stand gazing out at the water. Tim hovered above, watching her with a smile that said it all. Mary waved to Annie.

"Take a wild guess," I said as we picked our way between families to a spot that we innately knew was perfect without having to discuss it: close enough that no one could block our view of the teenage boys who would soon be throwing each other off the diving platform, far enough from the screaming kiddos at the city playground, and not so far that I couldn't conspicuously keep an eye on this unfamiliar creature that my little sister was becoming and the dopey blond boy beaming down at her.

We dropped our bags and unrolled faded beach towels. Annie produced a radio from her bag. When we were lucky, we picked up a rock station from St. Cloud, the college disc jockeys slinging edgy new music among hours of the Beatles and Bob Dylan, our very own Minnesotan hero. A fuzzy guitar solo broke through the static as Annie nestled the radio into the corner of her towel. I glanced around to see who might be watching and, seeing no appraising male eyes, tugged my shorts over the curves of my hips and flopped down on my stomach.

For the first time in what felt like weeks, it was nice to act like normal teenagers. No obligations or secrets or lovesick farmers' daughters, only a day lying on the beach next to Annie with the sun pulsing on my back.

"My mom thinks I should look for a job in town. Maybe Harry's will take me. At least I could score free beer," Annie was saying.

In addition to the Supper Club, Harry was the proprietor of the gas station connected to the Sports Shop, a one-stop shop for bait, tackle, gas, guns, and gifts. I suppressed a frown at the idea of Annie behind the bait counter. She wouldn't last one day at the Sports Shop.

What Annie didn't say was that we were two of the few girls in our class who hadn't applied to college or nursing school or something. I, at least, had a plan, a job to step into, whether I liked it or not. Annie had only vague ideas about running away with Prince Charming.

I turned my head toward her, maintaining a neutral tone. "What do you think?" I asked without opening my eyes.

"I think it sounds like a one-way ticket to getting stuck in Friedrich," Annie said. "But I might pop over there tomorrow and try anyway. It wouldn't be so bad to have some money this summer."

"Good point," I said. "Then you can pay me back for all the love charms I made for you this spring."

"Hey now," Annie said, nudging me lightly with her shoulder. "I'm no freeloader. But those were a best-friends special, right?"

"Always," I said, opening one eye to grin at her.

"But maybe working at Harry's isn't such a bad idea," Annie said quietly.

I could tell we weren't joking about free beer anymore. "Is that what you want?" I asked seriously.

"It's either that or the Sports Shop, or I end up like my mom."

I pondered for a minute. She wasn't wrong. Annie's mother had jumped from job to job and boyfriend to boyfriend ever since it had ended with Annie's dad when we were eight. Those were our choices. We could become our mothers or try desperately to break the mold. If Annie had a way out, she had to take it.

"You might meet some out-of-towners if you get to work weddings," I said, signaling my approval.

She pursed her lips and nodded, but I could sense her excitement. We lay quietly for a few minutes, listening to someone's magical hands sliding over the guitar strings through the static of Annie's radio. *Hendrix*, I thought dreamily.

"Hey," Annie said at the end of the song, nudging my shoulder with her own, which was slicked with baby oil, all the better for baking to a perfect, crispy brown.

I opened both eyes and pressed myself up on one elbow, watching her expectantly.

"How's it going with everything else?" she asked cautiously when I met her eyes.

Oh, Ann. If only you knew, I thought. I shrugged and lay back, closing my eyes to avoid her worried gaze.

"Oh, fine. Just fine," I said, sounding for all the world like my taciturn Dutch father.

"Really?" Annie asked, nudging me one more time.

As much as I loved Annie, and as much as we had been through together, getting in trouble every which way in and around Friedrich, I couldn't tell her the truth. She wasn't family. As complicated as things were with Magda and my mother, I couldn't break ranks. I couldn't air our dirty laundry to someone outside the family. My anxiety grew as I struggled to keep my face impassive. *Can she see it on my face? Do I look like something's wrong?* I was tempted to charm her into believing me, but I had promised myself I would never do that to my best friend. I thought of Magda and Cousin Mildred.

"Really," I said.

I sat up and swung around to face Annie, hugging my knees to my chest in both arms. I nudged Annie back with my knees, holding her gaze steady for as long as I could stand it.

"Really, Ann, I promise," I said, as earnestly as I could. "It's different than I expected, but I'm getting used to it. You know me, I'll do whatever Magda needs, and I'll have my fun with you and John and it will be the same as ever."

She nodded. Her long brown hair with soft blonde highlights fell across her face, obscuring her expression. *She's worried that I'll be too busy for her,* I thought. *Afraid of change, like everyone else. She's worried I'll abandon her too.*

A shout from the lifeguard stand interrupted us. I turned to see Karen Cooper standing with a wide stance on top of the platform. She was yelling into her megaphone at two boys scrapping on the diving platform. The boys, twelve or thirteen, scrawny but starting to fill out from the hormones coursing through their bodies, had each other by the shoulders and were attempting to hook each other around the ankle to tip their opponent into the water.

"No roughhousing!" Karen yelled into her megaphone.

The boys didn't look up.

"Hey!" she shouted again. "On the diving platform! Cut it out!"

Mary wandered out of the lifeguard station at the commotion, and other beachgoers began to watch. Tim followed behind Mary at a respectful distance, then stood beside her in the sand below the lifeguard stand.

Karen sighed with her whole body and swapped her megaphone for a red rescue tube.

"What's she doing?" Annie asked.

Karen climbed down from the chair, jumping the last rungs. She was more athletic than her gangly, freckled limbs suggested.

"She's gonna go give those brats a piece of her mind," I said.

As Karen took to the water, the boys squabbled on, red-faced and hurling insults at each other. I couldn't make out the exact words but could only imagine the variety and creativity of a twelve-year-old's profanity. As Karen deftly ducked under the line of buoys that marked the border of the deep-water swimming area, the furious shout of "Twat rocket!" reached us on the beach. I glanced at Annie over my shoulder; she met my eyes, and we simultaneously burst into laughter.

As Karen closed in on the platform in a tight front crawl, the Twat Rocket, buzzing with indignation, finally succeeded in hooking the other boy and toppling him into the water. The whole beach echoed with a wet, sucking *thunk* as the boy's head or elbow or some other solid part connected squarely with Karen Cooper's head. She instantly went limp in the water, buoyed only by the red float across her back. The boy in the water sputtered and flailed wildly.

The Twat Rocket burst into tears on the platform, leaning over the edge and gasping helplessly, "Oh my gosh! Are you okay?"

Mary and Tim were in the water in a flash, their own lifesaving devices across their backs. Barely a word passed between them, but they moved as if choreographed.

Mary expertly laid Karen's limp body across a float and slowly made her way back to shore. Tim coaxed the flailing boy in the water to take his float while the Twat Rocket whimpered. I saw Tim beckon—*come on*—to the Twat Rocket, who joined them in the water. Both boys flanked Tim closely in a sad doggy paddle, as if Tim had them by the ears.

On dry land, Tim scolded the boys with a stony face and, after confirming that the Twat Rocket's victim was uninjured, sent them marching with a firmly pointed finger to attend their fates outside the lifeguard shack. For a sixteen-year-old, Tim played the part of disappointed father well.

Mary tried unsuccessfully to rouse Karen in the sand. As Tim came to stand over her shoulder, I noticed a number of beachgoers, mothers in particular, swiveling their heads between Mary and me. *The other Watry-Ridder girl is here*, I could hear them thinking. *Why isn't she doing anything?* Or worse: *Look how useless these Watry women are in a real emergency.*

But the calm on Mary's face and steady movements of her hands as she pumped Karen's chest would've been enough to keep me at a distance. I also knew, though, that appearances were important in Friedrich. I glanced at Annie, then pulled my shorts over my swimsuit. I felt eyes on me as I crossed the sand to where a small circle was gathering around Mary and Karen. I stood facing Mary so she could see me clearly.

"I got this," Mary said without looking up. Her tongue poked between her teeth in concentration.

"I know," I said. *I'm here if you need me, for their sake*, I pulsed at her as I glanced at the mothers' faces raw with concern.

I closed my eyes and cast out the ice floe. Mary's sunny yellow light drew me in immediately. She hovered over Karen's faint pink energy, the color of a drop of blood spreading through water. I saw that Mary's hands were a charade for the beach, and I was twistedly proud. *Mare knows how to keep up appearances too, then.*

Karen's heart was pumping, albeit faintly, but she was fighting against consciousness after the hard blow in the water. While Mary outwardly made a show of performing CPR, her energy field was frantically searching for Karen's, visible only in the faint pink vestigial traces around Karen's physical form. Her life force had fled the building.

I got this, Mary pulsed at me.

Before I had a chance to plunge in myself, Mary suddenly pulled Karen's energy out of thin air and stuffed it back into her limp form, a blanket of warm orchid-pink energy spreading through her body.

I felt Mary whisper the words of protection—*Bisch wiff. Bisch wusle. Bisch gliebt*—as I opened my eyes to see Karen coming to. She gasped for air and her eyes rolled around wildly, searching for something familiar.

Mary stroked Karen's fiery red hair and kept her in place as the life slowly returned to her. The small crowd applauded and crossed themselves, their prayers answered in the form of Mary Watry-Ridder, earth angel. Someone had the foresight to run off and get Karen's mother, who arrived shortly after. She insisted on taking Karen to the hospital in St. Agnes, and Mary shrugged.

"If it makes them feel better," she said to me as they drove away.

* * *

After Karen's mother took her away and Tim sent the thoroughly scolded boys packing with their tails between their legs, the crowd quickly dispersed. People were unsettled. The few that stayed kept out of the water. It reminded me of a few summers prior when a water-skier had hit a rock during a show on the river outside St. Agnes. He was okay, but the last thing people wanted to see after he was pulled from the water was more trick jumps and pyramids.

Annie, however, was unfazed.

"Why would I let this ruin a perfectly good beach day? Besides, if I have to join the working world, I might as well enjoy my last days of freedom," she said as she lay back on her towel, face turned up to the admittedly perfect June sun.

"Fine," I said, and sat down again.

Mary remained kneeling in the sand long after Tim and Mrs. Cooper helped take the stunned Karen away to the Coopers' waiting station wagon and Annie and I went back to our towels. I watched Mary rise slowly to her feet and could see the exhaustion pouring from every inch of her body, but to the layperson she looked cool, calm, and strong as ever. She leaned against the base of the lifeguard stand, one knee bent and a bare foot pressed against the whitewashed wood. To the outside world, Mary was already back on duty, watching the few kids splashing in the shallows. But I saw that stack of wood holding her up.

One of the remaining mothers on the beach reached out and squeezed Mary's hand in passing. The mothers would tell of what Mary had done there that day. Mary Watry-Ridder had pulled a girl's soul back from the other side.

I, on the other hand, saw another perfectly capable Watry woman with the beginnings of a strong magic rising in her, and I seethed to think that Magda didn't see it in Mary too. And once I saw it, I couldn't leave it alone. For the rest of the afternoon, as Annie chattered on about some boy beside me, my drumbeat beneath the surface went, *Mary is perfectly capable. Why am I stuck with the family burden if Mary can do that?*

Ten

When I left to greet the water on Sunday, there was a box of hand-painted china with a delicate floral trim on the front step—presumably a gift from Karen Cooper's artist mother. I set it inside the door and crossed Lake Street.

The sky was overcast, but the lake was smooth and surprisingly warm from a heavy humidity in the air. I swam from the end of our dock to a buoy that warned boats of an enormous underwater boulder. It was a rite of passage for local kids to swim to the rock and stand on it when they finally had the stamina and guts.

As I swam, I couldn't wrap my head around what it all meant. I had been trying my entire life to live up to my name, to be the perfect Watry-Ridder girl that everyone told me I was—but if my mother hadn't wanted this responsibility, why should I? Why didn't Magda want Mary, when she was clearly becoming so skilled? Why did I feel like I was a cog in the machine of my family? I felt claustrophobic every time I thought about my future in Friedrich, John, the family business. I didn't know what other life I might choose for myself, but I desperately craved the opportunity to find out.

Every question propelled me forward through the water. By the time I pushed myself up on the dock, muscles blissfully tired, I was resolved to find the answers for myself. It would have to wait until after church, though.

I shook the water from my hair like a dog and exhaled deeply. *Thank you for bringing me back down to earth*, I whispered to the lake. I slipped my feet into the abandoned buckskin moccasins that were my preferred summer footwear and crossed Lake Street wrapped in a towel.

Inside, my family were in various states of preparation for church. Mom was fully dressed in a navy cotton dress, long blonde hair pinned up neatly, reading the newspaper at the table with Sam's white paws draped around her neck. Magda was beside her in her housecoat. Mary was parked on the davenport in front of the TV in a yellow dress and white stockings, her long, raven curls still a rat's nest from sleep, Mickey at her side, tail twitching. I had almost forgotten about Grandpa and Grandma Ridder's visit until I saw Mary's stockinged legs, something we only ever did for Grandma Ridder. My father was nowhere to be seen, presumably dressed and ruining his clean shirt with some greasy chore around the yard.

I ran up the back stairs two at a time into the shower. As the water washed away the mineral scent of lake water, I was calm. *Mom didn't want it, so they're stuck with me. I don't have to be nice about it*, I thought. *If they need me so bad, they'll have to deal.* I smiled as I worked the last of the conditioner through the length of my hair. The hot water was a delicious contrast to the lingering chill in my muscles.

In my room, I combed the knots from my hair and dressed in a pink paisley dress with neat bric-a-brac trim. I strained to button the rows of tiny buttons up to my throat and finally wrestled them closed over my chest. I blatantly skipped the stockings and garter belt as I slipped my bare feet into the black Mary Janes I reserved for church and school functions.

I clomped down the front stairs, legs jellified after the long swim. Without a word, I sat down on the floor in front of Mary. She sent Mickey skittering away as she sat up and bookended my shoulders with her knees. Without lifting her gaze from the TV, where they replayed the footage from Bobby Kennedy's funeral for the umpteenth time, Mary raked her fingers through my damp hair and began to braid the sides back away from my face. Her hands flew with a magic all their own, weaving my hair into two overlapping braids, the occasional sigh escaping her lips as she came across a knot.

This was one of the few rituals we shared. I had watched Mom braid Mary's hair from a distance when we were young, and when Mary was old enough, she began to do mine without comment. Before that, Magda would begrudgingly do mine, giving me one thick plait down my back to match her own. Mary finished as she usually did, with a firm squeeze of her knees on my shoulders.

I stayed on the floor, lulled by Mary's fingers, letting the morning news wash over me in silence. Mary braided her own crown to match mine. Magda's voice called from the kitchen, "Girls, let's go."

Magda had swapped the housecoat for her good green dress, which she wore every other Sunday all summer, and Dad reappeared with a telltale smudge on one elbow and his blazer slung over his shoulder. We walked the nearly two miles to church in pairs, Magda leading the way in front, Mom on Dad's arm. Dad spoke to Mom in a casual low tone about who knows what, and Mary and I brought up the rear. We walked slowly, Magda setting the pace as she waved to the folks emerging from their houses on Lake Street like she was the grand marshal of the Weekly Parade of Catholics. It was better than when we had to squeeze in the station wagon in the winter. In the summer, we walked through town and picked up Cousin Mildred and other neighbors on the way to the church built by our forebears on the hilltop west of the lake.

When Father Kevin bowed to the altar during the processional hymn, his back to the congregation, a thought suddenly popped into my head: *I could give Father Kevin a tail right now. And there'd be nothing they could do about it. They need me.*

I smiled to myself at the absurdity of it all. That would really give the newer families who sat in the back something to talk about.

"Don't," Mary whispered next to me. "Don't do it."

Quit reading me, I pulsed back at her.

I cast a shield right then and there to cloak myself from my nosy sister and grandmother. If they couldn't give me a little privacy, I would have to take it for myself.

* * *

After mass, we gossiped outside in the shadow of the spire. The lake was tranquil, but the sky darkened by the minute. I stood with Mary and Annie, scrutinizing outfits and enjoying the breeze that blew in ahead of the coming storm.

Annie asked in a stage whisper, "Did you see Tillie Matthews's dress today?" She widened her eyes in mock horror.

I raised an eyebrow toward the poor girl in question. She was going to college in the fall at Winona, a small school, but getting out of Friedrich nonetheless, which made Tillie a natural target of Annie's jealousy. I was jealous too, but I'd never admit it. Mary rolled her eyes at us and relocated to lean against the kelly-green double doors of the church. Mary had never much been one for gossip unless it was about us. Then she was all in, listening in the ladies' room at Sharp's or among unsuspecting beachgoers. More often she read the energy of what wasn't said when the conversation suddenly stopped the moment the Watry-Ridder girls walked in.

I watched her, curious, as Mary leaned her slender swimmer's body back nonchalantly. She surveyed the churchyard from the top of the steps, one hip cocked above the other, and it was clear as day to me that she was looking for a boy. Anyone else might have seen Mary as a tired, moody teenager needing space. But I immediately saw Mary on a mission.

Annie dithered on in my ear without so much as taking a breath, one hand gripping my arm above the elbow—"Tell me what's happening with John . . . I heard . . . Is it true? . . . It must be true . . ."—as I scanned the yard myself.

Quit it, Mary pulsed at me. *Don't read me.*

But I didn't have to read her to see what was happening. Mary tossed her head in that casual but practiced way I knew all too well. Her braided crown didn't move an inch as she blinked and looked around deliberately to see who might be watching. As she opened her eyes, I saw who she was looking for. *Did he see me? Is he watching?* Mary telegraphed with every ounce of her.

Tim made his way across the yard, saying hello to one group of kids, then another. Lo and behold, he worked his way toward Mary. *So that's Mary's plan for the summer, then*, I thought before I was distracted as John caught up to Annie and me.

As the crowd began to thin, John hooked his arm through mine.

"Having a good summer, Johnny boy?" Annie asked him with a suggestive raise of her eyebrows.

"Yep, pretty good," John answered Annie casually, but his eyes were on me.

"Having fun with our girl here?" Annie shot a pointed look at me and raised her eyebrows at John, who showed the slightest hint of a blush above the collar of his shirt.

John glanced at me sideways and couldn't help himself: a close-lipped smile spread across his face. His eyes were soft. He looked at me like I was the best thing that had ever happened to him, and I suppressed a shudder. *He's stuck with me too.*

"That good, huh?" Annie asked with a smirk.

"All right, goodbye then, Annie. That's enough of that. We're at church, for chrissakes," I play-hissed at her, extracting my arm from hers and giving her a little shove.

She laughed, a throaty sound that could have been coming from a downtown lounge singer instead of my boy-crazed eighteen-year-old Annie Holbrooke.

"Bye, then," she said with a fake pout.

"Goodbye, Annie," I said too brightly, turning my head subtly to catch a glimpse of Mary and Tim.

John's gaze followed Annie as she trailed her mother down the hill before he turned and crossed his eyes at me. His eyes ticked over my shoulder, and I followed John's gaze to where Mom and Magda were talking to Father Kevin. Sometimes the most Mom said all week was in those chats with Father Kevin. That was her role in keeping up appearances around town. I turned to watch, standing comfortably shoulder to shoulder with John.

There was always publicity work to be done to avoid drawing the gaze of those who might take offense at our work. It was hard for anyone not to notice the steady flow in and out of our kitchen and the unseen hand of Magda Watry's influence around town. But luckily there were charms to shoo anyone who would get in the way, and besides, who could question the work of such good, upstanding Catholic daughters as Magda Watry and Helene Watry-Ridder? It wasn't lost on me that people like us—that old W-word—normally operated outside the letter of the Church. When we read *The Crucible* in tenth grade, Magda had made sure to point out that it was those haughty, careless biddies who missed Sunday communion who were hanged first.

Magda took a package from her handbag and passed it to Father Kevin. His weekly migraine remedy, treated with a heavy dose of memory charm, just enough to keep the family business running smoothly without any objections from the parish office. We and all our grandmothers before us sat in the front pew every week, and as far as Father Kevin could remember, our family business was botany. No witchcraft or funny business, nothing that could possibly offend the Lord.

Dad stood beside John and me suddenly, watching the exchange. "John," he said with a growl.

"Mr. Ridder," John squeaked. He managed a manly nod.

My father couldn't stand his ground in front of Magda Watry at the breakfast table, but he could certainly put the fear of God into my teenage boyfriend. Both embarrassed and honored by my father's protectiveness, I wondered if Dad too had noted the time when John dropped me off the other night. I wondered what Dad thought about Mom's lack of participation in the family business.

"Elisabeth, better get going," Dad said as he continued his progress to gather Mary, Mom, and Magda behind him. It was time to prepare for Grandpa and Grandma Ridder.

I turned to graze John's shoulder with the tip of my nose, the most intimate touch I could muster in front of our parents and all of God's good people. I caught sight of John's parents beaming at us, trying not to look but unable to stop watching their precious baby boy. Mrs. Weseloh wore the faintest hint of a smile on her face, which was normally so etched in worry for John's brothers on the other side of the world. Mr. Weseloh tipped his head as my father passed, a silent acknowledgment between two of the last patriarchs of the families still making the Sunday rounds.

John's parents, like mine, like the whole damn town, assumed we were getting married, that this was it for us. Never mind that young women were going off to college and becoming writers and scientists and what have you. Two years of going together was proof enough for them that John Weseloh would be the one to stand beside the elder Watry-Ridder girl. John would follow in my father's footsteps, the man about town, the flimsy yet necessary front for our business, smiling and shaking hands and making plans for cards or fishing with the important men in town. Maybe John would take over at the Ridder Family Company. My uncles Ridder were both childless. The quiet, serious farm boy with the easy smile would seamlessly fall into that role, and I was overcome with shame and sadness that John had as little choice in the matter as I did.

John said, "I'll call you tonight," his lips practically brushing my ear.

I recoiled involuntarily for a split second before recovering myself, appeasing John with a roll of my eyes at our surroundings.

But inside, John's attention made it feel like the walls were closing in on me.

I fixed an appropriately pious smile in place and waved goodbye to John and his parents. As I turned to follow my family down the hill, visions ran through my head of a quiet, staid future with John at my side while Mary beside me hummed with possibilities.

Eleven

Mom set out a plate of summer sausage on fluffy rolls to tide us over until dinner. They weren't as good as Cousin Mildred's bread, but the butter was sweet and the sausage from the Nelson farm was rich and salty. Mom shooed us out of the kitchen with one stern look, and Mary and I slipped outside, a roll in each hand. Dad disappeared to his shed the moment we got home. The phone that normally hung on the kitchen wall had recently vanished, my father's presumed project for the weekend.

Magda retreated to her bedroom for a nap and liquid fortification. She had shown up three sheets to the wind and full of fire for a visit from the Ridders before, tired of defending our business to the family that had seemed so innocuous when she pushed Jacob Ridder on my mother all those years ago. Their spats were entertaining to me and Mary and, secretly, to our father too. He could never say so in front of his parents, though. My mother kept her head down, more than usual, during those meals.

Mary and I sat around the fire pit on the side of the house. We had a good view of the lake, which was starting to churn with crests of white on choppy waters. I felt Mom's eyes on us through a window in the side door, watching as we were blown to bits by the wind, worrying we would no longer be presentable to the in-laws. Mary's braided crown barely moved, but my own braids were whipped loose into a fine tangled mess.

I glanced at Mary, deep in her own little world, a dreamy smile between deep dimples.

"Anything you want to tell me?" I asked, wincing at my false-casual tone.

She straightened up and shrugged as if to say, *Of course you would ask.*

"No," Mary said firmly, but her smile held firmly in place. "Tim is just a friend."

"Sure, a friend." I rolled my eyes. If she wasn't ready to tell me, I wasn't going to press.

The first raindrops fell then. With an undignified squeal, Mary and I sprinted to the kitchen door as the sky split open and the rain—much needed in what had been a dry spring—came down hard and fast.

Inside, the air in our old house was damp with rain already. I could feel the wooden joists swelling around us, and out of a deeply ingrained habit, I whispered a fortifying charm under my breath. I pulsed my hands outward, and the house instantly stood straighter around us.

Mom glanced at the kitchen clock and sighed heavily as Mary and I took turns evaporating water and wet grass off each other by the door.

Mary said gently, "They're already halfway here." As if this sudden torrential rain might have been enough reason to cancel dinner.

Mom sighed and nodded.

Mary surprised me then. She closed her eyes and cast out the ice floe. Curious, I followed along through the ice floe past the edge of town. Mary found Grandpa Ridder's sensible Buick on the edge of Renville County and surrounded it carefully. *Gaume sia, gaume sia. Tuesch sia Parabli, Parabli gisch,* I felt her whisper through the frozen energy currents, clear as day. I did the same, adding my voice and energy to Mary's sunny yellow.

I opened my eyes and gave Mary a quizzical look.

"Just a feeling," she said, shrugging.

Mary stepped forward to put her arm around Mom's shoulders as Mom fussed over the potatoes. Mary sighed dreamily and leaned her head on top of Mom's head, a natural fit with their almost-six-inch height difference.

As Mom softened under Mary's embrace, my chest tightened with jealousy. *What is happening here?* It was suddenly impossible to breathe in the sweltering kitchen.

I retreated into the living room and collapsed on the stiff floral davenport. I tucked a brightly colored afghan around my legs and sat idly for a few mindless minutes. Mary followed me after a while. She nudged me with her knees to sitting and automatically began to loosen my braids, reworking them to make me proper for Grandma Ridder. I was too tired to fight her. I felt, once again, like the little sister and not the elder example that I was supposed to be.

But the rise and fall of the wind and the steady drum of the rain and the pervasive smells of blueberry cobbler and roast beef had a soothing effect. After a hypnotically calm hour, Mom appeared in the doorway to the living room. Without so much as a blink from our mother, Mary announced, "Mom wants us to set the table. And call Dad."

I rolled my eyes but stood to help. *Is everyone reading each other all over the place now?*

I knew I was being unfair. Mom was spent after her weekly chats with Father Kevin. It might take her two full days before she mustered the strength to speak again. Still, the secret language between Mom and Mary was unbearable.

The formal dining room on the north side of the house was mostly unused. As far from the kitchen as possible, it was ludicrously impractical for levitating the heavy Thanksgiving turkey to the table. Maybe that had been intentional when the house was built. The Watry women belonged in the beating heart of the house in the kitchen to the south, so the dining room was never intended for use anyway. Except on Christmas, Easter, and Thanksgiving and for dinners with Grandpa and Grandma Ridder.

We laid out silver and the good china, which had belonged to Great-Grandma Dorothy's mother Clara, and folded napkins. When Mom's pewter goblets were secured on the table, I asked Mary, "Should I call Dad, or do you want to?"

She gazed at me across the table with the same dreamy expression that had followed her since mass. "Oh, go ahead," Mary said.

I clucked and shook my head at the smitten teenager before me. I threw my energy like a lasso wide around the house, tightening it as I navigated the familiar topography of the backyard and the shed. Snaring Dad's orangey marigold energy, I tightened the loop and pulled him toward home. *Chunsch nooch Huus, nooch Huus chunsch*, I beckoned. *Ish cheldi dusse, chunsch.* I saw his light start to move toward the house at a quick pace as he jogged through the rain in his church clothes. Moments later, we heard Dad burst into the kitchen.

"Can you at least help me fill the water glasses?" I asked with more sting than intended, snapping Mary from her daydream.

She shot me a look with lips pursed into a practiced pout—*Fine*—and waved a hand over a goblet in front of her, her palm flipped up toward the ceiling over the bowl. Her fingers drew together and downward, pulling invisible purse strings over the lip of the goblet, pinching water from the air. There was an abundance of water to be had, as the storm hung heavy over the house, the wood and walls damp with it. As Mary pulled her fingers down five, six, seven times over the cup, cool, clear water slowly rose from the bottom to the brim of the goblet.

"Good," I said, wowed by her efficiency.

"I've been doing this for sixteen years too," Mary said plainly as she filled the goblets on her side of the table.

"I know," I said quickly, turning away to hide my face as I filled the goblets on my side of the table. Mary's skills needed some polishing, but I suddenly felt guilty that I had missed her recent improvements, that I had only noticed her skills when they were on public display at the beach.

If Mary is so skilled, why does she get to do what she wants all summer? I felt my cheeks burn as the question quickly supplanted any feeling of guilt. I turned my back and hustled from the room so Mary wouldn't see the tears spring to my eyes. *Why am I the only one without a choice in this family?*

I heard the sound of Grandpa Ridder's Buick in the driveway, saving me from my thoughts. I took a deep breath, rearranged my face, and straightened my dress. Mary followed me into the foyer, smoothing her hair and dress. Only a raised eyebrow from Mary indicated that I wasn't all that good at hiding my feelings. I wondered if I could shield myself further as we stood together to silently await Grandma Ridder's judgment.

We watched through the front windows as Grandpa Ridder got out of the driver's side and walked stiffly to open the passenger door for Grandma Ridder. I could barely see him through the thick sheets of rain, but feeling the need to show off, I parted the sky just a little, as if there were a protective dome, an invisible umbrella, over his head. Grandma Ridder glanced up nervously at the water parting over her head, but she made it to the front door completely dry, even if she wasn't all that happy about it.

Grandpa Ridder, a nearly six-foot-three Dutchman, bent awkwardly to kiss me on the cheek.

"Elisabeth," he said, pronouncing the hard *t* like my father and Magda did.

I heard Dad mutter over my shoulder, "Sure, you keep them dry, but not one of you could have done that for me?" I flashed him a grin, catching the twinkle in his eye. He wasn't really mad. Dad liked to tell us there was already enough magic in the house—literally holding the place upright—but he complained when there wasn't enough magic either. I rolled my eyes and turned back for my judgment.

"Hi, Grandma Ridder," I said as she embraced me lightly, her hands like crayfish on my back.

"Elisabeth," she said with a downward glance that told me she had indeed noticed my lack of stockings in mid-June. In spite of myself, I felt my face flush with shame. Grandma Ridder had a special way of doing that.

Grandpa Ridder bent with a kiss on the cheek for Mary and Mom and a firm handshake and shoulder clap for my father, who stood almost as tall as his beanpole of a father. Grandma Ridder, meanwhile, continued her tour of disapproval. Magda was noticeably absent.

After Mary took Grandma Ridder's handbag, Mom announced in a forced, halting voice, before we could make our way to the living room, "Dinner's ready." *Get them in and get them out,* I read on her face quite plainly. I smiled, and Mary and I followed her to the kitchen to help serve.

I carried the roast beef on a bed of carrots on Mom's good silver serving platter, usually reserved for Thanksgiving turkey and Easter ham. Mom followed with mashed potatoes and spinach salad with warm bacon dressing—Grandpa Ridder's favorite. Mary carried fresh butter and more silver-dollar rolls enveloped in a warm linen napkin in Great-Grandma Dorothy's silver bread basket. I knew the inscription on the bottom by heart—*Für Brot und Glück*—for bread and happiness, or love, or luck, depending on whose translation you believed.

When I realized Magda hadn't shown herself, I slipped away during the hectic settling into chairs and filling of plates. I found her lying on her bed with a lavender pillow over her eyes, fully dressed in her good green church dress, shoes, stockings, and all. A shiver ran up my spine. Her hands were folded serenely over her chest, and it made me deeply uncomfortable.

I reached out a tentative hand to shake her. Her arm was warm and solid as ever, I realized with relief. Magda rumbled slowly awake, then stretched all at once, raising her arms above her head and making the screeching yawn shared by all the women in our family. She whipped the lavender pillow off with one hand and rolled her eyes at me in an exaggerated way that immediately recalled where I had picked up that particular habit.

"Let's get this over with," she said.

I smelled whiskey on her breath and was jealous.

*　*　*

Grandpa Ridder led grace, our full plates growing cold under bowed heads.

"Mm, doesn't this look good," Dad said from the head of the table when everyone had crossed themselves. "What a treat for a stormy day." He loaded his fork with gusto.

Mom beamed around the table with a smile that faltered only slightly at Grandpa and Grandma Ridder. On the other side, Mary tried to make small talk with Grandma Ridder about lifeguarding.

I heard Grandma Ridder ask, "Are you planning to run around in a bathing suit in front of the whole town, then?"

Mary's face blanched. "I saved someone yesterday," she muttered into her potatoes, then fell silent and sulky.

After a few minutes of all of us chewing in near silence, the only sound in the room the rain pounding down on the house, Grandpa Ridder leaned in with purpose from the other head of the table.

He turned to me and said, "Elisabeth, we wanted to come by today to congratulate you in person on your high school graduation. Well done." He parted his lips in what might have been a smile. "Now that you've finished, you might come work in the front office of the mills. If not here with your father, with one of your uncles, Joseph or Daniel."

Oh hell no, I thought.

Dad's face went beet red at the other end of the table. "Pop, that's enough. I told you she wasn't going to come work as an office girl," he said before I had the chance.

Magda, on the other side of Mom, chuckled to herself.

"What's so funny?" Grandma Ridder snapped. Mary shrank next to her. "What's so funny about the idea of Elisabeth having a normal job like a normal girl until she marries her sweetheart like everybody else?" She practically spat the word. *Normal*.

That I certainly was not.

Magda viciously jabbed a long, slim finger in Grandma Ridder's direction. "I know it's hard for you to understand, but this girl has a gift. There is nothing normal about it. She is extraordinary, and she's right where she needs to be, so you can shove your office job."

I can speak for myself, I thought, even as I couldn't get a word in edgewise.

Magda shoved her chair back from the table and stood in a huff.

Grandpa Ridder stood too, carefully, as if to not waste any energy.

"Now then," he said in his formal Dutch way, "I think we should all take some breaths and consider what is best for Elisabeth."

Magda let out a pointed "Ha!" and then everyone was on their feet, except me and Mary, who was quietly observing this all with a mix of wonder and horror, mouth agape.

As my father began to raise his voice, Magda cackled with abandon, Grandma Ridder's voice rose to a shrill above the din, and my mother sighed beside me, managing a quiet "Oh for Pete's sake" under her breath, I found my feet. To Mary's obvious delight, I slowly levitated the contents of the table, another favorite party trick with little practical application, until forks laden with pot roast and Mom's heavy pewter water goblets danced at eye level. I held everything just so until the room was completely silent, save for Magda's hiss: "Elisabeth Ann Watry-Ridder, so help me if you break my grandmother's china!"

"I think I am the best person to decide what is best for Elisabeth," I said, speaking in a clear voice, quietly so that everyone had to lean in a little to hear me. "My place is here."

I said the words confidently, but I didn't know if they were true. I knew my place certainly wasn't at the Ridder Family Company offices, twiddling my thumbs until I married John. I didn't know exactly what I wanted, but an office job wasn't it.

With a wink to Mary, I gently rested everything back into place. Grandpa Ridder's mouth hung open. My father looked prouder than I had ever seen him, a familiar twinkle in his eye.

Magda dropped heavily into her chair. "There," she said. "It's settled." She picked up her knife to cut a bite of roast beef, laboring to saw through the gristle.

Grandpa Ridder remained standing, unsure of himself, debating whether to speak again. Finally, he pinched his lips into a straight line until they nearly disappeared altogether. But my magical display was too much for Grandma Ridder—she fainted, missing her chair entirely. Grandpa Ridder made an ineffective attempt to catch her, barely snagging her wrist to soften her fall as she went down.

"Oh!" Mary exclaimed. Her eyes caught mine across the table. *Something's wrong with Grandma Ridder*, they telegraphed.

"Mother!" Dad shouted from his end of the table. He made a move to go to her but stopped and looked to me. "Lisbett?"

I closed my eyes and cast out, feeling simultaneously Mary's sunny yellow energy and Magda's amethyst—her interest piqued. But they were waiting for me: the Watry-Ridder girl, the special one who would inherit the empire, called to action at her own supper table.

I heard Mary say aloud, "Oh my," as we both realized the problem. Grandma Ridder's blood pressure was so low, her heart so weak, I could barely believe she had been standing at all a moment before.

Panic rattled in my chest. I took a deep breath to clear my field. I had very rarely treated people I knew so intimately, let alone an actual family member. The pressure nearly swallowed me whole. *Breathe*, Magda pulsed at me.

"I know!" I snapped.

But then my training kicked in: I took another deep breath, cast out the ice floe, and sent my energy through Grandma Ridder's. I was relieved when instinct took over from there.

I tapped rhythmically on everything in my path—*one-two, one-two. Tub-thump, tub-thump.* I pulsed the sound of a healthy heartbeat throughout her very small, very still pale-green energy field. *Folge mir, mir folge,* I urged, the words coming to me from God knows where. I felt her heart give a weak attempt to pick up the pace. It sputtered for a moment but slipped into its old tempo after a few beats. Grandma Ridder's heart wouldn't be able to take many more surprises.

Knowing there was nothing else I could do, I wrapped my energy around Grandma Ridder's and whispered the words of protection. *Bisch wiff. Bisch wusle. Bisch gliebt.* I felt Mary and Magda following behind to do the same, wrapping Grandma Ridder in layers of protection. *You are safe. You are whole. You are loved.*

I urged her, *Wachst auf. Come back to us. Wake up, stay a while.*

I opened my eyes and waited. A moment later, Grandma Ridder opened hers from the dining room floor. She blinked hard and shook her head. Mary crouched beside Grandma Ridder and helped her slowly back into her chair.

Grandpa Ridder at her elbow pushed a goblet of water toward her. "Take a sip of water," he said.

"I feel . . . wonderful," she said, with a pointed look at Grandpa Ridder. She turned to scan the table slowly in wonder. Her eyes landed on me. "You. You did this, didn't you?" Grandma Ridder asked.

I didn't know what to say. Was it an accusation or an accolade? I sucked in my cheeks with an upward flick of my eyes that said, *Guilty as charged.*

"Well," she said. "Well, then." Her cheeks flushed, but she looked as pleased as I had ever seen her.

Magic did this, I wanted to tell her, but I didn't think she could take it.

We finished the meal in near silence, typical for passive-aggressive Dutch families after a blowout-knockdown-drag-'em-out fight, only the sound of rain above the tinkle of silverware on china.

As Mary cleared the plates to the kitchen—by hand—Grandpa Ridder reached into the breast pocket of his brown gabardine blazer. He produced an envelope and presented it to me with a sigh. The envelope said *Happy graduation*.

"We hoped this would be used for a new wardrobe for the front office," he said.

"Thank you," I said firmly, biting my tongue. Even after a firsthand show of my capabilities, he had to make one more dig at me. I didn't have the energy to state my case further and simply pressed the envelope into my lap.

"That's enough, Pop," Dad said from the other end of the table.

And no one said any more on it, the conversation turning blandly to the weather and the much-needed rain over coffee and cobbler. But after Grandpa and Grandma Ridder departed under still-dreary skies, Mary hugged me tighter than ever before.

"That was incredible," she whispered.

*   *   *

Something nagged at me later that night as I waited for sleep. *Mary's protection spell wasn't bad*, I thought. In fact, it had been pretty good. Thoughtful. Skilled, even, to cast over such a distance. When Mary said she had a feeling, had she known something was up with Grandma Ridder even before they arrived? Could Mary sense something I couldn't?

A quiet resentment started to take hold in me: *Why, if Mary is so perfectly capable, is this my sole destiny? Why is Magda excluding her? And what in the world happened that Mom didn't want this?*

Twelve

When I was a little girl, I was tormented by terrible nightmares, always the same: hands ripped me from my mother's arms and carried me away, a flash of bright light, then darkness. I was lost in impenetrable darkness, like being at the bottom of a well, but I couldn't see the sliver of light from above or find the sides to pull myself out. I was lost and alone.

I barely slept in early grade school. It certainly didn't help my short fuse with the other kids. I probably wouldn't have slept for years if Magda hadn't stepped in when I was seven.

I woke up sobbing one night, sweating in a web of tangled bedsheets. Mary, five years old, sat up in her bed beside me. She regarded me in the glow of the night-light that did little to keep the terrors away.

Rubbing sleep from her eyes, Mary tried to comfort me in her still-baby voice. "It's okay, Lisbett. It was just a dream."

I sat shivering in my own bed, gulping for air, trying to shake off the remnants of the dream world. Those hands snatching at me. A voice in my ear that I couldn't quite make out.

At the time, this was a nearly nightly occurrence. Mary, immune to the drama, snuggled under her covers and drifted back to sleep. I lay awake, staring at the ceiling, until the first light of morning through the curtains brought me back to awareness. I was so groggy it was hard to tell if I had slept at all.

Our bedroom door opened a crack. Magda's voice cut through the darkness. "Lisbett, come."

Too tired to object, I got out of bed and followed Magda. She led me in my pajamas straight into the waiting station wagon, and we drove the nearly three hours to Minneapolis to see Magda's friend, the Ojibwe healer Peter Omiimii, to whom I would forever be indebted.

Because of my sleep-deprived state, that visit was always hazy in my mind. We returned that evening with a beautiful dreamcatcher that would always hang above my bed after that, its powerful magic an extra safeguard against the nightmares that had haunted me.

*   *   *

But that night, after the visit with Grandpa and Grandma Ridder, I was revisited by my old nightmare for the first time in many years, the long-forgotten details coming back to me in startling clarity.

Unseen hands snatched me backward.

My mother was there, reaching for me, as I was torn away from her.

I kicked my legs in the air, flailing wildly for purchase.

The night was dark and heavy; the thick shroud of the paranormal around me obscured my sight.

I was alone at the bottom of that deep well.

I couldn't see the top, the hands gone, nothing but darkness.

A voice, familiar but far enough away that I couldn't make out the words, whispered into dread-choked air.

A flash of light blinded me, and the words hung overhead and all around and rained down over me.

The voice, the words, were so close but so far over my head as I reached, reached, reached for those unfamiliar hands, grasping for anything to pull me out of the darkness.

Where was my mother?

Take her, then. She's yours.

My mother's voice, small and resigned, receded into the darkness.

* * *

I jolted awake, burning hot all over. I had kicked all the covers off, and I shivered as the night air chilled the sweat on my back and arms. I thought my gasping for breath would've been loud enough to raise the dead, but when I glanced over, Mary slept on peacefully beside me.

It was nearly three AM. *The witching hour*, I thought, panic rising in my chest.

Adrenaline coursed through my veins. I had never remembered that last part. *Was Mom there when I had the dream before?* It was definitely my mother's voice, but not as I knew her. *Did she always say that?* I couldn't remember, but somehow it felt right. It fit.

I lay perfectly still, afraid to move. The feeling of those hands snatching me up, carrying me away, was fresh on my skin.

Was it real? I wondered for the first time since I was a little girl.

My heart pounded in my chest. I focused on the rise and fall of my breath, and minutes passed into hours as I stared at the ceiling. When I closed my eyes, that voice, those hands, haunted me.

In that delirious place between sleep and wake, another voice called to me. I awoke suddenly, not aware that I had been sleeping, with the words of protection in my ear.

Bisch wiff. Bisch wusle. Bisch gliebt.

I blinked hard to let my eyes adjust to the predawn light filtering in through our cotton curtains. The words came through again. But who spoke them? I heard them as if from far away.

Bisch wiff. Bisch wusle. Bisch gliebt.

It was a woman's voice with the elegant gravel of Magda's, but it wasn't familiar to me, just a voice calling to me from the dream world. But I knew better than to think it was just a dream.

Thirteen

I slept fitfully late into the morning and woke with my dream-mother's voice in my head. *Take her, then. She's yours.*

I returned after greeting the lake and was pleasantly surprised to find the house empty. It was a bridge day for Magda in town. She liked to get gossip straight from the source, untainted by the filter of Mildred. I sighed at the thought of Cousin Mildred. I had no clue where my mother might be but figured that if she was shopping or had been called away, she'd be gone long enough. It seemed like the perfect day to uncover some truths about my mother, and hopefully Magda, for myself.

Alone, I ditched decorum, poured myself a cup of coffee, and pushed open the door to Magda's room in my damp swimsuit. I had two hours until Magda would be home, and I had no idea what I was looking for. On a whim, I opened the door to Magda's closet and stared at her clothes, all hanging neatly pressed in order from dark to light colors. My fingers trailed across each fabric until something sparked my interest, and I removed a black silk robe embellished with thousands of tiny iridescent black beads in geometric flower patterns, flowers with four equal quadrants, the four elements, four cardinal directions. It was a pattern I had seen many times, a symbol of the earth and the building blocks of life itself.

I slipped the robe over my bare shoulders, and the hem grazed my ankles. It felt cool as a breeze and warm as a hug at the same time, like sunbathing naked. *Perfect for digging up family secrets.*

I knelt on the concentric circles of Magda's hooked rug in front of the cedar chest and unlatched the surprisingly well-oiled hinges. I extracted, one by one, Magda's overstuffed grimoires, full of inserted leaves and handwritten notes scribbled in the margins or stuck in the bindings. I breezed quickly through the ones I knew well—charms, energy charts, and the like. I had practically memorized some of those pages as a child as soon as I learned to read the Alemannic-English pidgin of my grandmothers. I was looking for something older. Something that would tell me why my family was the way we were, the real reason why my mother had refused the responsibility, why my future had been chosen for me.

I laid the books and crumbling pages in neat rows on Magda's rug and the next layer of dusty artifacts on the bed, ignoring the thick grease and grime that streaked the pristine quilt. Becoming frantic as the seconds ticked on, I flipped through the pages of a crusty old book with a strange corklike cover that I had never seen before. The book fell open to a drawing of a tree sketched by hand across two pages. The tiny leaves swept to the topmost corners, where the pages had disintegrated over time. I sighed as I realized it was an illustration of the various uses of beech trees and not the family tree that I hoped for.

Soon the cedar chest was nearly empty, its contents covering every available flat surface in Magda's room. Despite its size, large enough to hold me and Mary folded together as teenagers—not that we had ever tried—that old chest contained more in its depths than I had ever imagined. In my desperation, I cast out the ice floe to feel for a spark, anything that could guide me. The magical paraphernalia snaking across the floor shuddered, then rested uselessly in their places.

I was about to give up, the clock ticking toward noon, when Magda would return. But then I saw it—a faint glow of energy around the edge of the cedar chest itself, an illuminated trail of handprints, a ghost of magic. *Chunsch use*, I urged. The wood of the cedar chest itself glowed with a light from within its very fibers. I pushed further, with more hurt and desperation than I realized had been brewing in me since Cousin Mildred's visit. *If I'm on the hook for this family, show me why. Use, chunsch.* The chest hummed, as if it could levitate itself on the wings of pure energy. Then . . . it did. It began to rise.

In that instant, an eerily familiar flash of white light came from my own beating heart. That same glow around the cedar chest lit me from head to toe, until I too was consumed by light, made of light. Magda's room disappeared around me. There was nothing but blinding white light, so hot it glowed red at the center, like looking at the sun through your eyelids. My heart raced at first, that familiar dread from my old nightmare thrumming beneath the light. But as I began to glow myself, my heart pulsing in time with the cedar chest, I became unafraid. It felt as natural to me as breathing, even as I didn't understand it.

What the heck, came my own fuzzy thoughts from somewhere beneath the white light.

I had a vision suddenly of Magda standing over me as I lay in the bottom of the cedar chest as a child. I was so, so small, and scared. It was so dark and Magda's face was barely visible, like she was looking down at me from a great height. The smell of cedar was overpowering. I felt the rough, unsanded wood of the bottom of the chest and was curious about the feeling on my skin. Magda's hands, the hands from my nightmare, I realized, reached for me—but were they scooping me up or dropping me further into darkness?

My heart burned brighter, and I knew then that my nightmares were actually memories.

Bisch wiff. Bisch wusle. Bisch gliebt.

I heard the words of protection again, clear as day, as if someone were standing right next to me. The voice sounded familiar, but I couldn't place it.

Enough, I whispered to the cedar chest and the room and myself and Magda too. Through the blanket of light, I shoved my hands forward through the air, pushing it all away. The light dissipated, drawn back into the wooden fiber of the cedar chest. The dusty old books and yellowed papers sat tamely in their places on Magda's carpet and quilt and dresser. The room was hopelessly dim after the brilliance of the white light.

My mother's voice over my shoulder scared the breath out of me.

"Don't," she said. "You won't like what you find."

I whipped around, crackling with adrenaline. My eyes searched hers for answers. *But it wasn't Mom that said the protection spell . . .*

"What was that?" I asked her. My mind raced from Mildred— *you were right to choose this one*—to the sensation of my heart beating with the light from the cedar chest. Made of that light. Born of that light. *How? Why did Magda's hands rip me from my mother? Why did my heart beat with the cedar chest?*

"What did Magda . . . ," I wondered aloud. *What did you do to me?* I couldn't bring myself to say.

My mother cast her eyes around the room as if searching for the answer herself. Her eyes found the floor, her head hanging at an unnatural angle. Her avoidance, her silence, filled me with fire. *Speak up!* I yelled at her silently. *Why can't you be like a normal mother when I need you? What was so bad that it took your voice away?*

I stared, waiting for her to say something real, something that would explain why we were the way we were, why I was the way I was, why she'd let Magda take away any choice I could've had in determining my own future.

But she said nothing and turned away, one hand reaching for the wall to support her, as if she couldn't stand on her own two feet anymore from the sheer effort of that one sentence. I heard her slowly climb the front stairs, cross the landing, and haul herself up to the attic bedroom.

I was shaking with frustration, filled with sadness and a burning disappointment in my mother. I felt like I was going to explode if I didn't get some answers, and every answer seemed to unearth another question.

I gave a sloppy wave of my hand to direct everything back into place, a conductor of flying books. A second wave cleared the dust and grease smudges from Magda's quilt and rug. I snapped the hinges of the cedar chest shut with a satisfying *click-click*, sighed, and closed the door.

Fourteen

I sat quietly at the dinner table, still tingling from the startling white light of the cedar chest. It had felt so natural to me—*why?* Dad rambled on about the record low water levels and the "damn county dam regulations, even after Sunday's rain." I usually liked exchanging town gossip with him; sometimes I'd have a tidbit that he hadn't heard at the mill yet from our clients. But that night I felt like I was floating above myself watching the whole scene. I pushed mushrooms around my plate in their stroganoff cream and kept my mouth shut—even though I had seen the county regulator from St. Agnes himself just days prior.

Magda, on the other hand, was unrestrained. She loved to complain about the dam and milfoil with the best of the old-timers, and that night she was on the blitz. It was as if she were filling every possible silence lest I dare ask her anything in front of the family.

"Can you believe those idiots up at Medayto won't open the lock today? We're going to dry up down here," she said, waving her fork for emphasis.

"And George Klaperich isn't doing a dad-gum thing," Dad added.

"He hasn't been up to Medayto himself in weeks. What's the point of a regulator who doesn't regulate?" Magda said.

She was putting on the show for me. I did my best to tune her out and ate in silence, feeling the sting of tears threatening to fall if I opened my mouth.

When the plates were cleared, the remnants of my mushroom cream handed over to the cats—*waste not, want not*—Magda disappeared immediately into her room. I wondered if it was as obvious to everyone else that she was avoiding me.

I wasn't sure I was ready to hear what Magda had to say as Mom's warning rang in my ears—*you won't like what you find*. But I knew I couldn't leave it alone for another day. Lucky for me, Mom had made a rhubarb pie that afternoon—Magda's favorite. I cut two generous slices, doused both with fresh cream—presumably from Mr. Dellson's farm, where Mom must have been that morning—and carefully levitated everything to Magda's room.

I didn't knock on Magda's door but pushed it open with my hip, kicking my energy ahead of me to announce my visit, like how Dad had taught us to shuffle our feet through brush in the woods to scare away snakes and other undesirables. Magda was lying on top of the covers with one hand draped over her eyes. A frisson of déjà vu ran through me. The curtains were drawn, but the bright summer evening peeked around the edges, lighting the room dimly.

I set my hopeful offering on the bedside table next to Magda, then crawled in next to her. It almost felt cozy despite the tension.

"Rhubarb," I said.

"You were in my room today, Elisabeth," she said, pushing herself up.

Should've known she wouldn't accept a bribe.

Deep down, I had known she would know. Maybe I had wanted to get caught to force the conversation we had been avoiding for days.

We ate our pie in silence. But when the sweet, vegetal filling hit the rich stroganoff in my stomach, I felt suddenly ill and set my plate aside. The sound of Magda chewing and swallowing was deafening.

"I feel about a thousand years old," she said suddenly, setting her fork down.

I felt her energy shifting. Sheer exhaustion radiated from Magda, and I felt her guard dropping. The wall between us began to fall away, and my brewing anger was replaced with pity. My indomitable grandmother was an old woman, choosing to show me her vulnerability for some reason.

It was now or never.

Magda closed her eyes, sitting ramrod straight against the headboard, ankles crossed beneath her chiffon skirt. I thought of the black silk robe hastily shoved back on a hanger in her closet.

"Why didn't Mom want to do this?" I asked.

Magda blinked measuredly. "Why were you in my room today?" she asked, matching my tone.

Oh no. She's not going to tell me, I feared.

Magda stared straight ahead, avoiding eye contact. We sat staring into the space above the cedar chest at the foot of Magda's bed, until—miracle of miracles—she started talking.

"Lisbett," she said, pausing. "All the Watry women, from me and your Great-Grandma Dorothy to all of our grandmothers before us, have been sworn to protect our abilities. Our magic. The ice floe energy. My mother Dorothy passed the safekeeping of the cedar chest to me, along with its secrets, the words, the charms within. There has to be a guardian of the cedar chest, and in return, the guardian is gifted with all the secrets of the grandmothers. Someone many generations ago cast the first bonding spell over the cedar tree the chest was carved from, so it became part of the chest itself. That is how our grandmothers made sure their legacy will survive."

She glanced at me, gauging my understanding. I remembered that faint glow around the edges of the cedar chest. I innately knew it was powerful magic. I felt it flowing within me.

"What do you mean the guardian is gifted?" I asked when I found my voice.

Magda sighed. "Whoever is bonded to the cedar chest receives all the knowledge, all the spells, that came before."

I nodded, half numb, and Magda continued.

"So while we spend hours copying the notes for our daughters like your mother to memorize, the guardian doesn't need those. She knows the words, the charms, already in her heart and in her fingers from the moment she is bonded to the chest. The grimoires are there to help us, to teach our daughters, but our clever grandmothers ensured that our secrets will never be lost."

I thought of all the times I had seen Magda whisper words out of nowhere, pulling a spell out of thin air. And I remembered all the times the words had materialized for me brand new, like when I was a little girl attempting plagues of frogs, and the way the words didn't come to Mary like that even as she was growing in her abilities. I knew that my mother certainly didn't do that. She followed the rules and read the recipes and cast her rare, albeit adequate, charms to the letter of the book.

"Tell me why I can do it and Mom can't," I said.

"All magic comes with a price, my darling. You know that," Magda said simply, watching for my reaction. "I had to protect our legacy. When Helene made her choice, when she wasn't willing to sacrifice for this family, I had to make a choice too. I had to make sure the cedar chest would have a guardian."

"What did you do?" I whispered, already knowing the answer. I felt the ghost of Magda's hands dropping me into the darkness of the cedar chest.

Magda sighed and looked away. "Even the purest of magic requires sacrifice. When a guardian is bonded to the cedar chest, it requires the whole heart."

Magda sat up a little straighter against the headboard, as if to bolster her self-righteousness. "I was born into this life, like my mother before her and hers before her. It is our birthright and our burden, one we all inherit."

Not Mary, I thought. *Not Mom.*

"When Helene defied me and our grandmothers, I knew then that she would never be the guardian. And she had to face the consequences. I had to do what was best for this family."

Two versions of my grandmother were emerging—the Magda I knew, the strict but loving teacher I had admired and emulated my entire life, and this new version who had punished my poor, silent mother for whatever she had done that was so terrible. The two versions of Magda fought in my mind, like a staticky, double television image refusing to come together. There was so much that Magda wasn't telling me, so much she had kept from me. I had known I belonged to Magda, but my mother's voice haunted me: *Take her.*

I struggled to keep my face neutral.

"What did you do?" I asked again, my voice stony. I felt surprisingly calm.

"I was beginning to worry that after countless generations," Magda said, "I would be the end of the guardians, with no daughter responsible enough to inherit its secrets. But then you showed up in a burst of brilliant green energy under a moonless sky on the darkest day of the year. You started levitating so early, and when I looked into your little heart and saw your enormous energy, I knew. I knew you would be the one. And by the time Mary came along, you were ready."

She openly winced at Mary's name. I didn't know what to make of it. My trust in Magda was quickly waning.

"I started the binding process the night of the autumnal equinox, an auspicious day. I needed to ensure that the fiasco of what I went through with Helene never happened again. It was my sworn duty to the grandmothers. I bound half of your heart to the cedar chest that night, alongside my own. The other half has been yours to grow and nourish—until now. Until the binding spell is complete, which we will do on the equinox this autumn. It's time for me to retire and for you to be bonded to our magic for good, to ensure our abilities are always protected, forever."

Everything that I thought made me special, that made what I did worth it, was a lie. It wasn't innate talent coursing through me but words unearned from a stupid magic box.

"You gave my heart away," I said quietly. "And now you're taking the rest."

All magic requires a sacrifice. Mine would cost me my heart, my chance at true love, and my freedom—and it wasn't my choice to make.

"Why can't Mary—"

Magda held a finger up to stop me. "We have already talked about this. Your sister is like your mother. She doesn't have the gifts that you have. And when the magic is so divided, we are at risk. We are exposed, vulnerable to dividing it so far as to peter out."

"But—" I tried.

"No," Magda snapped. "This is just for you and you alone, like I carried this alone for the thirty years before you came along."

I felt defeated. There was no use in arguing with Magda. The cold realization dawned on me, though it didn't shock me an ounce: Magda, who had been making decisions for me my entire life, had already given away half my heart and planned to chain me irreversibly to the cedar chest and its secrets, all when I was too young to have a say for myself. And my mother hadn't stopped her. Magda had just confirmed what the nightmares had already told me—but I hadn't realized it was Magda's own hands that had put me there.

I had always felt like I didn't love John as much as he loved me—and there it was: I *couldn't* love John. I couldn't love anyone. My heart was not my own to give. My heart, my life, my future—all belonged to Magda. As much as I teased Annie about getting stuck in Friedrich, I was even more trapped than she was. Magda had made sure of that.

I was halfway out of the room before I registered what I was doing. Since I had no choice in the matter, or anything in my life apparently, there was no point in talking about it further.

"One day, you'll see," Magda called after me, her voice rising. "This was the only way!"

I shot straight up the front stairs, avoiding Mom and Dad and Mary watching TV in the living room, feeling like I was floating in a cold fog. I looked down at my feet—*are they even mine? Or do they belong to Magda too?*

Fifteen

As soon as I heard Mary's breathing fall into the light, even tempo of sleep, I opened the window and climbed fully dressed down the crabapple tree.

I had been doing it for years. Around age six, Magda had sent me to my room for talking back. I had said a rudimentary protection spell, heaved my stubby leg over the windowsill, and shimmied down. Magda was livid when she saw me waving insolently through her first-floor bedroom window.

By junior high, Annie and I were always sneaking out after dark, one of my small rebellions against Magda and her decorum. Annie's mom, usually soaked in gin, was less observant. Annie walked right out the front door at any time of day or night. Once, we found a door open to a construction site and explored every inch of what would become a new shopping center on the edge of town, with its wall frames exposed and nails everywhere. Otherwise, we biked to the Springs in the middle of the night and spied on the necking teenagers, until soon enough we became those teenagers.

I loved the thrill of sneaking out, so much that I had long ditched the protection spells. Each time my breath caught in my chest as the tree decided if it would hold me. Every branch was a surprise, dipping precipitously under my weight or rising to meet me when I felt on the verge of crashing to the ground—which I did eventually, landing flat on my back. I would say that luckily, nothing was broken, but luck had nothing to do with it. I threw out a hand at the last second and levitated myself enough to take the real momentum out of my fall. But levitation was mostly for books and small objects, not teenage girls, and I wasn't able to stop my fall entirely.

At eighteen, I swung down by the thicker branches closer to the trunk. My heart pounded in a way that thrilled me—*you are alive*—when my feet hit the ground.

That night it took me over an hour to bike the nearly ten miles to the Weseloh farm west of town. I needed the physical release to tamp down the words inside me before I said the wrong thing to my sister, or worse, my grandmother. I needed a distraction. I would've never admitted it to myself, but I needed a specific kind of distraction to wipe my mind of the horror of what Magda intended for me.

The wind whipped my hair into my face, and I was cold despite the residual heat of the summer night. There were few cars heading west at that time, and I was glad, because in the high visibility of the waning gibbous moon, I would've been immediately recognizable: *There goes that Watry-Ridder girl running around after curfew with her hair all undone, looking witchy as ever.*

In that slippery silver moonlight, I stood under John's window, my chest heaving from the exertion, sweat streaming down my face and slicking my hair to my neck. With my mother's coloring, I knew I would look a mess: my cheeks and chest flushed a hot red, tinged purply pink at the center, like the special tomatoes John's father grew. I cast out my energy to lasso John's energy where he lay blissfully asleep—early to bed, early to rise and all that. I paused to brush my energy against Lucy's where she lay next to his bed. *Don't bark, girl,* I whispered to her as my energy slipped past. *It's me.*

I wrapped my energy around John's and nudged him awake. I summoned him silently: *Wachst auf, wachst auf. Your lady awaits.*

Moments later, John yawned in the window. When he saw me in the yard below, his face cracked into a wide grin that made my heart flutter. He held up his peace fingers. *Two minutes,* he mouthed.

"I hate when you do that," John whispered when he was safely through the kitchen and out the back door. But like the few times I had shown up unexpectedly before, John didn't turn me away or say anything more.

"I know," I whispered against his lips.

I motioned to where the El Camino was parked around the side of the house. In the moonlight, John rolled his eyes at my haste.

"I got this," I whispered.

I mouthed the words to a simple protection spell—*Chunsch Stilli wie hnai. Stilli, chunsch*—and with a circular sweep of my hand, I cast out a small energy field around us and the truck, thickly blanketing us in slow, heavy air. The buzzing insects and whisper of swaying cornstalks disappeared, as if my ears were stuffed with cotton; John raised a hand to his ear involuntarily, even though it wasn't the first time he had experienced it. He sighed and picked up my discarded bike with both hands and rested it in the flatbed. John's measured movements told me he didn't quite believe the sound blanket was complete.

Once we were out of the driveway and on the open two-lane highway heading west toward nowhere, I let the charm fall all at once. My ears were suddenly filled with the sound of John's chuckle, deep and slow, over the rushing wind through the rolled-down windows.

"You're crazy," John half shouted over the wind.

Don't call me crazy, I thought instinctively. *But what else do you call a witch who bikes ten miles at ten* PM *and lures a young farmer from his bed?*

But I didn't say that. I smiled a tight smile, blinking hard, and reached for the radio. Anne Murray's brassy voice filled the air, making me smile. John didn't have much of his own taste in music, just listened to the latest releases of the mainstays from the Cities. I scanned for something fresher, despite a playful protestation from John.

I found the frequency and turned it up. A voice that defied definition, gravel and silk, filled the cab of the El Camino. When the last chords of guitar ripped through the air, a sleepy young man announced, "That was the Rolling Stones coming to you from way down here at the bottom of the dial, 89.1, the Loon. We've got Dylan and Hendrix coming your way next." He signed off with a decent approximation of a loon call as a harmonica started to whine.

I turned it down. "Wow," I said, a little stunned. "That was something else."

John looked at me sideways in the moonlight and smiled at me, a curiosity. I didn't need to read him to practically see him thinking, *Who is this girl in my front seat, who breathes rock music and wakes me up in the dark and has magic in her fingers? Who is this girl with the wild hair and wild heart, and how did I come to be in her orbit?*

But when John looked at me like that, I felt like I was going to drown and take him down with me. John had said he loved me. And I finally knew, after two years, why I felt like I didn't love him enough. I couldn't. My heart was not my own to give. But my body—that was still my choice, one of the few I could make for myself. I wanted to feel normal for one night—and stop thinking— just a girl and her high school sweetheart doing what everyone else was doing. Magda thought I had already done it, so why not? Magda had already made every choice in my life for me. For one night at least, I could choose for myself. I could choose what to do with my body.

I reached for John's hand. He pressed his callused palm over mine. When he kept driving, oblivious, I reached over and traced a finger from behind John's ear down to his collarbone.

"Pull over," I said over the music. Dylan again. So much Dylan.

* * *

Annie wanted to believe there was some storybook *Seventeen* magazine perfect romance between me and John, and I would never be able to tell her it was anything less. I had a reputation to uphold, and I knew I would never tell my best friend that my first time with John Weseloh was just sweaty and fast. That truth was reserved for Mary one day.

I lay on my back in the flatbed of the El Camino with the dirt and grime. John moved slowly at first as kissing led to more. When he asked, "You're sure?" I nodded. We frantically removed our clothing, awkwardly stopping to fight with zippers. The flatbed was warm from the heat of day, although the night air was chilly. John cushioned my head with our discarded clothing. I thought I was ready, but it hurt when he pushed into me. The sensation surprised me—full and tight, a sort of pinching.

As I found my mind wandering—*Do all boys sweat this much?*—John grunted away between my thighs and suddenly stopped.

Is that it? I thought, but doubted myself and my inexperience too much to say it out loud as John rolled to the side. *Is that all there is?* I asked my grandmothers silently.

*   *   *

Mary turned over in her sleep as I attempted to sneak in. Mickey jumped down from his place on Mary's pillow and swirled around my ankles, engine revving, before he turned his head and nipped my bare calf with his sharp little fangs.

"Ow!" I cried. "Get away!"

Mary stretched in her twin bed and said sleepily, "Why are you yelling at my cat?"

"Why did your demon cat bite me?"

"I can't tell you what my cat is thinking," she said, an old joke between us, since Mary was one of the few people on the earth who knew exactly what the cat was thinking.

I didn't answer her, and Mickey slid through the cracked door to his nighttime prowling. When she realized I didn't want to talk,

Mary turned over to go back to sleep. I kicked my jeans off and crawled between my cool sheets in my dirty T-shirt, the dust and sweat and John still on my body. I wasn't ready to wash it away yet, or to tell Mary. I needed a day to myself to process.

But as I waited for sleep to come, keenly aware of the unfamiliar ache between my legs, the thought found me again: *Is this all there is?*

Sixteen

That night, in the dead-to-the-world sleep of sheer exhaustion, Great-Grandma Dorothy came to me in a new dream.

*　*　*

Mary had said Great-Grandma Dorothy haunted the attic bedroom of our house. I had brushed it off as my pesky little sister showing off for attention, calling spirits on her own when Magda wouldn't include her. But for Mary to commune with Magda's mother Dorothy, whom Mary had never seen alive in her lifetime, that should've really been something, but Magda didn't have the time of day for Mary.

I was ten days old when Great-Grandma Dorothy died. That year also took Grandpa Earl. Mary came along about a year later. Before that, Great-Grandma Dorothy lived in the attic bedroom up the back stairs. Mom and Dad moved into the attic a few months after she was gone. When I was little, I pictured Great-Grandma Dorothy hanging upside down like a bat from the rafters when Magda spoke of her toiling over her grimoires up there. That room smelled like cedar dust, even after my mother covered the scent with lavender and sage. I associated that cedar smell with Great-Grandma

Dorothy, even though I wouldn't have known her scent in the few days we crossed paths on earth.

Mary said that Great-Grandma Dorothy hovered at the top of the stairs outside Mom and Dad's door. She stood just there, her hand pressed against the door like she was feeling for fire or life, like the door was anchoring her in place. She called Mary sometimes in the middle of the night, and obedient, sweet Mary would go to her. Mary said when she got too close, though, Great-Grandma Dorothy would fix her with a ghostly stare and disappear.

She only appeared to Mary and, to my surprise, to Annie once, the first time she slept over when we were ten. Annie asked me the next morning, "Who was that old lady outside your mom's room last night?" I never asked what Annie had been doing there, but I knew there was no way she had seen the framed cameo of Great-Grandma Dorothy on Magda's dresser. Dorothy appeared another time when Dad's cousin Glenda and her husband stayed with us once, visiting from Milwaukee on their way to a funeral in Grand Rapids. Glenda saw an old woman draped in black, bright-blue eyes staring, one hand poised on the door to the room of her grand-daughter Helene, waiting, waiting, waiting for someone to see her or to ask her what she was waiting for.

*   *   *

But that night, after my conversation with Magda and my excursion with John, I saw Great-Grandma Dorothy for myself. In my dream, I was seven years old again.

I hadn't yet learned to respect the barriers between the physical and spirit worlds.

I skimmed like a fish in a stream, slipping between the worlds brazenly, recklessly.

But suddenly I had gone too far.

The river turned white around me and flowed backward.

I was drowning in the infinite depths of the spirit world on the other side, where I—a living child—did not belong.

But there, on the horizon, through the rocking waves of white light, I saw a familiar glow of amethyst purple on the horizon—Magda.

Spirits rushed at me from all sides, hungry to tell a living soul their stories, threatening to overwhelm me.

The purple light blinked and was gone in the tangle of white light and souls returning to pure universal energy.

I tried to push upriver but was borne back by the current of energy.

Help me, grandmothers, my seven-year-old self and my eighteen-year-old-self whispered as one. *Help me.*

I smelled smoky rosewood oil suddenly, reminding me of Magda, and the white light began to part, a teensy, tiny bit at first, enough for my energy to inch back upstream toward the world of the living.

Magda's amethyst purple glowed brighter on the horizon again.

I came to the place where the spirit worlds flowed away from each other, the living energy lines stretching away in a rush of vibrant color that hurt my eyes—the crossing-over point between the living and the dead.

Suddenly, I felt myself borne forward on a warm, white light, carrying me toward the side of the living.

Here, mein Liebling, Great-Grandma Dorothy whispered.

Thank you, Grandmother. Protect me, Grandmother, I radiated back at her.

Always, she whispered. *I can't go with you there, but I'll be here to catch you.*

She pushed me through the whirlpool of white and rainbow flashes of light that burned bright before losing their color, until I could grasp the lip on the side of the living.

I reached toward Magda, a hand stretching toward me in the dark.

Not that way, Great-Grandma Dorothy whispered. *My daughter lost her way long ago.*

She pushed me forward then into the world of the living; brilliant color exploded all around me in life, life, life.

*   *   *

I awoke gasping with the memory of Great-Grandma Dorothy whispering the words of protection; they settled around me like Friedrich's thick blankets of winter snow. I was stunned, but somewhere underneath the adrenaline, I was relieved that it was a different dream waking me this time, relieved that it wasn't Magda's hands tearing me away.

As my breathing slowed, Great-Grandma Dorothy's voice fell from my mind, leaving me cold and bitter. *Thanks for the warning. But what the hell am I supposed to do now?*

There in the dark, when my brain quieted and I strained toward sleep, from the safety of my heavy quilt, hand-tied by one of Mom's talented cousins on Grandpa Earl's side, I knew what I had to do. Magda wanted me to be her perfectly docile Watry woman. No one had asked me what I wanted. I didn't know exactly, but I knew I was done having decisions made for me. I was going to have to be everything Magda feared I already was—reckless, loose, brash—to make my point.

Seventeen

Harry didn't have any openings at the supper club, but he gave Annie a job at the Sports Shop. After she made it only one squeamish day behind the bait counter scooping night crawlers into Styrofoam cups with her eyes closed, Annie had the bright idea to ask my dad for a job in the front office at the mill.

Seeing Annie twiddling her thumbs, filing invoices, and chatting with old men all day while she waited for her Prince Charming, I felt the walls closing in on me in Friedrich. I knew I didn't want what Annie chose—I felt she was settling, biding her time. That left me to be like Magda, the queen of a small domain, or I could be like my mother, a ghost. I didn't want any of it. At night I dreamed of Europe or New York or even Minneapolis, anywhere but Friedrich and what I was there.

In the busy June days leading up to Solstice, an idea started to take shape.

*   *   *

Friday was the summer solstice, an important day for our family, when *Fiir* and *Wasser* were more abundant than ever and the ice floe was recharged with that abundant, positive energy returning to our world from the other side. Our grandmothers had always known the power of that day, and it had been a key day in our service to the community since the Watrys first settled in Friedrich. It was our busiest day of the year, with a steady stream of clients asking for charms to augment their luck using the extra solstice energy—perfect conditions for changing just about anything in one's life.

That year we had been asked by the county farmers to do something about the drought threatening the area farms. At the end of the day, we would visit the inlet that brought the flow of freshwater into Clear Lake and see what we could do. The solstice was for the most powerful of our charms, the most difficult cases, the day we were most visibly of service to our neighbors. While we spent the year showing the town how respectable we were, Magda liked to remind them—especially the ladies who talked about us and the families that avoided us at church—how powerful we were, how dangerous we could be if we ever so chose. It reminded them that we were more than the innocuous healers on the north side of the lake.

I had long been afraid that Solstice the year I was eighteen would be the day that would bind me to the Watry-Ridder house forever. That fear became crushing after I learned Magda had already bound my heart and was coming for the other half. The family business—duties and privileges and all that went with it— was something I had been told to want, and I had wanted it, on some level, since I had first set that box turtle on Randy Hayes in first grade. But I could no longer ignore the question that haunted me: *What else is out there?*

*   *   *

The days running up to Solstice passed in an endless blur of water charms. Magda avoided me behind closed doors, and I was determined to avoid her too as I weighed my options. While I daydreamed about leaving it all behind, what I really wanted was to stand up to Magda, to show her that she couldn't control me. I started to wonder: What if I defied her publicly? What would she do then? Would she still want to bind my heart if I wasn't the sweet, obedient Watry girl she wanted me to be?

I saw little of Mary except during supper each evening. But when she crashed into her bed next to mine at night, I could feel she was changed since the incident at the beach. She had a new power, her abilities waking up all at once. I wanted to shout at Magda for not taking Mary's freedom too. I wanted to shout at her for giving my heart away. I wanted to shout at my mother for letting her.

I lay awake many nights listening to Mary's light, even breathing. Sometimes I wanted to wake her up and tell her everything about Magda, about the cedar chest, or about going all the way with John. Pride stopped me. I was supposed to be special, chosen—how could I complain to Mary, the passed-over little sister? I felt more alone in my burden than ever, alone in my own family.

In my sleep-deprived delirium, all thoughts of Magda and the cedar chest and our familial duty kept pointing me to Solstice. *I could leave*, I thought one night. *How awful would it look for the fearsome Magda Watry if I'm not there to do her bidding?*

A new but somehow familiar jolt of energy ran through me.

Yes, mein Liebling, a high, gravelly voice whispered in my ear.

Great-Grandma Dorothy? I thought. I felt her presence, an energy around me in the night. I couldn't see her but I felt her there, like a hand resting on my shoulder. After she had warned me in my dream, I knew in my gut it was her.

It wasn't always this way, Great-Grandma Dorothy whispered.

What do you mean? I asked her silently, starting to understand how we could communicate. Was this how Mary talked to her too?

She didn't answer, leaving me to mull it over for myself until morning. But I swore I felt the lightest pulse of energy every time I thought about ruining Solstice, about embarrassing Magda. *Is that what you want from me, Dorothy?* I asked the darkness.

*   *   *

At first, I didn't know exactly what I was going to do. But in those days leading up to Solstice, as I stewed in resentment and hurt, the desire crystallized: I kept picturing myself walking away from Friedrich, riding off into the horizon, leaving the town and my family and responsibilities in the dust. But it felt like a foolish fantasy. *How will Magda ever let me go?* I asked myself in despair. Our whole family's legacy hung on me. How could Magda ever let me walk away?

I wanted to defy Magda. I wanted to stand up to her, to make her look foolish, even. If I couldn't escape entirely, at least I could mess with her. When the house was quiet, I began to practice, thinking of ways to mess up Solstice. I practiced shielding myself, cutting myself off from the ice floe for seconds, then minutes, at a time. It was like holding my breath underwater, fighting the urge to shoot up and open my eyes. What would Magda do if I just disappeared during Solstice, the moment when she needed me most to show off for our neighbors?

I grew braver as my resentment swelled, practicing sound and visibility blankets in the corner of the room as I watched TV at night with my parents. If Dad had turned his head, he would've seen an empty armchair and thought I'd left the room when he wasn't looking.

Good, Dorothy whispered to me as I got stronger.

I didn't understand why Great-Grandma Dorothy was troubled enough to stir from her eternal rest and get involved, but it felt good to have her in my corner. Whatever Magda had done that Dorothy so disapproved of—*My daughter lost her way long ago*—I was grateful to have my great-grandmother's guidance from the other side. It reassured me that it wasn't all in my head. Magda had overstepped, and Dorothy knew it too.

*   *   *

John called or stopped by some nights, and we snuck off a few times to the cornfields for quick, sweaty encounters with the steering wheel digging into my back—better than the dusty flatbed, at least. But I found myself disappointed every time, waiting for it to be over, my mind slipping back to Solstice. It was easier to say that I was too tired after reading agitated housewives' energies all day, easier to watch TV with my parents instead. When John joined us, he sat in the armchair next to my father like he was already part of the household.

One night my mother gazed at John, then back at me. Her face changed, worry flashing across her face so quickly with the subtlest downward tug of her brow that I could have imagined it.

"What?" I asked her, too sharply, from my position on the floor near John's chair. I was nervous that my mother, or worse, my father, had somehow seen the change between us—that they knew we were fooling around, that they knew how disappointed and trapped I felt.

Mom said nothing and gave a small shake of her head. She pressed her lips together firmly and that was that. John tightened his grip on my shoulder, and I wondered if he too had seen the look from my mother.

Is this all I have to look forward to?

Eighteen

There was already a growing line outside the kitchen door when I returned from the lake on the morning of Solstice. It was just after seven AM.

Self-conscious in front of our queued clients, I pulled my towel tighter around my body as I tried to wave nonchalantly to the regulars. I was surprised to see Mrs. Andersen, Cousin Mildred's nemesis, among the early risers. I called out as I passed, "Give us a few minutes, and we'll be ready for you all soon."

Mrs. Andersen gave me a dazzling smile. "No rush. It's a lovely morning."

I slipped in the kitchen door and pulled it shut behind me. It was shaping up to be another infinitely beautiful summer day, I noticed, despite some wind from the east. There was a lingering coolness, the scent of dew and freshly mown grass heavy in the air. The birds sang, sweet and smug at the same time, as they confidently announced the perfect day.

I was annoyed, thinking their song was a little premature. *Who can possibly know how today of all days will go?*

Mom was in the kitchen making coffee in the multi-gallon carafe reserved for days like this. I eyed her turned back, disappointed that she hadn't said two words to me since she'd caught me in Magda's room but resolved to let it slide; I had more important concerns. She gave me a hesitant smile and flicked her eyes toward the stairs, as if to say, *Hurry up.*

"I know, I know," I said, taking the stairs by twos.

My hands, cold from the lake, buzzed with energy. I was twitchy with pent-up anger and ready for trouble. A small thrill ran through me regardless. I had a job to do first for the good people of Friedrich, and whether I liked it or not, I had a twisted sense of loyalty to the town, even as I dreamed of walking away from it all. Magda had made it clear that I was expected to shoulder the toughest cases needing an extra burst of solstice energy, and in spite of everything, I was excited to see exactly what I was capable of now that I knew I had the cedar chest's secrets behind me and the solstice light further magnifying my abilities.

My stomach clenched with anxiety as I dressed and attempted to braid the wet, tangled mess of my hair with unsteady hands.

"Here, let me," Mary said, suddenly in the doorway to our bedroom.

I turned and obediently slid to the floor in front of her bed.

Mary had previously been relegated to serving coffee and restocking supplies and charms on Solstice. But as Mary's fingers worked, I wondered if things could be different for her after what had happened with Karen Cooper.

Mary wove my hair into two overlapping braids with her light, magical touch, and I felt the unfairness again of her burgeoning powers that were suddenly rivaling my own. But I tried to tell myself it wasn't Mary's fault that Magda overlooked her. All blame came back to Magda.

Later, Dorothy whispered.

Mary squeezed my shoulders with her knees, and I stood to face her.

"Ready?" she asked, giving me the once-over.

"As ready as I'll ever be," I said, more seriously than intended.

"It will all work out," Mary said calmly, running a hand over the crown of my head to smooth the persistent flyaway hairs that refused to be tamed by her magical braids. I knew she wasn't talking about Solstice.

I hugged Mary tightly, suddenly overcome with gratitude and wonder at the woman my little sister had become.

*   *   *

Downstairs, the living room was packed with clients from all over the county shifting awkwardly in their seats and sipping coffee. The impossibly tall Mr. Gruen the science teacher bounced with nervous energy from one foot to the other in the corner. They all knew one another, and they all knew the others were clients in some way or another—the majority of the town was—but they only ever saw each other on Solstice.

Mary was already in the kitchen making love charms. It was all hands on deck for Solstice, and Magda had put Mary to work. Even Mom would see some of the animal cases out in the yard, Sam at her side. Magda was out of sight, likely treating a regular in the privacy of her bedroom already. We would all set up in separate corners of the house to talk to clients discreetly, hustling them through their treatments as quickly as would seem decent. Everyone in town knew the drill. No one was offended on Solstice.

The most serious cases, or at least the most serious clients, came first thing in the morning, when they guessed the magic was better for the getting. Better to be treated by fresh hands, at least. From the front stairs, I peeked into the living room at the folks waiting. Mary appeared in the doorway to watch as I organized the room.

"Mrs. Andersen, you're up first with me in the dining room," I called, stepping into the living room. "Mr. Gruen, you're next in the kitchen." *Better get his jumpy bones out of here and let everyone relax.*

"Then Mrs. Marsh is on deck for Magda. Mrs. Walsh for me next in the dining room, and Mr. Tate on deck for Mary in the kitchen. And so on *und so weiter*," I said, imitating Magda for effect.

As the first tingle of Solstice ran through me, I clapped my hands with forced enthusiasm. I couldn't give any signs that this Solstice was different than usual. As I waited for Mrs. Andersen to gather herself, I caught a glimpse of Mary's face, determined and nervous.

You got this, I pulsed at her as I pointed Mrs. Andersen toward the dining room with an open arm.

Mary squared her shoulders and picked up her face as I turned away.

I had chosen Mrs. Andersen for myself out of curiosity. We'd seen her mostly for small things—sleep remedies, immunity tinctures—but a beetle repellant for her garden wouldn't require a seven AM visit on Solstice. Mrs. Andersen followed me past the front stairs to the dining room. As I motioned for her to sit at the table opposite me, her worried expression caught me off guard.

I collected myself, sitting up straighter in my chair, and said in as soothing a tone as I could manage, "What can we do for you today, Mrs. Andersen?"

Mrs. Andersen's eyes twitched back toward the foyer. "Perhaps I should speak to Magda?"

I blinked hard and suppressed my immediate impulse: *What, I'm not good enough for you?*

I pushed on, speaking as casually as I could manage. "I'll consult with them if you'd like, but I promise Magda has taught me everything she knows, and I'm going to take good care of you. What can I do for you, Mrs. Andersen?" I repeated firmly.

She sighed and looked me over. Her expression was kind, but I felt judged.

"Okay," she said at last. "The thing is, I don't want any more children. I have five already and . . . and I could've had six, but I lost the last one early. I was so panicked the whole time. Harold's never home. I'm alone in the house with them all day. I got Julie potty trained and was starting to think I'd be free this decade, and then William came along."

Mrs. Andersen paused, taking a deep breath, and looked me squarely in the eye. "I was relieved, I guess, when I lost number six. And I'm so ashamed that I was relieved, but I know the truth now. I can't have another child. Please," she pleaded in a small voice. "Please, help me not have another child."

I drew in a shallow breath—there wasn't enough oxygen in the world—but held Mrs. Andersen's gaze steadily. Her eyes were a bright, sparkling green, intense and pretty in her perfectly made-up face.

Behind my cool facade, my heart fell into my stomach. Panic and bile rose in the back of my throat. I had no idea what to do, all of my bravado instantly falling away. I certainly couldn't ask Magda for help after projecting such sureness to Mrs. Andersen moments before.

The moon will be her guide. The words popped suddenly into my head. For the first time, I knew they came from the magic of the cedar chest.

"We'll help you with that," I said firmly.

"Thank you," Mrs. Andersen said. "And my husband can't know. Whatever it is, it can't be something that Harold will ever notice." While women all around the country were experiencing newfound freedom through family planning with the pill in the late sixties, change had been slow to come to our corner of very Catholic western Minnesota. I instantly understood why Mr. Andersen wouldn't approve.

So lying naked in the light of the full moon is out.

I nodded. "I understand. I think I have a solution for you," I said, trusting that the magic of the cedar chest and my grandmothers would direct me to the right answer. "I'm going to gather supplies. Back in a jiff," I added, hating myself as I said it.

Mrs. Andersen flashed me another dazzling smile that outshone the string of fake pearls at her throat.

"Thank you, Elisabeth," she repeated as I stood and tried to walk confidently from her sight.

My feet carried me through the house to hover in front of Magda's door. I recalled suddenly the image Mary had described of Great-Grandma Dorothy's ghost outside Mom and Dad's bedroom, one hand to the door as if feeling for fire. With a sharp inhale, I shook off the déjà vu and rapped my knuckles on the door.

Magda took her time answering. I willed myself to be patient, not knowing who she was with or what I was interrupting. Finally, Magda cracked the door, and her face, round like the moon, filled the space between door and jamb. I glimpsed old Mrs. Gary over her shoulder, likely realigning her fortunes for an extra bit of Solstice luck at the bingo hall.

"What?" Magda snapped. She narrowed her watery blue eyes at me.

I couldn't help it: I narrowed my eyes right back at her. I knew she would hate that, but I thought, *Tough. You bound my heart, this is your fault.*

Magda took in the serious set of my jaw and brow, sighed, and stepped into the hallway, closing the door behind her. She softened in the face of my unchanging scowl.

"Take a deep breath. You know you can't practice today with fear and"—Magda paused, giving me another once-over—"darkness in your heart. Clear yourself for your clients."

I hated that she was right. I took a deep breath and pushed the impatience and resentment from my energy field. I felt my annoyance drain into the ground beneath my feet. *Take it, take it away from me.* The lake alone wasn't enough to keep me grounded that day.

"Good," Magda said. "Now tell me. What do you need?"

"Nothing," I whispered, practically hissed, knowing we were within earshot of innumerable busybodies in the living room. "I need pennyroyal from the cedar chest." The words spilled out of my mouth. "For Mrs. Andersen."

Propelled by an impulse that I realized must have come from the cedar chest, my hands moved of their own accord in front of me.

I felt myself tying the strings of an imaginary pouch and innately knew that linen sachets of pennyroyal were what Mrs. Andersen needed. I couldn't recall ever witnessing Magda with a similar case, but I was sure it must have happened. She must have handled such delicate matters between women behind closed doors. But the cedar chest showed me the way. Generations of grandmothers gave me the charm, despite my inexperience. And for the first time, I truly understood how it worked as I witnessed with awe how the knowledge came to me out of nowhere.

"Oh, good," Magda said with a nod. Her face was impassive.

Magda cracked the door open a little wider, holding up a *one minute* finger to Mrs. Gary. She rifled through the cedar chest and produced pennyroyal. With a jerk of her head, which again reminded me of the moon atop her long, elegant neck, she motioned for me to take it and scram.

As Mrs. Andersen watched, I bent over the linen sachets laid flat on the dining room table, my wrists delicately lifted and my fingers loose and ready. I felt Magda's energy around me and was annoyed that she was checking up on me from the other room.

I got this, I pulsed back at her, pushing her away, so sick of the lack of privacy in our house.

I closed my eyes and waited. Like in so many other treatments, I cast out my energy in a close field around the room. But then I waited, feeling for the guiding solstice light to illuminate the way. I felt with astounding clarity the weight of Mrs. Andersen's decision and focused all my energy into imbuing the tea sachets with her choice, then called on the all-encompassing wisdom of generations of women to magnify it.

The words came slowly to my consciousness, buzzing through me from my very core. *Isch Mondwäg, Mondwäg isch. Isch in dini Sterchi, Mondwäg isch.* I felt my own voice longing to join the chorus. I whispered, *Mond bisch Leitere, Leitere Mond bisch.* I had never used those words before, but I knew they were powerful and true.

I opened my eyes and smiled, feeling energized by my own accomplishment instead of drained like I did after typical readings.

"Steep and drink this every morning after you are with your husband. Come back and see us when you run out. Don't let it run out," I said, the words coming to me from thin air as I instructed this middle-aged woman about things I had barely experienced myself.

Mrs. Andersen watched me expectantly for more. I forced a smile.

"Bathe in moonlight whenever you can. Especially during your cycle, leave the curtains open and let the moon into your bedroom. Let her know your intentions, and she will guide you," I said, the unplanned words tumbling from my mouth. *Whoa.*

Mrs. Andersen blinked. "I can do that," she said. "That's it?"

"That's it," I said. "Come back and see us, and we'll keep an eye on you."

As I showed Mrs. Andersen out, Mrs. Gary was making her way out through the living room, clutching a beacon to burn later.

I accepted a final, overpowering smile and a rare cash payment from Mrs. Andersen and steeled myself for the growing crowd.

* * *

The next few hours were a flurry of activity. Mary treated Mrs. McInerney's painful bone spurs in the kitchen while Magda did an energy reading for Mrs. Rose in her bedroom. I treated Mr. Stanley's sleepless nights with an energy reading, a problem I was all too familiar with myself. Mary provided water charms for Mr. Henry, Mr. Salzburg, and Mr. Pettrich. Magda tripped over sixteen-year-old Katherine Mayger as she sat on the living room floor patiently waiting for a love charm from Mary. Mom ran her hands over the belly of Mrs. Quinn's beloved schnauzer Princess, magnificently pregnant with eight puppies—they would arrive after midnight that night. Mr. Carroll took home a year's supply of fencing beacons to bury along his property lines to keep his cows from wandering out—and county officials from wandering in as they surveyed land for subdivisions and a new highway. I did an energy reading for Mrs. Kostych in the dining room while Mary made love charms for Sue Jensen, Jackie Tillman, and Lisa Vonderbaum.

At some point in the afternoon, I became aware that Magda's line wasn't getting any shorter. I was about to go see what the holdup was when I was surprised to see John walking through the door from the kitchen into the living room. I glanced at the clock on the mantel opposite the television, which showed three PM. John held a covered offering in front of his broad chest, and I was suddenly, acutely aware that I had nothing in my stomach except the distant morning's coffee and was running on caffeine and adrenaline.

John cracked a wide grin, and the folks in the living room—Henrietta Adams, Miss Mason the junior high school secretary, Mr. Johnson, Mrs. O'Malley and her daughter Lilly, the elderly Mrs. Shaw, and Mr. Gunderson, who were all pretending not to watch—fell away.

"Mom sent corn bread," John said by way of a greeting.

Glancing around the room, I thought, *Screw it*, and waved for John to follow me.

"I'll be right back for you, Miss Mason," I called over my shoulder as I led John through the foyer. "Henrietta, you're up next with Mary."

I hesitated in front of the front stairs, glancing at John. If the house hadn't been full of the watchful eyes of busybody neighbors, I might've been tempted to lead him upstairs for a private moment. That itchy, reckless feeling in my fingers almost made me do it. *Damn the neighbors*, I thought.

But Mary's eyes caught mine across the room. *I know, I know*, I pulsed at her.

She rolled her eyes toward the ceiling.

"Can you check on Magda please?" I asked her. "She can take Mrs. O'Malley next. Thanks, Mare."

I pulled John into the dining room, collapsed into a chair, and ripped the still-warm plate from his hands. He smiled down at me in amusement as I stuffed two large squares of corn bread into my mouth, filling my cheeks like the chipmunks that frequented my father's bird feeders.

"I figured you might need reinforcements by now," John said, casually dropping into the chair next to me. "I didn't know you'd need it this bad."

I smiled and slapped his arm in mock offense with the easy familiarity of having slapped it a thousand times before, then pulled back, suddenly self-conscious. I wasn't sure how I was supposed to act around him anymore or what was expected of me after the new physicality of our relationship. Still, as John watched me chew, my heart ached freshly for him, and I finally knew why. My heart was not my own, and all John could ever hope for was half.

I wondered as John watched me with those kind, hazel eyes if he had been able to feel it all along, my half-heartedness. I was starting to think John could feel that I didn't—couldn't—love him the way that he loved me. Somewhere, underneath the fresh wounds inflicted by Magda, I wondered if I secretly wanted someone who would demand my whole heart. I deflated every time John settled for half. *What kind of person would accept half love anyway?* I sighed inwardly.

And what could he expect after the equinox, when Magda bound my whole heart for good? I was too young to remember how Magda and Grandpa Earl had been. Had she been able to love him at all? John's future with me was looking dimmer by the minute.

"Thank you," I said, as lightly as I could manage, when I had choked down what was in my mouth.

Still, I was glad he was there, his presence a comfort to me. John reminded me of my father in that way, showing up at the precise moment of maximum helpfulness, supporting the Watry-Ridder women in the exact ways we needed it. *Bending over backwards for us*, I thought guiltily.

"How's it going today?" he asked.

"Fine." I shrugged. I guessed it was, anyhow.

"Good," he said. "Think you'll have time to come by town before tonight?" He grinned eagerly. John's father was one of the farmers who had asked for our help for his rain-starved crops. John knew how important our work that evening would be.

I dropped my eyes to the floor. "I don't know. I barely have time to breathe. I'll be lucky if I make it to the inlet by sundown."

His face flashed dark. "I was hoping you'd come say hi to the guys before. Nelson got a few cases. They'd love to see you today," he said.

There it was. John was expecting his spoils, the honor of showing off his Watry woman to his friends.

"I'll see what I can do," I said, knowing I wouldn't have time and would disappoint him. "I should get back there."

I leaned forward and kissed his cheek to soothe him. "See you tonight?"

"I'll be waiting," he said. John smoothed a stray lock of my hair back into place and let his hand rest on the side of my face for a beat too long. I resisted the urge to bat his hand away.

"I don't know what I'd do without you," he said into the top of my head. Heartbreaking and chilling, it felt like a threat. John turned away without expecting me to respond.

"Tell your mom thanks for the corn bread," I called after him lamely.

I allowed myself to sit there for one more minute and stuffed one more piece of corn bread in my mouth before retrieving Miss Mason from the living room. By the time I did, Magda was back in operation, her line moving again, and I almost forgot about the near hiccup in the afternoon.

Nineteen

Just after six PM, I showed Mrs. Grundahl out the door, accepting a cherry pie and fancy sugared almonds in exchange for ginger root tonic for her delicate stomach. I found Mary barefoot in the kitchen attacking a chicken chow mein hot dish. Any other day this would've been a grand offense to Magda's tightly run ship and our mother's spotless kitchen, but on Solstice, anything goes. It was a tradition, in fact. I grabbed a fork and squeezed in next to Mary. We were a matching set of Watry women with cream of mushroom soup and soy sauce dripping down our chins.

"Good, huh?" Mary said through a mouthful of noodles and chicken. "Mr. Berg brought it straight from home, still hot."

I nodded but couldn't manage words through the salty, creamy, crunchy noodles in my mouth. Mom slumped at the table with a mug of stale coffee and one hand over her eyes, looking for all the world like her mother. Magda was noticeably absent from our Solstice foraging, she who usually led the charge with a fork raised like a triumphant banner.

The counter in the kitchen overflowed with casseroles, pies, and bars; garden-fresh beets, cucumbers, green beans, leeks, greens, garlic, peas, radishes, rhubarb, and handpicked blueberries;

packages of beef and pork ribs, roasts, and fresh sirloin steaks from the butcher, Mr. Pettrich. The casseroles and baked goods and meat would go in Dad's enormous ice chest in the garage. We spent the days after Solstice pickling most of the vegetables and storing them for the winter, except the rhubarb and berries, which would be baked into pies.

There were also a handful of new feathered friends in residence in the chicken coop, and Mom somehow ended the day with a new kitten. The ball of orange fluff sat in her lap, stunned to be there, as Mom absent-mindedly held strings of beef jerky from a Tupperware container to its sweet pink mouth. Sam the cat, who operated as Mom's ears around town, eyed the scene suspiciously from the top of the refrigerator, refusing to give up his perch while the interloper was in Mom's lap. The kitten told Mom that his name was Fred, and his auspicious appearance on Solstice begged Mom to add another familiar to her clowder.

Mary strategically scooped all the crunchy noodle topping off half of the hot dish, then collapsed dramatically into a kitchen chair. Only when the pan was reduced to celery and cream clinging to the sides of the pan did I relinquish my own fork and set the pan on the floor for a special Solstice kitty treat for Sam and Mickey and the tiny orange newcomer.

As much as I wanted to rest with a coffee, I knew if I sat down for one spare minute, I might lose my nerve; I might never stand up to Magda. And if I didn't, I might as well shut up like my mother, let John claim me, and let Magda pull the invisible strings of my life forever.

I trudged upstairs to dress alone in Solstice white, the better for calling water to the county that evening. I pulled a short white macrame dress over my head with hands that wouldn't stop shaking.

*   *   *

"Let's go," I said to Mary as I breezed through the kitchen and out the side door, not waiting for her to catch up. I wanted to show that

I still had some authority. I carried a backpack with a few things, intending to sleep over at Annie's after I embarrassed Magda thoroughly in front of the farmers at the water calling.

Mary wore a sleeveless white macrame shift to match mine, gifts from the talented Mrs. Conlin. As much as Solstice was a time to wear white and set intentions for the coming season, it was also a time to honor youth and bare skin, to expose long legs and feet and shoulders to the moonlight on the shortest night of the year.

"Oh." Mom made a small sound behind us.

I hesitated outside the kitchen door but couldn't make the words come out. *It was supposed to be you. You chose my future for me. You gave my heart away.*

"We'll see you there," I said instead.

Mary walked beside me toward the inlet on the east side of town, even as I knew she must have felt the fire radiating from me. But she said nothing and matched my pace, our footsteps sounding like one against the sun-warmed asphalt.

The sight of the lake on our left, a blinding mirror under the magic-hour evening light, did little to calm me. I moved as if in a dream. The trees barely swayed; the wind out of the east had settled since morning, I noticed through my fog. *A good night for a fire*, as my father and his brothers would say. There were more boats on the lake than normal at that hour, making their way toward the inlet to watch the water calling as the sun slipped behind the tree line to the west. My fingers ached with anticipation.

As we neared town, cars passed us along Lake Street on their way to the inlet. A truck with a handful of boys in the flatbed honked when they recognized the Watry-Ridder girls on their ceremonial progress. One of them, a boy who had been a year ahead of me, leaned out the window and yelled something unintelligible under the roar of the engine. I didn't need to hear it; it was never anything good.

That familiar fire simmered below the surface. It was intended for Magda and my mother, but I impulsively raised a hand at the passing truck and flung my arm toward the lake. *Baumöl*, I thought. *Chunsch, Baumöl.* The truck skidded wildly, careening across Lake Street. There were no cars coming in the other lane, luckily, but the boys in the flatbed were thrown hard to one side.

Mary pushed my shoulder roughly and raised a hand to set it straight, whispering the words of protection.

"What the heck was that?" she asked, whipping around on me, incredulous, as the boys drove on.

None of them so much as looked back, so they must've blamed the driver and whatever beers they had certainly consumed in advance of the Solstice proceedings.

My power is infinite. I thought of that morning with Mrs. Andersen and the time with the raven's feathers and all the times the words had materialized on my lips, that guiding energy in my hands. I was itching to test the boundaries of my powers, break all the rules of magic Magda had taught me. If I had all the wisdom and spells of generations of witches from the cedar chest at my disposal and the auspicious Solstice light at my back, I could do anything. There was nothing Magda or anyone could do to stop me.

"What?" I barked at Mary, burning with resentment.

Mary cut her eyes at me.

"I slipped," I said, daring her to challenge me. She didn't even know how lucky she was with a whole heart to give away.

Mary shook her head and started walking slowly, waiting for me to catch up.

"You can talk to me when you're ready," she said. "I have your back."

I softened instantly. I wanted to take Mary's hand, but I couldn't make myself do it. We were born of different elements, and water and earth can only mix with fire for so long before the flame is smothered.

Another honking truck passed and broke the spell between us.

*   *   *

We crossed the bridge over the inlet that connected Clear Lake to the nearby Blackfoot River. The town beach and Harry's Supper Club were on the other side, separated by a strip of swamp and scraggly trees. A small crowd had gathered along the edges, lining the banks of the inlet. It was mostly farmers, their families, other old-timers, and a handful of teenagers—Annie, John, and his basketball teammates among them.

They shifted before us, parting the way toward the place where the inlet met the lake as the sky streaked pink. Our father greeted us, beaming.

"Ready, girls?" he asked, glancing behind us. "Where is your mother? You didn't come together?"

I shrugged and felt Mary's eyes boring into me. "They're coming," I said flatly.

He turned away, distracted. "Well," he said, running a hand through his thick, dark hair. "You've got a few minutes . . ." And then Dad was off, his attention turned toward shaking hands with his friends and the other important men in the agricultural fabric of Friedrich.

In the long golden minutes before sunset, the sky burned bright in shades of pink and red and orange. Mary scanned the crowd.

"I'll be back," she said, spotting Tim near a knot of boys impatiently waiting for something interesting to happen. Her hand went automatically to smooth her hair. "Wave me when Mom and Magda get here."

Mary said Magda's name softly, delicately, and I thought suddenly, *I don't know how or what, but Mary knows something.*

I turned slowly in her wake, taking in the crowd—about eighty people so far—and letting them see me. To heighten the effect when I ran out on Magda, I needed everyone to know I was there, highly visible in my bright-white dress. I stomped through the long grass in my moccasins, as a few children, farm kids invested in the outcome for their parents' sake, played tag between people in the crowd. The old-timers watched from afar, setting up folding chairs on the stable ground back by the road. I made sure they all saw me.

John was talking quietly with his father, his teammates nearby. After I had worked my way from one end of the marshy land around the inlet and back again, I focused my energy on John's turned back, lassoing him effortlessly. He turned quickly, unsmiling. It took him a beat too long to find a smile for me when he saw me standing apart from the crowd. My heart caught in my throat. *He knows he deserves better*—like my father, and Grandpa Earl before him. I had a feeling that all the patriarchs in our family were used to settling for less, but John was starting to crack as he got a glimpse of his future that summer. And I couldn't blame him.

I felt the air go out of my lungs when I thought about the future that Magda had dictated for John too. He was as trapped as I was, and I was racked with guilt thinking that he would be stuck with me like I was stuck with Magda and the cedar chest and the house on Lake Street. Embarrassing Magda would mean embarrassing John too. Was the honor of being next to a Watry woman enough for John? Would he support me when I stood up to Magda? Or did he want her future for us too?

As I deliberately turned my eyes from John to scan the crowd, my heart ached for all the women before me who had carried the same terrific burden. *Did Grandpa Earl know that Magda's heart wasn't for him? Did he mind? What about Dad? Does Mom get to love him with her whole heart?* My insides burned at that thought—that Mom, even like she was, was free to love when I wasn't.

Mary drew my eye through the crowd as she leaned into Tim's side, their fingers entwined as they stood where the swampy land around the inlet gave way to the pebbled beach. I sighed, flaring further with resentment and hating myself for it. Mary's heart was whole and hers to give. I found it devastatingly unfair that only one of the Watry-Ridder girls would know true love.

John found me as day faded into dusk. He glanced around to see who might be in the vicinity—my father and uncles, Mr. Weseloh, Father Kevin, or the many town gossips—then kissed me squarely on the mouth, marking his territory in front of all of them.

I looked away, distracted. "Thank you," I mumbled after a moment, torn between feeling guilty about John being wrapped up in my family's secrets and feeling uncomfortably like John's prize.

"For what?" he asked.

"For being here. For everything," I said, before choking up.

"I'm proud of you," he said, blushing, the sweet, shy farmer-tinker who'd had the guts to steal his brother's snowmobile peeking through.

I drew back and leaned my chin on top of his solid, warm shoulder.

"Mm?" I murmured, afraid my voice would crack if I spoke.

"You were so in charge today. Running the show. Like you've been doing it forever," John said.

I have been doing it forever, I thought.

I didn't answer John, as I spotted Mom and Magda making their way toward us. Magda, as always, looked like the queen of the Black Forest fairies—as intentionally far from that stereotypical Wicked Witch image as she could manage. Long white skirts grazed her ankles, and her arms were covered by a gauzy white blouse and stacks of silver and gold bangles that tinkled when she moved. Her silver hair fell loose down her back from under a white silk scarf dotted with red posies. Gold earrings of tiny rows of bells swung from her ears. My mother's look—a flowing white tunic over slim white pedal pushers—was a bit more understated. But she too wore a number of bangles and let her long, blonde hair flow free.

I was practically twitching with nerves. I was about to stand up to my grandmother in a very public way to show her that I wouldn't accept her future for me. I didn't know how she would react—would she punish me? Would she decide, God forbid, to not bind my heart on the fall equinox after all? Would she let me go? I wasn't thinking about the consequences. All I was thinking about was not doing what Magda wanted for once in my life.

I buried my face in John's shoulder, breathing him in, thankful for his presence despite the guilt that threatened to consume me.

"Ready for a show?" I asked in a tight voice.

"Always," he said, grinning.

An exuberant energy zapped through the crowd as neighbors greeted one another, sharing flasks of whiskey or cans of beer. I pressed John's hand one last time, then turned to seek Mary. Across the crowd, she touched Tim's arm lightly, completely unaware of the outside world, her face flushed with the pure joy of a first crush. I pulsed at her—*It's time.* She looked up immediately, squeezed Tim's arm once, and moved toward me.

My path up to that point had been determined for me by my mother and grandmother. It ended that night. I would choose for myself. As Mary cast one more look at Tim, an easy smile on her face, I slipped between groups of neighbors with their backs turned—and disappeared.

I had been practicing, but I didn't know exactly how long I'd be able to hold my shield, so I moved quickly. It was more difficult to maintain than the sound shields I used when I drew John from his bed in the middle of the night. I was completely invisible, walking among my family and neighbors unseen.

I moved toward the lake, where the crowd thinned, positioning myself to watch the drama unfold. Behind me, the lake was dark and beautiful and dangerous. Like us. Like me. A hush spread as Mary joined Magda in the center of the marsh. A wall of people closed in around Mary and Magda, clamoring for the best view.

I watched, nearly dizzy with adrenaline, as Magda whispered to Mary with a forced smile on her face.

"Where's Lisbett?"

Mary scanned the crowd.

"She was just here," I read on her lips.

Mom seemed to notice that something was amiss and turned to look.

Please, be enough, I whispered to my shield from where I watched.

I felt Dorothy's presence like a warm hand settle on my back.

It wasn't always this way, she reminded me.

Magda's smile faltered. "Your sister is supposed to lead the water incantation tonight," she hissed to Mary. Suddenly I was Mary's problem.

Mary kept her composure. "We walked over together. She was just with John."

Magda's eyes snapped to find the aforementioned Weseloh in the crowd, where he and the basketball team had started to push closer to the inlet.

Our neighbors were starting to notice.

"What's the delay?"

"Where's Elisabeth?"

"She was here, I saw her . . ."

"Is this part of it?"

"I don't think so, look at Magda."

The gathered crowd, silent only a moment before in hushed anticipation, broke out in scandalized whispers. Then they didn't even bother whispering. Seconds stretched into minutes as Mary stood inert, faking a smile, waiting for Magda to decide what to do. Proceed? Cancel? Even in the dwindling light, I could see Magda's eyes turn to ice. I was ecstatic.

John dared to stride forward, breaking the line of spectators. Magda glared, and Mary rushed forward to talk to him. John scratched his head and waved an arm where we had been standing. Magda was turning an unseemly shade of pink, almost as purple as her energy. It had worked. Magda was furious, and I was delighted. She deserved it after what she had done to me.

As full dark settled and the moon began to rise, Magda turned to face the lake, waving Mom and Mary close to her with raucous speculation at their backs. I stood on my tiptoes under my shield, waiting to see what would come next, overjoyed that I had made it so far. I thought I would watch Magda flail for a few minutes more, then slip away to Annie's.

But then Magda began to cast out. I felt my shield waver. "She's still here, I can feel it," she hissed. Magda threw an arm out in a wide arc and whipped it above her head, setting aside all decency. She was incensed. The crowd exclaimed in surprise as the ever-poised Magda Watry absolutely lost it.

Before I could react, my shield split in half. There were gasps and hesitant exclamations from the people nearest me as I was suddenly visible next to them.

"Is this part of it . . . ?" someone loudly wondered.

Magda's head snapped in my direction.

"Elisabeth," she said with an eerie calm, regaining her composure. "Come here right now," she barked through gritted teeth, betraying how furious she was beneath the cool exterior.

"No," I said, my feet solidly planted beneath me. "I'm done being your puppet." Shock erupted from the crowd.

"Excuse me?" Magda snapped. "That's enough. Let's go."

"No," I cried, "I said no!"

I caught a glimpse of John's face as it fell. With my defiance, he lost his special status and privileges. I was ruining his future too.

Magda waved away the fractured remnants of my shield and motioned for our neighbors, who watched us with bated breath, to stay back. Her hands kept working, the words unspoken beneath the surface of the ice floe. I felt a force unseen wrap itself around my feet and legs and hips and drag me forward.

"Magda!" I gasped. It was unthinkable to cast to control another individual's movement, let alone that of a family member, another

Watry woman. I threw up my hands to protect myself, unintentionally showering sparks down on the marsh. Magda met my sparks with a fiery rope around my waist.

Up to this point, our neighbors had been watching warily, shifting in place, unsure whether it was safe to move. At my shower of sparks, they exclaimed and shielded themselves with their arms, and a few started to edge toward the road. But our neighbors couldn't tear themselves away from the scene entirely—they watched us with fascination and fear, a real-live family feud before their own eyes, wincing and exclaiming at every fiery charm. I felt John and my father and my uncles and Annie and Cousin Mildred nearby and shivered. All I wanted was to restore my shield and get away.

Watch out! Dorothy urged.

Before I knew what was happening, Magda's fiery rope dragged me to my knees in the mud. I floundered, trying to work my hands free as Mary let out a shriek. She instinctively threw out a hand toward Magda, but stopped short of actually touching Magda or casting. Even in her fear, Mary knew better than to get in the middle of it.

Magda pulled me toward her, and the weeds whipped my bare legs like knives. *What was I thinking, wearing a dress?* came the ridiculous thought in the back of my head. *What are you doing? Fight back!* I told myself, letting all the rage and resentment of the past weeks break through to the surface. I finally broke one of my hands free and let it rip.

I had never dreamed my grandmother would dare to physically cast on me, nor that I would cast sand and wind and rain back at her—let alone in front of the whole town. But as I struggled to my feet, the words leapt to my tongue unbidden. I threw charm after charm at Magda, anything to make her release me. I heard exclamations of shock and fear from our neighbors.

Magda cried with surprise, "How dare you!" She threw up her arms to drag me down again, and I dug my moccasined feet into the silt.

"That's enough!" Mary yelled above the din as my father looked on in horror.

Magda snapped her head to glare at Mary but kept her hands trained on me.

"You stay out of this, girl, or you will regret it," Magda hissed.

I tried to shield myself in that moment, but Magda kept going. She was throwing fire at me, and I knew I had made a grave mistake. I feared for my very life.

The crowd scrambled away from us, giving us as wide a berth as the narrow strip of land around the inlet afforded, when Magda threw a charm that took my feet out from underneath me. I fell to my knees again.

Mary made a sound of distress but didn't move, leaving me to deal with Magda alone once again, and in that split second I saw any future for myself outside of Friedrich slipping away. Magda was never going to let me walk away from the future she'd chosen for me. If I wanted a different future, I was going to have to take it for myself.

Get up, Dorothy whispered.

I had never cast the words before, but with the enormous solstice energy, adrenaline, and Dorothy's presence around me, I felt unstoppable. I felt out of control. I cast fire at Magda, and she threw it right back.

"Lisbett!" Mary cried above the gasps and screams, her voice full of fear. I didn't see her. My eyes were only for Magda.

Our fire charms met in a violent burst above the inlet. A gust of hot air flattened the weeds to the ground, and the lake, serene moments before, was whipped to a frenzy behind us from the wind and flame kicking back from our charms, each larger than the last. There were terrible screams from our friends, family, and neighbors as our energies met in the middle and exploded in a brilliant tower of fire, shooting gaseous green flames a hundred feet high, an enormous flare in the night sky through the narrow gap in the tree line. I thought I heard John's voice in the din cry out, "What are you doing?" But I couldn't stop it.

"Oh shit." The words tumbled from my mouth reflexively.

The column of fire stood between me and Magda, blocking her from view. The only thought I had in that moment was to get out of there. I didn't want to *fight* Magda, but she'd attacked me first. I didn't want to risk hurting anyone else. But there was no stopping it; it was too late. I threw up a shield and made a run for it.

I didn't get far, though, in the chaos of the moment. The fire sent people running, shoving and scrambling over each other to get away from the eerie green embers raining down on the swampland. The heat was immediately unbearable. I had already lost track of Magda, Mary, and my parents, leaving them somewhere behind me. My only thought was to get away before I antagonized Magda further and risked my friends and family in the balance. But it was slow going in the sudden crush of bodies seeking safety on Lake Street. I inhaled sharply, starving for breath in the smoky air.

Time seemed to slow down as I looked over my shoulder from where I was caught, unseen, in a group of old-timers from the VFW clambering their way toward the beach and Harry's. The column of green flames was surely visible for miles in any direction; if I hadn't seen it with my own eyes, I would have thought there was a nuclear bomb dropped on Friedrich. I felt guilty for the terror ripping through my friends and neighbors, especially in a time when everyone feared nuclear war with the Soviets. Would they blame me? Or would they blame Magda? She'd cast first, after all—but did our neighbors see that?

Before I could finish the thought, the wind changed, picking up unexpectedly. Maybe it had been there all along and I hadn't been paying attention, as focused as I was on breaking Magda's charms on me. It happened so quickly that I couldn't have stopped what occurred next if I wanted to: across the sand, Harry's Supper Club ignited. My eyes followed the embers carried on the wind to Harry's roof, which was quickly engulfed in an unnatural green inferno as cries of shock and one long wail went up around me.

"Oh God," I cried aloud.

A few heads turned in my direction, but for the most part, all
eyes were on Harry's, watching the blaze. I racked my brain—had
there been a wedding planned for Solstice? I strained to see—was
the parking lot full? I couldn't tell through the growing smoke. I felt
like I might be sick. *God, what have I done?*

Mary appeared, tearing down the beach toward Harry's. Magda
trundled after her, her duty to the community ever the priority,
even after attacking her own granddaughter in front of them. I felt
nauseous. I defied my grandmother, unprovoked, in front of our
neighbors. I didn't mean to hurt anyone. My whole body began to
shake where I was frozen in place beneath my shield, eyes glued to
the flames licking through Harry's roof as tar paper and shingles
ignited and flew off.

This wasn't part of the plan. I had wanted to embarrass Magda,
put a kink in her grand plans for me, show her she couldn't control
me. I should've known how hard she'd fight to keep me in my place.
I hadn't meant for it to go this far.

Even in the mad dash toward cars and the beach parking lot,
people stopped to watch Harry's burn. The sound of shattering
glass—the patio windows that looked out onto the lake—was audi-
ble above the roar of the fire. The fear on the faces of my neighbors
in that moment told me: all their worries about us over the years had
come to fruition. Their lake, Friedrich's agricultural lifeblood, and
Harry's, their social epicenter, were on fire, and I was solely responsible. I was afraid. I had to get out of there before I was blamed.

I couldn't wait to see if Mary and Magda were able to control
what seemed like an uncontrollable fire. I pushed through the
crowd, fervently whispering the words of my shield like a prayer
and letting the press of people carry me down Lake Street away
from Harry's.

But someone caught my wrist in the crush. I looked up to see
my mother's profile illuminated by the green flames. I hesitated,
wondering for a split second if it could be fixed, if I didn't have
to run, if there was any world in which I could feel at home in my

family knowing what Magda had done and now knowing what I
had done. But looking at my mother's face in that light was like
looking at a future version of myself. *How can we be so alike and
so different?* I thought in a daze. *It will only get worse.*

And in that moment, looking at her like I was looking at myself,
I knew I was always going to walk away. I had to find out who or
what I could be away from the Watry-Ridder house, away from
Mom and Magda and their secrets and that stupid cedar chest. I
hadn't meant for my departure to so explosive, but now that I had
fought so publicly with Magda and set the town on fire, I had no
choice but to go.

I wasn't surprised that Mom saw through my shield, even if I
didn't know how she did it. I had seen that look in my mother's eyes
before; she was guided by something more primal, ethereal. She
grasped my wrist with a strength I hadn't thought possible.

"Elisabeth," she said, a plea in her voice.

The tears I had been holding back for days broke free, stinging
my eyes. "It was supposed to be you," I spat back, saying the words
I had thought so many times, intending to hurt her. "Why wasn't
it you?"

Mom dropped my wrist suddenly, as if my skin had burned her
fingers. We were pushed together by the crowd on all sides, uncomfortably close in the blazing heat. Every retreating back was clear as
day in the night sky glowing green. I could see the fear in stunning
detail on each passing neighbor's face, but no one noticed us; my
shield had at least done that.

"I . . . we . . . Mother . . . ," she stammered. "We did the best we
could."

"You gave me away. You let Magda take my heart, and you
spared Mary."

"You don't know what you're talking about. You don't know
what she was like back then," my mother said. Her tone was defiant,
even as I could barely hear her above the roar of the fire.

But I had heard enough half-truths from my family. I shook my head. My mother's thin arms hung limply at her sides, and her entire body heaved in a sigh. I saw then that she would give me up, again. I burned with fury—*why won't you fight for me? Why didn't you help me?* I tore myself away from her, sparking with rage and disappointment.

"I had to protect at least one of you," I heard my mother say to my back, finding her voice as I shoved through the last of the crowd unscathed, the flame and ash and smoke parting around my shield.

Twenty

My heart pounding, I took a forgotten bike from the beach and whispered the words of a protection spell obsessively to ward off the prying eyes and headlights of fleeing townsfolk. I didn't know what I was doing. I just had to run.

What now? I asked Dorothy, praying she would answer.

She didn't respond, but a thread of white light illuminated in front of me, stretching toward the two-lane highway out of town. *Thank you.*

The shocking green glow from the fire above Friedrich gave way to relative darkness the further I rode from town. Fourteen miles later, I found myself outside the Greyhound station in St. Agnes. I stashed the bike in the bushes and went inside to look at the schedule. I felt Dorothy light up when I read the time for Minneapolis. *Better than Fargo.* At that moment, I remembered Grandpa Ridder's pristine envelope stashed in the front pocket of my backpack and was grateful. *Okay, Dorothy. Let's go.* In a daze, I bought a one-way ticket, then attempted to wash as much mud off my legs as possible and rinsed off my moccasins in the bathroom of the tiny St. Agnes station.

With soggy shoes, I boarded a bus toward the Cities in the early hours before dawn. I held my breath until I was safely on the

highway east, hoping the driver hadn't heard the news from Friedrich as I slunk low in my seat. I had no idea what shape the town
was in, or Harry's. I had no idea if anyone had been hurt. Behind
me was a burning town that would shortly know how I had lost
control and attacked my grandmother—and how Magda Watry
dealt with insubordination in her family.

The events of the evening were a complete blur barely ten hours
later. What had even happened? How had things gotten so out of
control? I had wanted to stand up to Magda, not hurt anyone. Had
she meant to hurt me? Had she known what she was doing? But no,
she had to. Magda didn't do anything by accident. She'd known
exactly what charms she was throwing at me, fire and all. And she
was the reason for it all.

With thirty miles to the next town, I watched the farms fly by
and replayed the events of the days since Cousin Mildred's last visit
had split my world apart. I was shocked to feel relief beneath the
guilt and fear.

I had wanted space to discover what else I could be, what I
would have been if all the choices in my life hadn't been made for
me. What would I be if I hadn't been born a Watry? I thought of
Mary, free to do with her heart as she wished, with a nascent power
and the spark of first love coursing through her. I could see her natural talent with my own two eyes, but I would never be able to see
my own. I would never know what I would've been if Magda hadn't
bound my heart as a toddler. I knew then that I needed to go, but I'd
never imagined I would leave in a ball of fire, a fugitive in the night.

The open road to Minneapolis blossomed with possibilities
before me. I had made the three-hour drive to Minneapolis with
Magda occasionally for special supplies, or that time as a child
when I had met the Ojibwe medicine man. But this was entirely
different. I was escaping, running away from my grandmother, my
family, my destiny.

I sat in nervous, guilty silence for most of the ride. When I
drifted off, I saw that green blaze consuming Harry's roof again.

My dreams were replaced by eerie green fire—and a deep anxiety. *What if I killed someone?* I'd dream, then jerk awake.

The towns began to cluster closer together along Highway 12, the Greyhound flew past the Minneapolis suburbs, dawn blossomed into morning, and a new excitement grew in me in spite of my guilt. I thought, *I'm free. I'm free, I'm free, I'm free.* Out of habit, I closed my eyes and felt the brilliant energy of Minneapolis burst open like a spring peony igniting into full bloom. The ice floe exploded into an unnavigable rainbow lake of tens of thousands of energies. The sheer volume was overwhelming.

But then the fire came back to me, and the fear in Mary's voice. I snapped my eyes open with a sharp inhale. *Can't do that anymore.* I could practically feel Magda creeping over my shoulder. Would she come for me? Did she already know where I was? I would have to be diligent about not using magic. Even shielding myself drew on the ice floe. I would have to cut myself off completely. I would have to be normal, perfectly normal—ironically what Grandma Ridder wanted—to avoid the long reach of Magda's influence. I needed to hide.

What did it feel like to not use magic? What would it feel like to turn away from everything Magda said was supposed to be mine?

But would I still be able to talk to Dorothy without the ice floe magic? I wasn't sure, and Dorothy didn't offer any answers. I'd have to wait and see as I arrived into Minneapolis unguided. I sat very still and practiced disconnecting myself from the ice floe.

What does a normal person do when she closes her eyes? What does a normal girl think? It made me itchy around the collar. I would have to practice more. *What does it feel like to not read everyone's energy in the room?* My fingers and toes tingled with excessive energy. I glanced at the few other passengers—*what does it feel like not to have burned a town to the ground?* In my mind's eye, I saw myself shove the living energy of Minneapolis into a small room.

I slammed the door shut and turned a skeleton key in the keyhole, locking the ice floe away—for how long, I didn't know.

The city rose out of the front window of the bus, and minutes later I was unceremoniously deposited in a grimy Greyhound depot on the edge of town. Empty coffee cups and candy wrappers blew like tumbleweeds between the legs of indifferent travelers waiting to return home after a visit to the Cities. Respectable-looking families sat beside worn-out husks of long-haired youths: *Older than me*, I thought. *Or maybe the city ages young people.* The air was damp and heavy with the smell of unwashed bodies and burnt coffee.

I bought a coffee, knowing it would be terrible, to stall. It nearly scalded me as I shuttled the flimsy paper cup uncomfortably from hand to hand. I scanned the room as I waited for a tired woman with silver-streaked hair to count my change. A beggar, or a drunk, slept heaped on a plastic chair in the waiting area, a stark contrast to the relative cleanliness of the small Greyhound stop in St. Agnes. This was not a side of Minneapolis I had ever seen before.

I stepped out into an overcast but pleasant morning. A warm breeze floated up from the nearby highways. With no help from Dorothy, I surveyed the street and wandered vaguely southward for no reason other than it led away from the bus depot.

Whatever nerves I felt—the anxiety of not knowing where I was or what I would do next, or the full extent of what I had done—I shoved down for the time being, projecting a confident exterior. *Be cool*, I told myself and squared my shoulders. *Like Annie would be*, I thought sadly, wondering what Annie would think of my and Magda's public sparring.

I strolled through the polished buildings and wide avenues of downtown Minneapolis without a destination or purpose in mind, driven by a constant drumbeat: *I'm free, I'm free, I'm free.* I was convinced that I looked like a criminal, or at the very least, out of place among the weekend shoppers and visitors: a big-eyed country girl with wild hair after a sleepless night among the chic downtown ladies running their errands in Jackie O–style sunglasses and brightly patterned dresses. I was jealous of the carefree day ahead of them, while my crime—as I was starting to think of it—and my escape were still fresh. I looked down at my own clothes smudged with ash and general grime, and sighed. *These are not my people.*

I found myself swept up in the flow of bodies and, too tired to decide for myself, surrendered to the gravitational pull of pedestrian traffic. I looked up from my shuffling when I recognized the Dayton's building. I had a vague recollection of Mom and Magda taking Mary and me there as kids for the first flower show, with its intricately detailed displays bursting from every inch of the first floor. I remembered playing hide-and-seek with Mary in the furniture department while Magda chose the davenport for the living room and a perfectly layered club sandwich in the fifth-floor café, a foreign delicacy compared to my mother's goulash.

My stomach—empty except for the bitter Greyhound coffee—grumbled at the memory of that beautiful club sandwich. While I had at least ninety dollars left of Grandpa Ridder's graduation money, I couldn't submit to the humiliation of the café turning me away for looking like such a ragamuffin. As I kept walking past the sparkling display windows, I felt the smallest nudge forward and followed Dorothy willingly.

So Dorothy is able to reach me, I realized, even after I had locked the ice floe away. I had been kidding myself to think I'd be able to close myself off completely to the other side—or Dorothy was stronger in spirit form than I understood.

After a few blocks, downtown gave way to industrial buildings. Beyond, the roar of the Mississippi River rose above the sound of city traffic, calling to me. In the last block before the river, there was a luncheonette among the warehouses. It was nearly empty except for a few old guys in the back. I bought a tuna sandwich from the man behind the counter and asked him to wrap it to go. The near silence of that place and the way the line cook eyed me through the pickup window were unnerving. Not a place for a girl alone.

I sat on a bench at the top of the steep riverbank and unwrapped the sandwich. It was the best tuna salad sandwich of my life, and I inhaled it so quickly that I thought I might be ill.

As I stared blankly at the river, the gravity of what I had done was setting in. *Is this what I wanted?* I asked myself, feeling very, very alone. *I need to know who I can be*, I tried to remind myself. *Magda was never going to let me walk away . . . I wish it didn't have to come to that. But Magda cast on me first, right?* I winced, starting to doubt my blurry memories of the previous fifteen hours.

But what's done is done, I told myself. No going back, not after the state I had left Harry's in. Still, I couldn't deny the relief I felt to be looking at the opportunity before me. Magic was my birthright, but I was tempted to give it up if it let me live a single day like a normal eighteen-year-old, with a normal heart, free to give as I wished. Free of the burden of my family and Magda's rules. *Even if it means hurting Friedrich in the balance*, I thought.

I watched the Mississippi River winding through the middle of the city like it had carved its way through a fully formed thriving metropolis instead of the city springing up around its banks in the previous century. It reminded me of the Ridder Family Company office nearby run by Uncle Joe, and I thought suddenly of my father, innocent in all this, and my heart dropped in my chest.

The rush of water filled my ears, blocking out the sounds of the city. I had a sudden impulse to ride the river all the way to the Gulf of Mexico. I felt unmoored and drunk on possibility. I asked the river, *What next?*

It wasn't the river but a familiar voice that answered. *Come, mein Liebling*, Dorothy pulsed at me, her voice crystal clear in my ear above the rush of water. She nudged me to stand and turn back toward downtown. A new path of white light illuminated before me. She hadn't led me wrong yet, so I started to walk.

*   *   *

I turned a corner, and suddenly there she was, the golden dome of St. Mary's Basilica rising above a green square in the bright afternoon sunshine, a dame on her throne. There weren't many people around midday on a Saturday. I felt disoriented and sluggish as I trudged up the stone steps.

Church? Really? I asked Dorothy silently.

I was looking to distance myself from my family, and Dorothy had immediately led me right back to their ways.

Go on, Dorothy urged.

I rolled my eyes as I tugged open the obscenely heavy door at the top and slipped inside. I had to admit the cool, dark interior was a treat after wandering in the bright June sun.

Humoring Dorothy, I made a slow revolution around the perimeter of the empty basilica. My footsteps were swallowed by the enormous stone arches.

And now? I asked Dorothy.

Just then, a hymnal crashed off a table near the door that led to the rectory. The movement sent the hundreds of glass candle votives tinkling against one another in their stands, flames swaying.

Okay then.

A not-quite-middle-aged woman with dark hair in a tight bun looked up as I pushed the door open into the parish office.

"Can I help you?" she said from behind the desk. She lifted her pen from her paper but hovered it over the page as if to get back to work as quickly as possible.

"Hi, Sheila," I started, glancing at the name tag pinned on the lapel of her plain black dress. The words came out in a rush. "My name is Elisabeth, and I'm from Friedrich, Minnesota, where I belong—belonged—to Our Lady of Grace parish."

Sheila, be kind, I begged silently. I tried to remind myself not to cast out and ease the conversation with magic.

"You see, I don't know where to go. I don't know what I'm doing . . . I thought the church might have resources? For someone like me?" *Runaways like me.*

Sheila smiled. "Well, sweetheart, you've come to the right place. I can't exactly help you here, but you go see the sisters at St. Kate's on Marquette Ave. It's a women's dormitory for good Catholic girls in the Cities. They'll fix you right up. Then come back and see us on Wednesday night for our ladies' group supper. We'll get you settled in no time."

She spoke with a nasally Wisconsin accent and unmissable cloying cheer. Sheila reminded me of Karen Cooper, and I couldn't wait to get out of there.

"Oh my, that sounds like just the thing," I said through my teeth. "St. Kate's on Marquette and Wednesday night, got it. Thank you."

Armed with directions, I was sent on my way with a smile from Sheila and the invitation to supper repeated several times. She reminded me of all the nosy church ladies back in Friedrich, but she was nice enough, and she did give me the dormitory as a solution, after all.

* * *

I stood outside St. Kate's Dormitory for Christian Women on a side street off Marquette Avenue, staring at the squat gray brick building. *Maybe these will be my people*, I thought.

A nun in full habit greeted me when I pulled the door open and stepped inside the entryway. I realized that she wasn't that much older than me, her unlined forehead hidden by the coif. *The habit adds ten years*, I thought, wishing Annie was there to hear that joke.

"Can I help you?" she asked.

"Is there a room available? Sheila at the Basilica said there might be."

She perked up at Sheila's name, and the young nun heaved a thick plastic binder onto the desk. She flipped to a blank form in the back.

"Fill this out," she said, turning it toward me. "It's thirty-five dollars a week. Breakfast and supper are at six on the bell. Don't be late or you don't eat. No visitors after nine PM. No male visitors upstairs. No alcohol, no smoking, no funny business." She smiled as she recited the rules like catechism.

I finished the form, giving them Annie's last name—Holbrooke—and information in case they'd actually call my family.

"It's thirty-five for the week," the young sister repeated. "Up front," she added when I stood there dumbly.

I dug in my backpack for Grandpa Ridder's envelope and pulled out a few crisp bills. It took a large bite out of my cash, but a clean bed and hot shower were worth it. I would only be able to afford a week or two there, so I would have to get it together quickly.

"Good," the sister said. She scooped up the stack and did a quick count. "Room two-sixteen is open. You can take your things up now, and we'll see you at six PM sharp. The bathrooms are at the top of the stairs. Two-sixteen will be down the hall on the right." She started to close the book and turned away.

I stood motionless, arms by my side. "Do I get a key?"

The young sister's face mimicked sternness. "No keys here. Open-door policy, and Sisters Margaret or Anne may do an inspection at any time. And I'm Sister Katherine," she added, to deny any association with the ruthless room inspectors. "Sister Kate of St. Kate's." She smiled to herself.

I nodded and headed to the stairs in the back of the first floor. I passed the open door to the dining room behind the front office and a poorly decorated sitting room for entertaining male visitors under the sisters' supervision. I found my room on the second floor—small, dimly lit by one hideous yellow bedside table lamp, desk, chair, twin bed made up in the same putrid yellow, and a small sliver of a window looking down on Marquette Avenue.

I had never been so grateful for a hot shower in my life. After, wrapped in a graying towel, I peeled back the scratchy coverlet to lay on the cool sheets. The shower had washed away the last traces of guilt and Friedrich and Magda's authority clinging to me, a clean break between everything that had happened in my life up to that point and the life I would choose next for myself.

But at the passing thought of Magda, I could've sworn I felt her tugging at me. It might've been my imagination, my fear, or maybe I wasn't as disconnected from the ice floe as I thought I was. Now that I had tasted my freedom, even for a day, I couldn't stand the thought of Magda or anyone else dragging me back kicking and screaming. I would have none of it.

I remembered seeing a potted plant at the reception desk and sat up. But I stopped—it would have done nicely for another shield, but I couldn't risk casting and further drawing on the ice floe in the process. With my heart already bound to the cedar chest, I wasn't sure if there was a safe way to completely sever the energy connection between me and Magda and the cedar chest. I shuddered to think of the consequences if I tried and something went wrong.

Can you hide me, Dorothy? I asked, realizing another option. The other side had strange powers and energy that I was only beginning to understand.

I'll do my best, she pulsed at me. *It may not hold . . . but I'll try.*

After a moment, I felt the energy around me dim. In my mind's eye, I saw the door where I had tried to stuff the ice floe shrink and disappear entirely. I fluttered my eyes open and tested the immediate energy field. I felt nothing, a peaceful blank slate like a bubble around me. Magda's energy was no longer tailing me. I was off the grid, for the moment at least. My actions were my own for the first time in my life.

*   *   *

When I heard the rising din of female voices from below, I attempted to smooth my hair into a bun like Sheila's and went to join them.

In the dining room, about thirty women were already seated at long rectangular tables. I worked my way through the line at the front where Sister Kate and another nun served lasagna, green beans, and Jell-O cups. I set a glass of milk on my tray and turned to face the room.

Is this what I ditched Friedrich for? I thought, eyeing the orange grease congealing around the lasagna. I scanned the downturned faces of the other girls, barely women, dressed for dates or other Saturday social activities—neat blouses tucked into form-fitting but appropriate skirts, sweater sets, a few in jeans like me.

It reminded me uncomfortably of the Friedrich cafeteria, but what choice did I have? I slid into an empty seat near the front of the room. Without bothering to introduce myself or make eye contact with the good Catholic girls sitting there, I shoveled limp green beans into my mouth. I could feel inquisitive eyes on me, but I didn't have the energy to make small talk, to give some fictional backstory to these girls.

A brunette across the table caught my eye as I approached the lasagna.

"Don't let the sisters see you start without praying first," she said in a low tone. I had a flash of Grandma Ridder's stories of getting her knuckles smacked by a ruler-wielding nun at parochial school in St. Agnes.

I couldn't suppress an eye roll as I crossed myself. This strange new sisterhood wasn't quite the future version of myself I had daydreamed about. I perfunctorily thanked the Virgin Mary and my grandmothers for delivering me safely, said a quick *Bless us oh Lord*, and recrossed myself.

I tried to remind myself that a bed and a hot meal weren't nothing. I tore through the lasagna and swallowed down the last bite with a sip of milk. I plunged a spoon into the Jell-O cup, but my stomach turned at the squelching sound it made. Resigned, I nudged the tray away. When I noticed a few girls were starting to bus their trays to the kitchen and filtering out to start on elaborate predate beauty routines, I quickly followed. I had the urge to do something new, something I had never done before.

After spending a few futile moments attempting to tame my hair, I gave up and headed out the front door.

"Curfew is at nine PM," I heard Sister Kate call as the door slammed behind me.

Twenty-One

I didn't know how long I'd have before Magda or my father would chase me down, before I'd have to face the consequences of my actions. I wanted to experience a completely different grown-up life in the time I had. I wanted to experience everything that had been deemed unbecoming of the granddaughter of Magda Watry. I wanted to let loose. I wanted to forget the look of terror on the faces of my friends, family, and neighbors.

Within a few blocks of St. Kate's, I saw a sign for Radgard's Neighborhood Drinking Establishment, and it piqued my interest. I had never set foot in a real bar before, the only option in Friedrich being the VFW. With a passing thought about what Dorothy might think, I pushed open the door and stepped into a dimly lit interior like a subterranean dungeon. For a Saturday evening, the place was surprisingly empty. I glanced at the Coca-Cola clock on the wall. *What time do people go to bars anyway?*

I hesitated, lost in the space between the dart boards and the row of barstools. My arms hung uselessly at my sides as I wavered. I closed my eyes tight, overwhelmed.

"Rough day?" I heard as I opened my eyes.

I blinked. A good-looking bartender, hard and lean with shaggy brown hair and a dimple you could lose a nickel in, watched me with curiosity.

"You could say that," I said with a shrug, immediately changing my posture. *Be cool*, I told myself. *Fit in.*

The bartender watched me intently as he polished a glass. His eyes were light brown, but they shone golden in the uneven yellow lighting of the bar.

"Pull up a seat. What can I get you?"

I hesitated, having only drunk beer before. "Seven-and-seven?" I said after a moment, my voice rising at the end. I wondered what kind of girls drank them. It was what my father drank sometimes. It was one of the few drinks I knew by name.

If it was a strange order, the bartender gave no indication, just nodded and took a glass from a rack above the bar. I liked him immediately.

He held my gaze with those golden eyes and set the drink in front of me. I tried not to wince at the burn as I took my first sip.

"Well," he said. "Are you going to tell me about your day?"

Since it was a day of firsts, I straightened my back and thought, *What the hell?* After years of the feeling of settling with John, a man's attention, any attention, sent a small thrill down my spine.

"No," I said impulsively, shutting the door on my entire life up to that moment. "Tell me about you."

His eyes glittered with surprise.

Another customer called him. The bartended nodded in that direction and said, "I'll be back for you." He stared for a beat too long before turning away.

I was uncomfortable. I was excited.

I watched him attend to the regulars at the other end of the bar. They were tradesmen by the looks of them, in crisp work pants and light-blue shirts with names stitched on breast pockets, having a few beers and one-upping each other with loud stories. The bartender poured them a few more, the firm curve of his bicep flexing under his plaid shirt. It made me think suddenly of John and his boyish physique, his arms the arms of a farmer's son, a body that had grown up knowing hard work. The bartender was different— lean and calcified and definitely a man, although he couldn't have been more than twenty-three.

I had rid myself of Magda's shadow, but the thought of John made my stomach sink. He deserved so much better than my half-heart, than my blatant destruction of our presumed future together and running off without a word.

The bartender turned and caught me watching him, and whatever cowardice and guilt I felt were buried beneath a new fluttering in my chest. He raised one eyebrow to appraise me and smiled a half smile at me, a sly thing that showed in his golden eyes and the upward curl of his lip, that dimple in his right cheek. After that, I didn't think about John anymore.

*   *   *

His name was Nick. We talked all night—but I could barely register time or what we talked about, everything from ice fishing and waterskiing to Coca-Cola's new distribution plants in St. Paul, and music, so much music. In the back of my mind, I knew I was ignoring reality, but in the moment, it felt amazing to pretend. It felt amazing to talk to someone who had no idea who I was, who my grandmother was, or what I had done. I could've been anyone, as far as Nick knew. I could be anything.

My mind went completely blank when his golden eyes met mine. It might've been from the whiskey. *I'm someone who drinks whiskey now*, I thought to myself, giddy with the newness of it all. I had never drunk so much in my life. Annie and I had shared warm beers at parties, but never enough to make my arms feel heavy and my laugh tinny in my own ears. I felt invincible. Everything was so funny, and I wanted to savor every unexpected, blurry moment.

Nick went to serve another customer, the place filling up in the peak hours between ten and midnight, and I sipped my drink through my teeth, ice cubes clattering against my mouth. I watched Nick lean across the bar and laugh heartily with a couple in their late twenties. I realized I was the only woman there alone, and by far the youngest. Panic swelled to the surface for one brief moment. But then Nick was back asking if I had seen the latest Johnny Carson, and I would've stood naked in Siberia to talk to that man, to talk to anyone who wanted to know what I thought about anything besides water charms and Magda.

I had flirted some with other boys to get a rise out of John. But that, and what I did with John, could barely be considered flirting. John was an inevitability, and there was never the excitement of the chase, the thrill of attention from a well-executed hair flip or a perfectly timed remark; there was just a settling into our roles, linking arms and getting on with it. No man had ever watched me as closely as Nick did that night.

I totaled the drinks in my head. At seventy-five cents each, I had had far too many already. But with each drink, I relaxed more in my body. I felt a new kind of power with Nick's eyes on me. I tested the limits of how he would react, feeling his gaze even when he was across the room talking to someone else: *if I move this way, his eyes do that; if I say this, his lips do that.* It was like he had an antenna tuned to me and me alone. I felt hunted and wondered drunkenly if the antelope ever enjoyed succumbing to the lion. I laughed at myself and my own ridiculous thoughts. Nick was a specimen to be turned over in my hands, his every move cataloged. There was something irresistible in his attention, something all my own that existed only in that moment.

The bar started to clear out, and through my whiskey haze, I suddenly felt exposed. My reckless confidence went out the door with the last woman on the arm of her beau, going home at a proper time with a proper escort. It was too much. Too much change in too short of a day, from Magda and the fire and the Greyhound to this. *This isn't right.*

"I've got to go," I mumbled in Nick's direction, wheeling around on the barstool. I stood and threw a few bills down, unsure if it was too much or too little, but I didn't want to lose momentum as I stumbled toward the door.

"Hey, wait," Nick said behind me as I reached the door.

I hesitated. Nick stood at the edge of the bar, rag slung over his shoulder, one hand poised on the edge.

He cocked his head to the side, watching me. When I didn't move, he said, "I'll see you soon, Elisabeth."

I melted when he said my name—the only name I had given him, anyway. But underneath, I felt the steel edge of fear and could only nod in response. My feet, and whiskey bravado, carried me forward into the night before I knew what I was doing.

The walk home—and I was already thinking of St. Kate's as home—was impossibly long and treacherous in my state, but somehow I made it. However, Sister Margaret must have noticed I didn't make curfew and was waiting up for me at reception. Fueled by whiskey and adrenaline, I was careless enough to cast a little memory charm at her to ease my passage. She smiled blankly and turned her attention to tidying the desk in front of her as if I weren't there. I tripped up the stairs and fell into bed feeling triumphant.

Twenty-Two

When I woke up with a start, one of many times that night, I realized that my dreamcatcher still hung in Friedrich. Even as the ice floe was undetectable during the day, the door to the other side was flung wide open when I closed my eyes. A flood of voices rushed at me to tell their stories that night, so many untethered spirits searching for a friendly energy.

Around that aptly named witching hour, I gave up on sleep and lay awake studying the room. My body was exhausted, but I couldn't make myself close my eyes and venture unguarded into the spirit world again. Without my dreamcatcher and without Magda's cedar chest nearby, I feared I wouldn't have the strength to draw the veil between worlds firmly back into place.

Streetlights outside on Marquette Avenue lit the room with a milky haze. It didn't look anything like it did during the day. An insidious shape hung across the second-floor window, swaying slightly. I reminded myself, *There's an elm tree there on the sidewalk.* An unidentifiable form occupied the desk chair, making it look like someone sitting there, like one old woman in particular come to hunt me down.

My heart raced as I told myself it was nothing, nothing at all in that chair. But I was alone in a big city, and I was drunk. The pit in my stomach grew and my eyes ached as I stared at the ceiling. But I refused to look at the chair and acknowledge who or what lurked there.

I must have fallen asleep at some point, because I was abruptly awakened by the clanging of the bell for breakfast. Solstice, Magda, the fire—it all came back to me in a rush. *That really happened* quickly followed by *Oh God, what did I do?*

Groggy and shocked that it was six AM already, I felt like I had a mouth full of cotton. I finally understood that phrase. I sat up slowly and forced my gaze on the suspiciously empty chair. I laughed unconvincingly at my fear and racing heart of the night before, but I knew all too well that an empty chair in the morning didn't mean I had been unwatched at night. I shook my head to banish the all-too-familiar form from my mind. *It was a dream*, I told myself with false conviction. *A drunken dream.*

My head pounding and with no responsibilities, no one waiting on me, I decided to forgo breakfast and closed my eyes again.

* * *

I awoke hours later to bright sunlight. The halls were quiet, as most of the other good Catholic girls of St. Kate's must have been off to mass and other Sunday doings. I hauled my body, heavy as lead, down the hall toward the showers. But when I saw the second-floor phone booth, I felt a jolt of energy from Dorothy. I hesitated, staring. *Do I have to?* I asked.

Images of Mary and our house on Lake Street zapped through my mind.

I didn't want to, but Dorothy was right. I should probably let someone know I was safe.

If you say so.

I pulled the door shut behind me, picked up the receiver, and recited the numbers by heart for the operator.

I was relieved when Mary answered the phone the way Magda insisted. "Hello, Watry residence. Who's calling, please?"

My mind scrambled for the right thing to say. My tongue froze in my mouth. *What must she think of me? Mary saw Magda cast on me first, right?*

"Lisbett?" Mary whispered on the other end of the line. Of course she knew it was me, even before I spoke.

"I'm sorry," I croaked. "Is Harry's . . . ?" I couldn't finish.

"It's not good," Mary said quietly. "Where are you? Magda's, well, she's mad, but it will blow over . . . It will be better to face her."

I was scared to ask, but I had to. "What . . . what happened at Harry's? Did anybody . . . ?" I couldn't finish the sentence.

"Harry's is gone," Mary snapped.

"What do you mean?"

Mary didn't answer, and I began to panic. "Mary! What do you mean?"

"No one died," Mary said finally. "But just barely. Mr. Raymond is in the hospital."

The mustachioed face of Harry's line cook flashed through my mind. "Oh God," I croaked. *What did I do?* "Mare, I've gotta go," I said in a rush. "I wanted to tell you I'm safe. Don't come looking for me. I love you. Be good."

"Lisbett!" Mary yelled as I hovered the receiver over the hook. I set it down like I was laying it to rest.

I stumbled back down the hall toward my room in a daze. It had been a mistake to call. What if Magda could trace me? What if they came for me? *Who am I kidding? Magda probably already knows*, I thought.

I can't go back there.

I needed a plan. I had enough cash for one more week at St. Kate's, but if I was going to stay in Minneapolis, I'd need to think of something, fast. I let myself lie back on the ugly yellow coverlet and mope for a half hour. I felt very alone and very far from home. My mind wandered back to Magda and Mom and Mary and what they all must be thinking about my out-of-control magic and Harry's and, God forbid, what the town must be thinking of our family in the wake of it all. Was my family safe? Would our neighbors try to run us out of town after such a dangerous display? But no, surely Magda wouldn't allow that, I told myself.

I was plagued, too, by the fear that Mary and Mom hadn't seen Magda cast on me first. Maybe they thought I was the aggressor. I felt a masochistic pull to cast out the ice floe for Mary and see what she really thought. But it would be like looking into the sun. I knew I shouldn't, but I couldn't tear myself away from the empire of secrets that was my family.

I was about to head to the showers when the dinner bell rang. I wanted to ignore it and hide out with my feelings, but my stomach gurgled at the thought of food. I threw on my same dirty jeans and blouse, the only outfit I had packed for Annie's, and headed downstairs begrudgingly.

The tables were full already with chattering young women in their Sunday clothes. I was hoping to blend in, mind my own business, but it was hard in such close quarters. I took an empty chair at a table already seating five girls, where the same brunette from the previous night watched me with mild curiosity. She elbowed her friend in the high-necked blouse and announced loudly to the table, "All right girls, we have a fresh body. What's she need to know?"

I felt myself blush as the other girls stopped their conversations and turned to me. *So much for going unnoticed.* I started to cut my chicken, waiting to be appraised.

A plain-faced blonde on my right leaned over and stage-whispered dramatically for the table's benefit, "The chicken's okay, but the Salisbury steak is crap. Make dinner plans for Wednesday nights."

A big-boned girl across from the blonde shrugged. "I don't think it's that bad . . ."

"The macaroni's okay," another girl admitted with a shrug.

"Don't ever expect to see a vegetable."

"Check your packed lunch before you walk away at breakfast. Sometimes girls trade or pinch things from the sacks."

"They pack us lunch?" I asked.

"Every weekday. Brown bag, peanut butter on white bread, apple, chocolate chip cookie," another girl answered.

"Sister Margaret farts," the blonde dramatically whispered again, "a *lot*. Don't sit next to her." That was met with a burst of giggles that drew the sharp eyes of the sisters at the front of the room.

I laughed genuinely with them. *This isn't so bad*, I thought. As the laughter petered out, I offered, "I'm Elisabeth."

The brunette gave a little wave across the table. "Bridget," she said, motioning for the other girls to introduce themselves.

There were three Marys, an Anne, and two Katherines. They came from all over the state, and a few, like the blonde, Diane, were from Illinois or Wisconsin.

Bridget's eyes wandered over me again as she sipped her coffee. "How old are you?"

"Eighteen," I said.

Bridget nodded. "I'm nineteen."

I tried to not show my surprise. It was hard to believe that this confident woman, who seemed to know things about the world, was barely a year older than me.

"Do you have a job lined up?" Bridget asked.

I shook my head. "Nothing."

She set her coffee cup down and seemed to consider me again, deciding if she liked me.

I must have passed the test, because she said, "I'm a full-time nanny for a family in Lowry Hill. They asked me to babysit Tuesday, but I have a date with Richie—that's my boyfriend. I can give them your name if you're up for it?"

Babysitting sounded like a dream, although I would've accepted anything in that moment for the money. "Yes!" I said with a little too much enthusiasm. "I mean, that would be great. Thank you. Really, it's so nice of you."

"Good thinking," Diane said. "I might be able to get you an interview with my department at Dayton's. I'm in women's ready-to-wear on the fifth floor." She frowned at me then. "We'll need to do something about your clothes, though."

Bridget laughed at that. "Well, she's right," she said with a broad smile, waving a hand in my direction for emphasis. "Or you can always borrow things for now."

"Thank you," I said, my eyes welling up with gratitude.

A wave of relief washed over me. These girls didn't have to be nice to me. They didn't have to help me. But here they were, welcoming me into their fold. I was grateful. It wasn't a long-term plan, but it was enough to buy me time to figure out what I was going to do, what I might want to do.

I forced myself to head for the showers first as I contemplated my next move. Standing under a stream of lukewarm water with my heart racing in my chest, I realized it was going to be harder to disown my magical birthright than I had ever imagined. Even though I had tried to disconnect myself from the ice floe and Dorothy was doing her best to shield me, the connection was still there, just beneath the surface, the minute I was careless or emotional enough. It was too easy to reach through and grab it again. I wanted to explore a life for myself that was entirely different from what Magda had wanted for me, but so far, every road had brought me right back into Magda's orbit.

As my heart rate slowed, my mind wandered back to Nick the bartender, the only bright spot in an exhausting twenty-four hours. The thought of Nick's hard, lean arms popped into my head, followed by those strong hands pouring a cold draft of Milwaukee's finest, and after that . . . those strong hands in my hair, on my body . . . Anything to make me feel better about Harry's and Mr. Raymond.

I shook my head to clear the thought. Nick and the bar would have to wait for another day. I needed to save my money. I would need money if I was going to get out of St. Kate's, away from where Magda already knew I was. I towel-dried my hair and wrestled it into a plain braid as best I could—*I wish Mary was here*, I thought with a pang to my heart—then knocked on Diane's door to see about borrowing clothes to look for a job on Monday.

Twenty-Three

I spent Monday poring over the help-wanted ads in the paper I borrowed from Sister Kate, who offered to put the word out to parishioners who might be looking for childcare. I hesitated—did I want to be a nanny like Bridget? Was that what I had fled Friedrich for? I had never taken care of kids before and couldn't see myself doing that for long. But I didn't have the luxury of being picky. Any job would do, at least at the beginning.

I knocked on a few doors, talked to shop owners and office managers who were hiring. No one seemed terribly excited to talk to an eighteen-year-old without a résumé. I made a mental note to ask the sisters if they had a typewriter and see if any of the girls could help me come up with something.

After I ate my peanut butter sandwich, I spent the afternoon wandering along the river in the mild sunshine. I was nervous that Magda would know I had used magic at St. Kate's and come looking for me, so I thought it best to spend as little time there as possible.

Watching the river, I thought again of the Ridder Family Company office in the nearby downtown, and curiosity got the better of me. Had word made it to the Ridder men in Minneapolis? I couldn't resist scouting it out for myself.

I didn't know the exact address, but I knew the office was a few blocks from the riverfront from years of Dad's stories. My uncles Ridder loved to joke about the over-the-top restaurant built right on top of the remains of the Standard Mill, which they could see from the office windows. Curious, I wandered over to the Washburn A Mill, the one that had been rebuilt after the infamous explosion in 1878, and started walking. I was looking for anything that looked familiar, any hint of the cross street that contained the Ridder Family Company office.

I knew it was risky, but since I had stupidly cast on Sister Margaret, I couldn't be a sitting duck waiting for Magda to come. I had to know if they were looking for me. I had to know how much time I had left, if I even had time to try to make a new life, one without magic, without the burden of my family.

Be careful, mein Liebling, Dorothy whispered as I walked.

Can't you hide me, Dorothy? I asked, annoyed.

You have to find your own path, mein Liebling, she pulsed at me, as if she had read my next thought, even when I didn't direct it at her. *And if you are going to keep using magic, there is only so much I can do, child.*

Point taken, I responded.

As I made my way north along the mill outbuildings, I spotted the sleek glass-and-polished-oak exterior of the new Fuji Ya restaurant that had my uncles so confounded—*A fancy restaurant right there by the falls; can you believe it!* I cut down a footpath back toward the riverfront and the restaurant, which was quiet in the afternoon. As I looked over my shoulder, all the tall buildings I saw in the area belonged to the Washburn Mill.

But as I rounded the front of the restaurant and crossed the parking lot, a stout tan brick building rose across the green to the north. I approached from the river side, and I was glad I did, because when I came around the side of the building, there was my father's station wagon parked in front of the main entrance. And there was my father a hundred yards away talking to Uncle Joe. I froze and slammed myself flat against the bricks. Dad stood on the sidewalk with his head braced in one hand, thankfully looking down.

I slid back around the corner of the building to face the river, praying I hadn't been seen, even as I felt I looked different in a borrowed A-line dress from Diane and my long hair slicked into a tight bun like Sheila's. Somehow I'd had a feeling this was what I would find, but I had needed to confirm my suspicions. It was too late. Here was my father to track me down, to drag me home to face the music.

Magda must have felt me cast in the city, but maybe she didn't know *exactly* where I was, I realized with a glimmer of hope. It wouldn't be like looking for a familiar energy in the well-known environs of Friedrich. It was nearly five o'clock. Dad could have spent the whole day looking for me. *Maybe this is him giving up, telling Uncle Joe to keep an eye out.*

Even if Dad had come to look for me, I would not give him, or Magda, the satisfaction of finding me. I was determined to have another day of freedom. I inched along the back of the building, toward Fuji Ya. *Am I safe, Dorothy? Is he coming this way?* I asked her.

Go, quickly now, she answered.

I hustled down a sloping footpath toward the riverfront, moving as quickly as I felt I could without drawing attention to myself. I stuck to the riverfront paths as I made my way south for as long as possible before crossing back into the city streets toward St. Kate's. None of the sisters said anything to me when I returned, so I figured my cover was safe for another day. Still, I slept fitfully, lest I slip into the spirit world unawares again.

Twenty-Four

Bridget's nanny family had a darling chubby-cheeked one-year-old girl, Vanessa, and a precocious three-year-old boy, Tyler, who asked me "Why?" all night but more or less listened to me. But Tyler was toilet training and managed to have two accidents over the four hours he was awake, and I was relieved when he finally fell asleep. It was nice to have a quiet hour to myself in a big house in an unfamiliar part of the city. But as I scrubbed Tyler's playclothes, I knew that nannying wasn't going to be for me. When Vanessa cried, I felt the same frustration I did with the animals of Kandiyohi County—*I wish you could tell me what you need.* And I didn't dare use magic to find out.

When Mr. Johnson laid a crisp ten-dollar bill in my hand at the end of the night, all I could think about was what Nick would be up to then. I wanted more of his rapt attention and the thrill of knowing that he had no idea who I was, who I had been before. I wanted to pretend I was a girl with a whole heart to give away as she pleased.

But when I pushed through the door of the bar, Nick wasn't behind the bar. My heart skipped a beat. *Stupid*, I chided myself. *What was I expecting anyway?*

I had started to turn to go, wondering how long I'd be safe from Magda at St. Kate's or if I dared used another charm to break curfew, when I heard his voice over my shoulder.

"You're back, huh? I must have made quite the impression."

There he was, muscles straining under the weight as he hauled a new keg up from the cellar.

I tossed my head back easily, instantly buoyed with a confidence that I barely recognized.

"I'm just thirsty is all. Nothing to do with you."

I strode forward and clambered awkwardly onto a barstool directly in front of Nick. I dropped my bag on the ground, which was sticky with sawdust and peanut shells. He grinned as he slid the keg into its proper place and tapped it smoothly.

"Well, all right then," he said, straightening up. "What'll it be, Elisabeth?"

He drew out the syllables of my name like he was savoring them, and I melted all over again. I was suddenly very sure of my decision.

I pouted and tapped the Cupid's bow of my top lip in mock concentration. *Seven-and-seven*, I almost said, but remembering the whiskey burn, I felt the spirit move me otherwise.

"What do you recommend?" I said with a smile.

He contemplated me for a moment. "Gin fizz," he said seriously.

I didn't know anything about it, but it seemed grown-up and ladylike to me. I nodded.

Nick smiled and reached for a bottle. "Coming right up," he said.

*　　*　　*

I didn't know what would come next, but I knew that I wanted it. I felt both completely in control of my actions and simultaneously like I was floating above my body watching the scene. John flashed through my mind briefly, but I pushed him away. I knew I was being careless, the kind of woman I teased Annie about lest she become one, but I didn't care. I needed to be anything except what I had been in my grandmother's house.

Nick was a musician. As the last of the Sunday evening regulars filtered out into the June night, he leaned across the bar and told me he played guitar in a band called Hiawatha Man, named for the fictional peacemaker of the Longfellow epic. They played on Saturday nights in Uptown. I smiled and nodded when he went on about music being like a physical part of him, as essential as his heart or liver. I didn't know what he was talking about, but I pretended I did because I wanted him to keep talking. It was easier than talking about myself. I could pretend we were falling in love for real if he kept talking.

As Nick spoke about the rhythm of a hot bass line and slide picks and developing his voice while growing up in Red Wing, Minnesota, I pictured myself standing in front of the stage while he played. I would wear flowing peasant sleeves like Joan Baez and wear my hair longer than it already was, and Nick would write songs about being tamed by his one true love, the wild woman whose heart matched his own. All the other girls would sway their hips to the music, and they would be so damn jealous when they realized Nick was singing about me. At the end of the night, we would go home together and crash up the stairs in one of those turn-of-the-century Minneapolis houses, barely making it to the bedroom before tearing off each other's clothes, and then . . . *and then what?* I caught myself thinking.

The last of the neighborhood crew said goodnight to Nick, their good buddy and ever-present sympathetic ear. He grinned at me, and I pictured his arms wrapped around my waist, lifting me effortlessly into the air like one of those kegs.

He met my eye. "Do you want to get out of here?" he asked. That dimple in his right cheek emphasized his devilish grin.

It was better than risking breaking curfew again at St. Kate's or drawing Magda's attention with another charm.

*   *   *

Nick reached around me to pull the front door closed—and locked it, I noted. We were in the kind of neighborhood where people locked their doors. Nobody did that in Friedrich. His home was not the charming little house I pictured.

Nick rented a room in the back of a house where I saw evidence of at least three other roommates. He led me through the kitchen to his first-floor bedroom tacked onto the back of the house. It should've been a laundry room at best, but sure enough, there was barely enough room for someone to walk around the perimeter of a full-size mattress on the floor. That mattress had never seen clean sheets, but I was thankful in that moment that at least it had sheets.

Reality broke through as I took in the room. Nick watched me from a respectful distance as I eyed the strangely neat row of guitars that lined one wall. A broken closet door hung open, revealing a mountain of dirty laundry. The room smelled faintly musky, like a man, like sweat and whiskey and cigarettes.

What am I doing here? I felt suddenly very sober, but I didn't want to leave. I was nervous and excited and scared all at the same time—and somehow calm about it all.

"So this is my place. What do you think?" Nick said softly, standing within arm's reach.

I leaned toward him, testing the touch of my hand on his chest. *I chose this*, I told myself. *I want this.*

"It's nice," I said in a low voice, trying to play the part. "I like your guitars."

Nick took my face in both hands and kissed me long and slow, more gently than I was expecting. I slipped my arms around his waist. A thrill went through me when I felt his flat, hard stomach beneath his shirt.

As I relaxed into the kiss, Nick's hands migrated. He twisted my braid, gathering my hair around his fist, and pulled my head back softly but firmly so that my lips couldn't reach his. I tugged against his grip, my mouth opening and closing softly as I was stuck, wanting him. He held me like that, immobile, and I opened my eyes to see him smiling down at me, enjoying my struggle.

"You like me, don't you?" he teased.

"Yes," I said.

"Good," Nick said. He kissed me hard as we tumbled to the mattress together.

In the back of my mind, I realized that Dorothy hadn't made herself known for a while. I was embarrassed to think she might be watching me, embarrassed of what she'd think. But . . . *she has no problem telling me what she thinks. She would have steered me away if she thought I belonged somewhere else,* I reassured myself.

I was surprised when Nick didn't immediately undress me. My hands went to the hem of his shirt—I thought that's what I was supposed to do—and he automatically lifted his arms as I pulled his shirt over his head. Nick's bare skin was beautiful, taut over lean muscles, and unblemished save for a crooked scar that snaked from his clavicle down the side of his heart. I couldn't resist tracing it with a finger.

"I caught a branch helping my dad remove a tree after a storm when I was thirteen," Nick offered.

His face fell in the ambient light through the uncurtained windows.

Before I could ask—*Did I do something wrong?*—Nick blurted out, "What do you think happens when we die? Like, after? What happens to us?"

"That's a big question," I said slowly, surprised.

I felt self-conscious of my hands hovering above his chest. I could feel the warmth off his skin.

"Come here," Nick said, tugging me toward him. He turned me over in his arms, pressing my back to his bare chest. Nick nuzzled his chin into that soft spot between my ear and neck. I complied, confused at the turn of events.

"I've been thinking about it lately," Nick said with a sigh, his breath warm behind my ear. "My dad died last month, and it takes me by surprise sometimes. Like it's such a trip to be here with a beautiful girl and breathing and thinking and my dad isn't here anymore. He's just gone. Poof, he doesn't exist anymore. Gone from earth." Nick's voice trembled as his words came out faster.

I shivered as he absently ran a hand across the softness of my belly where my shirt had inched away from my jeans. Nick whispered into my hair, like he was talking to himself, entranced as he traced shapes on my exposed skin, and I was flooded with tenderness for him.

I didn't know what to say but tried to make soothing noises. I started to think maybe we wouldn't do it after all and was vaguely relieved. I felt painfully awkward. *Does he like me, or does he need a sympathetic ear? What did I think was going to happen anyway?*

As Nick rambled on, I realized how vulnerable he was beneath the hard-boiled exterior, and I began to understand the role I was playing for him—a comfort, a distraction. It took immense self-control to not cast out the ice floe and read him, to soothe his energy in all the ways I had been trained. I decided to do the next best thing: I told the truth.

"I don't think that's true," I said cautiously when he stopped to take a breath. "The end is not just the end. People leave this earth, but they're always with us."

"Yeah, they're with us in *spirit*?" he said with more than a hint of sarcasm. "I've heard that one before. Like, what does some priest really know about me and my family and where my dad is now? He's with *God*? That's the best they can do?"

I wriggled out of Nick's arms and pushed myself up on one elbow to face him.

"I mean it," I said. "It's not exactly like they say in church. But it's definitely not the end. Spirits walk among us. We just can't all see them."

Nick mirrored my pose on my elbow, cradling his head in one big hand. He searched my eyes intently. "How do you know?" he asked seriously. "How do you know what comes next? What if we're all wrong and it's just over?"

"Because I've seen it," I dared to say.

Nick gave me a funny look, rightly so, and I couldn't bring myself to say the next part: *Because the spirits are there on the other side of the frozen energy river. Because my departed great-grandmother talks to me and may even be here now. Because I grew up in a house where magic is real, spirits are real, and we are stewards of this earth for a short time before we pass our learnings to the next generation.* I couldn't tell a man I'd just met all that . . . unless he had grown up in a place like Friedrich too, where the friendly county witches were around to take care of the town and the spirits and all that.

So I said the most true thing I could manage. "How do you know there isn't something after? Our existence on this earth is too random, too special, that we rose out of the bubbling swamps and dark forests, for what? It can't be random. There is something larger than us at play, something we will never quite understand. It's there, the spirit world, all around us; we can't all tap into it. It has to be there. Our little lives here aren't enough. There is more to this place than meets the eye."

I got chills as I said it, the soft blonde hair standing up on my arms and the back of my neck. If Dorothy was listening, I knew she was proud of what I had to say.

Nick nodded solemnly. "Maybe." He smiled and reached out to tug on a lock of my hair that had worked its way free.

I smiled, thinking that maybe we'd talk all night. Maybe that's what he needed.

But then Nick reached for me, pulling me close, and wrapped a hand in my hair. I laughed, surprised and unsure of myself, as Nick pulled me down on top of him by the shoulders, and I knew I wouldn't say no. He paused to retrieve a condom from the dresser, so nonchalant, and I tried to play along, hiding my inexperience. *Can he tell I don't know what I'm doing? That I'm barely not a virgin?* But then he made love to me, frantically, hungrily, like I could fill the void that threatened to swallow him whole when he let his mind get quiet.

*   *   *

I thought dreamily, after, that I had never once been remotely satisfied by what John and I did. I didn't know I could be. I wouldn't have known how to ask for that indescribable mix of pain and pleasure until Nick was above me, his forearms hooked under my shoulders, teasing me slowly toward an edge I didn't have words for.

With my legs still shaking, my whole body coming down from that edge-place, Nick gave me a full-body squeeze and rolled to one side. He lay back, and I snuggled into that spot that let him wrap his arm around me and let me press my cheek into his chest. Nick lit a cigarette with his free hand, the scent instantly clinging to my skin and hair.

"That was nice."

"Mm-hmm," I managed.

I didn't know if we were supposed to talk more. My brain was like jelly. I was content enough to dare think that even if Dorothy was watching us, she wouldn't be judging.

Nick finished his cigarette and stroked my hair absently.

When I thought he had drifted off to sleep, Nick must have felt that void opening up, because he asked in a small voice, "So do you believe in God?"

I considered. I knew what I was supposed to say, the good Catholic daughter and all that, but I was beginning to like this feeling of telling the truth after so many years of hiding my voice and deferring to Magda. "I don't know," I ventured. "I believe in spirits and people and some kind of grand plan. But is it like they say? I don't know."

Nick seemed reassured by that. "Me too," he said, burrowing his nose into my neck and hair. His lips brushed the back of my ear. "Goodnight," he breathed. I started to drift off, feeling a sense of wonder toward Nick, and I hoped I could pretend to have a whole heart for a while longer. If I didn't have a heart to give, at least I could give Nick the truth.

Twenty-Five

I woke with a start, sweating. My mind was blank for a moment as I came out of the dream world. I realized with a jolt that I had been dreaming of John. Try as I might, I couldn't recall the details of the dream. But John's face was fresh in my mind, his voice lingering in my ear, and I felt guilty as Nick snored lightly with both arms stretched above his head.

The early-morning sunlight flooded Nick's tiny room from the row of windows above his guitars, illuminating all the dinginess and mess I hadn't seen the night before. I closed my eyes and, nestled under the covers, itched to cast out the ice floe for John. But I wouldn't break my own rules again. I couldn't dare expose myself to Magda again. Besides, what would I even see if I looked in on John? He'd be awake and moving ahead of the world on the farm, and he would be as betrayed as Mary when I called home. I had forfeited the right to gaze upon his life when I boarded that Greyhound.

I closed my eyes tight. *I chose this. I wanted this.* I snuggled into Nick's side but couldn't fall asleep again. My body thrummed with energy—excitement and that persistent underpinning of guilt for John, for Solstice, for Harry's and Mr. Raymond, for the look on my mother's face when she turned away from me and the anger and disappointment in Mary's voice when I called. I thought once again, *Did they see that Magda started it?* But it didn't matter. I was still guilty for trying to embarrass Magda, for letting it get out of control.

Still, I felt undeniably alive as I listened to the steady rise and fall of Nick's breath. I was sure I had done something no woman in my family had done before me. This was all mine. It was difficult to imagine my mother or Magda as young, wild women, or as anything like me at all. They were supposed to be my people, but I had felt invisible among them, or worse, like an outsider. The Watry name was supposed to mean something, but I couldn't imagine any other Watry woman burning the supper club to ashes, running away from home, or spending the night with a strange man, let alone doing all three.

I sighed and pressed my cheek into Nick's chest. I willed him silently to wake up and hold me, or better yet, to kiss me again—so different from the fumbling in John's truck—but I was content to lie there against Nick's hot, smooth skin, brushing his scar absently with my thumb, further delaying whatever flack I'd catch from the sisters.

*   *   *

Nick awoke with a yawn and a stretch that pulled his whole body taut beneath my cheek. It was well after ten AM. I couldn't think of a time when I had stayed in bed that late on a weekday when I wasn't sick.

I felt Nick watching me, checking to see if I was awake, and turned to look up at him, digging my chin into his chest.

"There you are," he said.

"Here I am," I said, uncertain.

"What are we gonna do today?" Nick asked sleepily, surprising me yet again.

"Oh," I wondered out loud, "I wasn't sure if last night was . . . if this was . . . a one-night thing?"

His laugh came out a sudden, belly-shaking bark.

"Oh, geez." His golden eyes creased in amusement as he ran a hand through his hair. "Last night was nice," he said. "But I'd like to see you in daylight too. I have practice with the guys at three, then back to the soul-sucking pit at five for the evening shift. I'm yours until then."

I was relieved that Nick didn't ask where I was staying or what I was doing in the Cities. I didn't know what I would've said, and I didn't want to lie to him, but I also didn't want to tell him the whole ugly truth. Even as he slid over and made room for me in his life and his bed, I wasn't sure if he wanted me around to fend off his own dark thoughts or if he really liked me.

Dorothy? I asked tentatively, lest she have any opinions. But no, it seemed I was on my own. I briefly wondered how much trouble I would be in when I finally went back to St. Kate's, but I figured in for a penny, in for a pound.

"Let's start with breakfast," I suggested.

*   *   *

We sat on the same side of a red-plastic booth in a family restaurant near Nick's house, away from the roaring river and busy downtown. We drank scalding black coffee out of stained porcelain mugs and talked of nothing in particular.

When I hesitated to order, acutely aware of the last bills stuffed in my pocket, Nick said, "My treat."

I asked for pancakes. Nicked ordered an obscene amount of food for two people. We were quiet waiting for the food, two grinning, sleep-deprived idiots in the corner booth.

"I can't believe you're still here," Nick said, bashful in the light of day.

"Why wouldn't I be?" I asked in mock offense.

"Most girls leave before breakfast," he said, pinching my thigh under the table. "But you were crazy enough to suggest it. Bold."

My heart dropped into my stomach at the mention of other girls, but I tried to ignore it. What did I know of Nick's life anyway?

"I have never been so hungry in my life," I said, raising my eyebrows at him.

It was true. There was an appetite awakened in me like I had never known.

"And I . . . I thought I may have scared you off," Nick said, dropping his gaze.

"No," I said. "And I am sorry about your dad."

"Thanks," he said quietly.

A waitress arrived bearing hot plates heaped with golden-brown pancakes and pats of melting butter, blueberry syrup for me and maple syrup for Nick, eggs over-easy with crispy edges, fluffy scrambled eggs, and a mound of thick-cut bacon. We barely had enough room to navigate between all the plates and sauces and jelly packets, my elbow knocking Nick in the ribs as I cut my pancakes.

I watched as Nick doused his eggs with ketchup—reminding me of Mary, who did the same thing—and my heart ached again beneath the easy, flirty mood of the morning.

*   *   *

After Nick paid the tab, we wandered through the neighborhood hand in hand. Nick would pause to point out buildings or landmarks or local curiosities of varying importance.

"That's the WCCO station that broadcasts all of the Twins games."

"That's where my buddy Greg fell asleep in the bushes when he was drunk."

"That's the new record store where I've been jamming with the guys sometimes," he said with a proud smile, stopping in front of a large storefront plastered with album covers and promo posters.

A neon sign declared the head-scratching name that was yet to become a Minneapolis institution: Electric Fetus.

"Let's go in," I said. Scandalized as I was, I was intrigued.

My eyes could barely take in all the artist and band names announced in the window, a treasure trove of music new to me. I could imagine nothing better than wandering the aisles and discovering new music with the handsome musician on my arm.

Nick flashed that heart-stopping smile at me. "You're the boss. Lead the way."

A long-haired man behind the counter was deep in conversation with a young man with a magnificent Afro. Neither of them looked up when we came in, despite the peal of bells over our heads. The long-haired man—*Is he the owner? Could a man with hair like that own a store like this?*—smashed his index finger down adamantly on the glass display for emphasis. A few other young people browsed the aisles or flipped leisurely through the wooden bins of records. A few people listened to records on competing stereo sets in the back of the store, a guitar solo floating over a woman's folksy alto.

As the young Black man threw up his hands and admitted defeat in whatever greatest-musician-of-our-time argument he and the other man had been engaged in and stepped back, I saw the peace flag draped across the glass display. I had seen the flag printed in the papers or *Time* magazine before but couldn't remember seeing one in person, certainly not in any of the antiquated establishments in Friedrich. It struck me as an instant declaration of what kind of place this was and the free-spirited, opinionated young people who frequented it. I wondered if I could be one of them. I wondered if Nick already thought I was.

We spent over an hour lazily browsing through the bins. Nick smiled politely as I pulled out my favorites, the Righteous Brothers and that ubiquitous Minnesotan native son Dylan, but his eyes lit up when I held up *Aftermath*.

"This," I said. "I heard this on the radio a few weeks ago."

"You like the Stones?" Nick said with an eyebrow raised in scrutiny. "You continue to impress me."

We sank into mismatched chairs in the back of the store and listened to the first side straight through. Nick reached for my hand, and I let him take it. We weren't sitting close enough for a good grip, but I liked the gesture, holding hands by our outstretched fingertips.

I was struck by this strange microcosm of Minneapolis and how it felt worlds away from anything I had known in my small town. I had never before imagined the possibility of spending an entire day in a record store, doing essentially nothing all day. It made me feel itchy, like there was something I was forgetting. I tried to push the feeling away and lose myself in the music, but the magic of the moment was gone.

"Don't you have somewhere you need to be?" I asked Nick, attempting a casual tone to cover my rising anxiety.

He glanced at the scratched watch on his wrist. "Are you trying to get rid of me?" he said. "I have all the time in the world for you . . . well, another half hour at least." I recalled with a shudder John making an almost identical declaration in absolute earnest.

Nick made a face as a couple of teenagers—younger than me, anyway—started blasting Yellow Submarine through the second hi-fi. "On second thought," he said, "let's get out of here."

* * *

A few stores down, something in the window caught my eye. A mannequin modeled a slip dress with a scandalously low back that looked like something Jane Birkin would wear.

"Ooh," I marveled, then felt childish.

I had never been one for fashion. That was Annie's department. But images of my new runaway bohemian lifestyle flashed through my head, and that dress, everything in that window, appealed more than the conservative dresses and sweater sets of the St. Kate's girls.

Nick watched me, amused. "Let's check it out," he suggested.

Among the neat rows of clean linens and loose, flowing cottons, I felt more embarrassed than ever by the same dirty jeans that were all Nick had seen me in. I couldn't borrow clothes from the girls forever. The dwindling cash from Grandpa Ridder called to me.

"Do you mind if I get a few things?" I said to Nick in as casual a tone as I could muster.

He shrugged and leaned against the wall by the door.

"Take your time," he said.

I grabbed a few shirts, and when I was sure Nick wasn't watching, I stuffed a handful of underwear underneath the clothing slung over my arm, not stopping to confirm colors or sizes. I hesitated in front of the Jane Birkin dress, deliberating about the cost, which was nearly everything I had earned babysitting.

"I'll get it for you," Nick said, suddenly at my side. "It will look nice on you."

"Thank you," I practically whispered, too dumbfounded to protest, humbled by the man at my side, who was as kind as he was quick. I was sure he didn't have the money to spare either, which made the gift mean that much more.

With a large shopping bag secured over my shoulder, I was one step closer to my daydream of swirling in loose fabric with bared legs and shoulders in the front row at Nick's gigs, one step closer to a new life.

We wandered the neighborhood for a while longer before giving in to the subtle downhill slope toward the river, across the famous Stone Arch Bridge, to watch the water pour down the falls. Nick was quiet beside me as I took it all in—the river, the falls, Gold Medal Flour standing proudly over the riverbanks. The sound of the water was painful to me as it crashed over stone. The water wasn't clear enough to see fish or vegetation, but I could feel the energy of living things in the mist. My hands itched to cast, and the longing in my chest for magic took my breath away.

My body was telling me it had been four days since I'd swum in Clear Lake, four days without cleansing myself of the fire. Four interminably long days with only stagnant, captive water in showers and city pipes. Four days since Harry's had burned to the ground. Four days since that fire within me had become uncontrollable. Four days without the ice floe magic that flooded my veins.

Nick watched me, a curious look on his face. I reached over and
squeezed his hand, breaking from my reverie.

"What are you thinking about?" he asked quietly.

Fire and water and magic, I wanted to say. *I'm a witch and need
to balance the elements within me or I feel off-kilter and itchy, and I
need badly to bathe in living water. I need to atone.*

"This place is beautiful," I said instead—true, but certainly not
the whole truth.

He nodded, accepting that I wasn't going to tell him more.

"St. Anthony Falls," Nick said, pointing to the lock and dam.
"I like coming here to watch the boats pass through. Like, who was
standing here a hundred years ago and thought, *I've got an idea*,
and made this happen? It boggles my mind sometimes."

"It's amazing what men can do when they're not busy fighting wars," I said, before I could talk myself out of saying the first
thing that came to mind. I smiled and waited for him to think I was
weird.

But Nick smiled back. "Right on," he said. "Some very determined guy built this, and now the Mighty Mississipp' can take you
anywhere. Where would you want to go?"

I smiled again as Nick drew me from my reflection. "I needed
to get out of my middle-of-nowhere town," I admitted. "I never
thought about where I'd end up." That was the truth. I vowed to
myself that I would always speak my mind to Nick, no more of
the people-pleasing facade that I put up for Magda and John and
Friedrich.

Nick drew me close to him, resting his chin on top of my head
comfortably. We stood like that for a few quiet minutes before he
squeezed me firmly with both arms and tilted my chin toward him
with one hand.

"Now I've actually gotta get to practice," he said, and I was
scared that was the end of it, that I would never see him again. But
Nick surprised me, saying, "Meet me at the bar later?"

"Of course."

"Good."

Nick kissed me once, hard, and sauntered away—actually whistling—leaving me to contemplate the river.

You can lose yourself in a man like that. Dorothy's voice sounded in my ear. So she had been watching, at least for a while.

What do you mean? I asked. *I don't even have a heart to give away anyway.*

Be careful, mein Liebling.

I just met him. It's not like I'm thinking about a life together, I protested. Dorothy didn't answer, though, leaving me wondering, once again, what exactly it would feel like to be a girl with a whole heart.

Twenty-Six

Sister Kate was behind the front desk again when I returned to St. Kate's.

"Miss Holbrooke," she said quietly as I tried to scoot past the desk. She glanced at her watch. "Sister Margaret noticed you weren't home last night after babysitting. Is everything okay?"

The lies fell out of my mouth so easily. "So sorry, Sister. Mr. Johnson wasn't in a state to drive me when they got back, and I didn't want to spend all my money on a taxi, and Mrs. Johnson said I could stay on the couch, so I took her up on it, and then today was so nice out I told the Johnsons I would walk, and I've just been moseying my way back here. I guess I was daydreaming a bit and just taking it all in."

I tried to make my eyes big like the innocent country girl I was pretending to be.

Sister Kate blinked hard. I couldn't tell if she believed me or not, but she seemed to take pity on me. "Don't let it happen again, or at least call if your employer puts you in that position."

"Of course, Sister. I'm so sorry. It won't happen again."

I sighed with relief as I climbed the stairs. I needed St. Kate's to remain a sanctuary for me for a while longer.

But when I opened the door to my room, a strange sight stopped me in my tracks. A large raven sat on the windowsill, peering in. I froze in the doorway, and it looked me in the eye with eerily familiar light-blue eyes, unblinking. It looked like the fumbled charm I had cast over Sister Margaret had come back to bite me.

I had given myself away in one moment of whiskey stupidity. I hadn't been able to hide from Magda for even a full week. I felt so dumb. I had drawn on the ice floe to sneak in, and it had taken Magda a few days, but she must have been watching, waiting to see where my energy would pop up. And here was a raven with my grandmother's eyes, hunting me down.

I reached behind me to pull the door closed in case there were any inquisitive ears around to listen, not daring to turn my back on the raven. I took a cautious step into the room but left several feet and the pane of glass between us.

"Magda?" I asked the raven tentatively, my heart pounding.

The raven cocked its head and cawed sharply. I jumped but recovered quickly, grateful not to hear my grandmother's voice from its beak.

I narrowed my eyes at the bird and took another step into the room, feeling bolder. "So she sent you to find me for her," I said.

The raven blinked, finally, but said nothing,

I need more time, I thought. I had just had my first taste of freedom. Nick flashed through my mind involuntarily. I wanted more. "I don't think so," I said finally.

Blowing open the door to the spirit world, I cast a charm at the raven through the window, muttering the words to myself. I had never spoken the words before, but the cedar chest's secrets opened to me as always.

The raven blinked, and when its large eyes reopened, they were no longer that strange pale blue but the normal glassy black of a raven. It looked at me dully through the window, then took flight, unhurried. I wasn't sure if it was still bewitched and would return to Magda to tell what it had seen or if I had broken the spell completely, but I felt momentary relief that I had bought myself time—or at least the day or so it would take the raven to cover the hundred miles back to Friedrich. But if Magda's raven had found me, it was only a matter of time before Magda or my father or Uncle Joe showed up.

I thought about standing my ground, but what was I fighting for? I still didn't know what I wanted. I thought about the girls I had met, and they were all nice enough, but their lives felt so quiet to me. They were different versions of Annie, working until they married a beau.

I needed more time, and I'd have to give Magda the slip again to get it. I couldn't risk staying anywhere where I had used magic before.

And if Nick's bar wasn't exactly a safe haven, at least it would be an entertaining place to bide my time. Dorothy's warning about Nick flashed through my mind, but what options did I have? I thought I could get away with sleeping at St. Kate's, but I'd have to make myself scarce during the day.

Am I being stupid? I asked myself, that dangerous feeling rising under my skin.

I slipped on the new dress, shoved my feet into my moccasins, and let my hair spring free down my back. I attempted to smooth the fuzz at my crown, at least, thinking of Nick and his achingly sweet dimple.

Twenty-Seven

That evening after supper, I made my way back to Nick's bar, creeping along alleys and side streets for the few short blocks from St. Kate's. The last of the day's heat seeped from the concrete sidewalks, and my energy floated away with it. But as I pushed open the heavy wooden door to Radgard's, I shook it off and stepped tentatively forward into my new skin. Who was I going to be?

I was surprised to hear Dionne Warwick triumphantly belting from the jukebox. *The regulars have good taste*, I thought.

The local barflies were already parked at the far end, hunched on their respective stools. Nick looked up from behind the bar, where he stood pouring a draft, as I walked in. I smiled and met his gaze but suddenly felt like I was moving too slowly, only playing unconvincingly at fitting into his bohemian, carefree life. I shook it off, laughing out loud at myself, not caring if he thought I was childish.

This isn't you, whispered a small, familiar voice in the back of my mind. A tiny part of me feared it sounded like Magda, that she had eyes on me somehow.

No way, I reassured myself. *I can do what I want for once in my life.*

"Aren't you a sight for sore eyes?" Nick asked as I pulled up a stool in front of him. "What did you get up to this afternoon?"

Nick's easy manner, and that dimple in his cheek, quickly replenished my flagging confidence, and I leaned forward, lips pursed, to let him kiss me across the bar.

"Just catching up with my family," I said. It was almost true, depending on how you looked at Magda's raven. Nick's face registered faint curiosity at the mention of my family, and I asked, "How was practice?" changing the subject neatly before he could ask me anything else.

He flashed a smile. His dimple appeared, turning my legs to jelly beneath me.

"Hiawatha Man rocked today. This weekend's gonna be great," Nick said. "Will you, uh, be around for that?"

I knew what came next. *What's the plan? What are you doing here? Where are you staying?*

But Nick didn't ask me any of those things. He waited, watching me through dark lashes over his light, golden eyes. Nick was nervous, I realized, taking in the furrow of his brow, the downward turn at the corner of his lips. He was waiting for me to step forward into his life or else turn tail where I had come from for good.

I was struck with the distinct knowledge that I would disappoint Nick too, like I had John; it was the only option with my half-heart. True love would never be for me, even if I gave up magic. Could I hope for the next-best thing from Nick? What, companionship? Or at the very least, the bodily delights I lacked with John? I blushed, thinking of Nick's gorgeous body in the hazy light through his dirty windows.

I was tempted to cast out the ice floe and read Nick. *What will happen to you, golden boy? Will I disappoint you too?* I asked him silently with my eyes.

"Sure," I said, attempting coolness.

Even if he wanted to ask me those other questions, Nick said nothing. He must have realized by then that I had said nothing substantial about home or what I was doing in Minneapolis. Surely he'd noticed my scant funds, the hungry look in my eyes, and my dirty blue jeans. I feared I reeked of desperation despite my best attempts to put on the thick skin of a runaway. But if Nick noticed, he said nothing.

"You'll be there," he said, his brow smoothing again. "I'm sure of it."

"Sure."

Nick started making me a drink without asking what I wanted.

"A bourbon old-fashioned. You'll like it," he said as he set a low-ball with a fragrant orange twist before me, like he was already the authority on what I liked. This both annoyed and excited me.

One sniff nearly singed my nostrils. I took a sip and flinched at the burn, blinking hard.

"Where are you staying in town?" Nick asked gently, finally voicing that delicate matter between us.

Blood pounded in my ears. *This is it*, I thought. *I'm caught.*

"Technically," I said, looking away, "St. Kate's Dormitory. You wouldn't believe what a tight ship those penguins run." I grinned.

Nick grimaced in fake horror. "Well then. You must be giving them a run for their money."

I swallowed hard. What kind of woman did he think I was, breaking all the dormitory rules? But then again, wasn't I? I smiled, unable to speak—from the liquor burn in my chest, from the hot shame flushing across my cheeks.

Nick leaned across the bar and whispered in my ear, "I can't wait to take you home again."

I didn't know what to say and lifted my drink to my mouth to cover my awkwardness. I didn't want to admit it to myself, but I was afraid of what Dorothy had warned. I hadn't left Friedrich and embarrassed John just to lose myself in another man. As fun as it was to pretend I was a woman with a full heart, I wasn't. I had the distinct feeling I would only let Nick down too.

When Nick sidled away to serve another patron, I quickly finished my drink. Feeling sad, I made a lame excuse about being back at St. Kate's before curfew. I would try to save Nick from my half-heartedness, at least for another day.

Twenty-Eight

I spent the rest of the week away from St. Kate's as much as possible, asking about jobs or reading the classifieds at the Minneapolis Public Library during the day and babysitting or spending time at Radgard's with Nick in the evenings. I felt the weight of my half-heartedness and Dorothy's warning, but I couldn't stay away. As the days went on, I felt the stark difference between Nick and John. It wasn't the innocent, budding romance between Mary and Tim, and it wasn't the stalwart support that John offered. Maybe we were providing each other what we needed—comfort and a place to hide—but it seemed simpler, sweeter than all that. It was like nothing I had ever experienced before, and all I wanted was anything other than what my life had been.

*   *   *

That Saturday I found myself in a crowd of wall-to-wall sweaty bodies in another dank bar. It wasn't quite like I had imagined. I arrived late after waiting until dark to walk from St. Kate's—even after no signs of Magda or Dad all week. The place was packed with young people, high people, drunk people, people with long hair, people with big hair, all kinds of people in bell-bottoms and short dresses in flowy fabrics. Nick didn't smile at me through the crowd like in my daydreams. He couldn't even see me in my new Jane Birkin dress through the sea of people and dim lights.

I stood at the back of the crowd, anxious that Nick wouldn't know I was there, that he would think I had bailed. But then the band started and I found myself lost in the music. I let myself go, swinging my limbs long and slow around me. Energy zinged from the tips of my fingers through every inch of me and out into the bar with each swing of my hips or slow toss of my hair. The energy in that dark, sweaty room was enormous and young and rainbow bright, and I could've felt it even if I didn't have magical abilities.

I drifted toward the stage after the show, but Nick found me first, his hand suddenly on my hip as he emerged from the opposite direction, a magician in his own right. Nick turned me toward him with the slightest pressure on my hip, pulling me back into his orbit after being apart. I laced my fingers together behind his neck, and he smiled, pleased, as I leaned into him. Whole heart or no, my body begged for his. He didn't move, teasing me, making me strain toward him, and with each passing second my heart dropped, filled with the mixed pain and anticipation of wanting him and faint worry that my eagerness turned him off.

He relented at last, twirling a hand in my hair to pull me closer. Nick claimed me with a forceful kiss that gave way to gentler ones until our foreheads pressed together, grinning mouths like fools' centimeters from each other's. It was exhilarating.

"Let's go," he said.

"Where?" I asked.

"The band's going out. I want to show you off tonight."

A small thrill ran through me as he said it, at knowing Nick wanted to show me off for myself and not for my name or reputation or abilities like John had. I could think of nothing I wanted more.

One of the other guys in the band appeared, a tall, thin man with stringy hair to his collarbone. He and Nick engaged in an esoteric male ritual, greeting each other with a round of "Hey, man" and a handshake with hearty back pounding.

Nick slipped a guiding arm behind my back. "This is Elisabeth," he said.

"Mikey," the man said. He didn't extend a hand but dipped his head in acknowledgment as he was already turning away from me.

"Ready?" Nick asked as we watched Mikey slink down a dark hallway to the alley.

"Let's go," I said.

In the alley, Nick did a quick round of introductions, and I immediately forgot half the names. There was Mikey, bass; Jim, drums; Jim's girlfriend something or other; and Ronald? Rick?—somebody anyway, keyboard. A girl on Ronald/Rick's arm introduced herself as Kathleen. She was the only one who bothered to shake my hand.

The glamorous night with the guys of Hiawatha Man commenced with lugging their equipment into Jim's van. The stereotype was true—you couldn't be a drummer without driving a Handi-Van with a shag carpet.

But the guys had the loading down to a science, and before long we were pouring out of Jim's van and traipsing down to the basement where Jim and Mikey lived. I wondered if Jim's or Mikey's parents lived upstairs. The basement was grimier than Nick's mattress on the floor, but someone turned on music and a bottle of whiskey was thrust into my hands, and nobody seemed to mind the general shabbiness.

Sprawled on the floor on rugs or pillows or seated on the edge of unmade beds, the guys launched into a thorough breakdown of their performance. I was surprised to learn that Jim's girlfriend, Cheryl, was a junior at the University of Minnesota. She was prelaw and about to start studying for the LSATs and told me about her work organizing protests and rallies for SDS while she rolled a marijuana cigarette with expert dexterity. I was okay with observing, feeling uncomfortable in my body. I was unused to so much booze.

"What about Jim?" I asked.

"What *about* Jim?" she retorted with a laugh. "If he doesn't like me going to law school, he's not going to like me being a lawyer. Tough cookies."

"So is this just a summer thing?" I asked, genuinely curious.

She shrugged. "Everyone parties a bit in the summers."

I was impressed by her nonchalance, by how certain she was, and immediately wanted to be like her.

Cheryl perched on the sofa arm near Jim, and I had the feeling that she only let him think he was in charge. The guys were debating a twelve-string in a folk number with a backbeat that "ran away." I was content at first to sit by Nick's side with his arm slung casually over my shoulders, his fingers tapping some unknown rhythm on the bare skin revealed by the low back of my new dress. The way he watched me out of the corner of his eye, all the while vehemently making his case to Ron in favor of keeping the twelve-string, made me feel like the most fascinating creature in the world.

But the conversation turned to Vietnam and another Minnesotan native son and favorite topic, Hubert H. Humphrey, and I couldn't help myself. I wanted to speak my mind.

"H.H.H. had his shot," I said. "If he was gonna get us out of there, he would've done it already. It's time for him to go."

Jim laughed into his whiskey, and Nick looked at me funny, eyebrows raised.

"What?" I said, instantly worrying that I had said the wrong thing.

Nick shook his head. "Nothing . . . I'm just not used to girls saying what they think. I like it." He leaned into me, his words for only me. "I want to know what you think about everything. I want to know everything about you."

I might have only had half a heart, but Nick certainly had a whole one.

"Me too," I said, even as another mention of other girls from Nick's mouth made me irrationally jealous.

It had barely been a week, and I was blown away by the generous, adventurous man beside me. He was exactly what I would never find in Friedrich, and I wanted nothing more than for him to truly know me, the one thing it wasn't safe to give him.

Through my whiskey-fueled contentment, my fingers suddenly itched with uncast charms. When Magda and Lake Street seemed a world away and I dropped my guard, the magic that had always been a constant in my life bubbled to the surface. I was torn. I wanted Nick to like me for myself, not my reputation. But it hurt to think that he could never truly know me without magic, an enormous part of my life. It had been everything until then.

Feeling gutted and missing magic like missing a physical part of me, I gave in despite my better judgment. I leaned my cheek against Nick's shoulder, closed my eyes, and cast out the ice floe. It had been days since I had tapped into it so deliberately. But there it was, the energy of our world and the next unfurling before me, filling me with a deep vibration. I was overjoyed to see all the bright, young energy in the room. And then—there was Nick. God, what a beautiful energy, a deep turquoise. I wanted so badly to follow his energy forward and see what path he would take in life, but even in my drunkenness, Magda's frequent warnings against soothsaying came back to me.

Magda, I remembered with a jolt, opening my eyes. But it felt so good to cast, to feel the ice floe again, that I almost didn't care about the consequences.

Nick tugged on my hair playfully, bringing me firmly back into the room. When I looked up at him, all thoughts of Magda went out of my head. Whatever happened, I would deal with it tomorrow, I thought, reaching for the whiskey to drown out any fears.

Swept up in the energy of the night, I had the vague thought that I was going to stay out all night for the first time in my life. That made me want to stay out for the sake of having done it, stay up forever, keep drinking coffee and choking down whiskey with this loud, self-assured crew. As the first light crept in the basement windows, someone announced they were hungry, and soon enough we were sitting in a nearby diner, eating fries and grilled cheese sandwiches and eggs and pancakes with bleary eyes and voices raspy from a night of drinking and smoking. I watched as Nick dipped his grilled cheese in ketchup—the man put ketchup on everything, like Mary did—and felt young and happy and free.

Twenty-Nine

Before I knew it, it was the Fourth of July. I had been spending less and less time at St. Kate's, gravitating toward Nick and the band and the girls that ran with them. I was starting to think I could pick and choose my future—being brash like Annie, working hard like Bridget and Diane, taking or leaving a man like Cheryl.

Nick and I met the guys, Kathleen, and Cheryl in Powderhorn Park. The city was buzzing with an energy that felt familiar, yet wholly new to me. It reminded me of Solstice. Everyone was in a celebratory mood and had their own way of showing it—Nick with illegal fireworks procured from the back of a truck in Woodbury.

The smell of fresh-cut grass and hamburgers and gunpowder and the cacophony of fire trucks and honking horns and a brass band made me nostalgic for the Friedrich Fourth of July parade. I thought sadly of Annie, whom I hadn't spoken with since Solstice out of fear and shame. *She's not family.* I wondered what Annie thought of my act on Solstice, but I couldn't bring myself to call her.

It was the first year that I would miss out on our tradition of meeting late along the parade route past where the princesses disembarked from their floats to claim our spot in front of the dumpster. While Lake Street was otherwise packed with families and little kids and dogs in festive bandannas, like magic, our spot was always reserved for us. We sat on the curb and leaned our backs in tank tops against the dumpster's hot metal side and stretched our legs into the street, just in time to see the Shriners' big finale.

Minneapolis's Fourth festivities put Friedrich to shame, though, and I was dazzled by the city's budget and capacity for celebration. Hiawatha Man was playing an outdoor event in the park that evening, eschewing the traditional patriotism of the official city fireworks on Nicollet Island for a more raucous, grassroots affair. There were other bands and folk singers and antiwar speakers in the lineup from noon to midnight, and Cheryl had a group from SDS there.

I was impressed by the way the guys mobilized in the early afternoon when they wouldn't play until at least six o'clock. I wasn't prepared for the sea of people and patchwork of quilts and blankets covering the park lawn edge to edge. People were out in full force. It felt like pure chaos and I loved it. I was relieved that Jim had had the foresight to beat us there to stake our claim with a baby-blue bedsheet flanked by Styrofoam coolers and a tiny charcoal grill, undoubtedly borrowed from his parents' garage. Some traditions couldn't be shaken: we unloaded our all-American picnic of hot dogs and buns, condiments, and store-bought chips and cookies. One of the guys mixed plastic cups of whiskey and warm Coke, and we sprawled on the thin sheet over the parched midsummer grass as Nick and Jim charred hot dogs. Kathleen passed me a cigarette, and I took it with an inward shrug. I dragged on it slowly, trying not to cough, trying to look like Annie would.

Other people, friends, came and went as they made their way to their own picnics or made their way closer to the stage. Sometimes Nick didn't introduce me, or someone would stop by to talk to Mikey or one of the other girls, but I didn't mind. I was content to take in all the people. Besides, it was easier not to read them accidentally, to not be tempted to glance at their energies, if I didn't know their names.

A name could bring the thin veil crashing down between worlds. As much as I would've loved the energy of the vibrant, living, breathing crowd around us—it made me feel young and invincible—the act of accidentally reading that energy shackled me to Friedrich and Magda and my birthright, whether I liked it or not. But my hands relaxed as we played cards, and although I knew I was not entirely like the others in the group, I felt more at home with this band of misfit music geeks, hard drinkers, and unapologetic women than ever in my life. By the time of Hiawatha Man's set, I was more relaxed than I had been in months.

I didn't know yet how to fully be myself without magic, but I wished I could bottle the magic feeling of that day and wear it forever.

✳ ✳ ✳

A few days later, a newspaper headline caught my eye in my daily scouring of the classifieds.

"More Drought for Western Minn." announced the front page of the *Star Tribune*.

It bothered me all day, and when I returned to St. Kate's for supper that evening, I headed upstairs to the phone first, willing Mary to pick up.

Maybe it worked, or maybe my mother and Magda didn't answer the phone anymore.

"Hello-Watry-residence-who's-calling-please?" Mary exhaled in a monotone.

"Mare, it's me," I said. "I—I wanted to check on you. How are things there?" I asked.

"Not good, Lisbett," Mary said sharply. "Magda can barely keep up, but she won't let me help besides water charms. Folks are uneasy since Solstice, but we have a huge line every day for water charms."

I was relieved to hear there were still clients at our door.

"It doesn't sound so bad then, Mare," I ventured. "I'm sure it's not—"

"It's bad," Mary hissed, cutting me off. "Magda is cleaning up your mess, and the town is barely hanging on through this heat wave. I am defending you left and right to our neighbors, but it's getting harder to do that the longer you're gone. You should be here."

"My mess? But Magda—" I started.

"I've gotta go," she cut me off, uninterested in hearing my side of it or unwilling to. "If you're not going to come home and help, don't bother checking on us." She hung up without another word.

This is what I wanted, I reminded myself.

I couldn't help it, I still felt responsible for the people of Friedrich. It was our duty to care for them. I had wanted to loosen Magda's grasp on my life, but I didn't want the town to suffer. I hoped Mary was stepping up, but even then, it made me burn anew: *If Mary is perfectly capable, why isn't she good enough for Magda? Why won't Magda let her help?*

The longer I stayed away, the more I had to admit I missed my magic. My fingers were burning with uncast charms, and it was killing me to cut myself off from the ice floe magic. I was starting to slip up. After Magda's raven, she had left me alone, and I didn't know why. Maybe she was just too busy with things at home, but I found it strange.

And the more I got to know Nick, the more I wanted him to know the real me, which felt impossible.

When I headed back down for supper, Sister Margaret and Sister Kate were waiting for me outside the dining room. Sister Kate looked sheepish, but Sister Margaret was resolute.

"You've broken curfew too many times, Miss Holbrooke."

I got stares from some of the other girls heading into dinner. Bridget hovered near the dining room doorway to eavesdrop.

"We'll need you to pack your things by tomorrow morning," Sister Kate added with her eyes on the ground.

I stared, waiting for them to say more. When Sister Kate didn't look up, I impulsively said, "Fine. No need. I'll be gone tonight." Deep down I had known St. Kate's wasn't for me. I wasn't a good Catholic girl like Diane or Bridget. I was becoming something else.

I couldn't bear the idea of answering questions from the other girls at dinner, so I headed back up to my room, rolled my few belongings into my backpack, and left St. Kate's in the dust.

*   *   *

When I showed up at Radgard's with my backpack, Nick didn't bat an eye. Maybe he didn't realize I was carrying everything I had to my name at the moment, or maybe with all the time we had been spending together, he had expected this at some point. I had the feeling he was used to transients of all kinds flowing through his bar and his life. *Maybe nobody has ever stayed*, I thought sadly. But Nick looked at me like he was ready for me to slide right into his life and said nothing as I waited for him to lock up for the night.

We had starting walking back to his place when, after a few blocks, I tripped over something soft. I squinted into the midnight shadows, and there was Sam, my mother's big gray tabby cat, his white paws practically glowing in the streetlight. His fur was dirty and thick with sandburs, but it was definitely Sam.

"You've gotta be kidding me," I said.

"What's that?" Nick asked, his hand finding my waist.

"Look," I ad-libbed. "There's a stray cat." Sam revved his engine and swirled around my ankles like he hadn't been sent there by my mother, like he was a normal tabby cat. I wondered how long it had taken Sam to find me.

"Right on," Nick said with a shrug.

"Do you mind if I bring him home? I think he likes us," I said. Sam helped by rubbing Nick's ankles too.

"Whatever makes you happy," Nick said. He leaned down to scoop up Sam, and I was relieved when Sam cooperated.

I instinctively reached out to take Sam from Nick, tossing his long front legs over my shoulder like my mother would. Sam scrambled up my shoulder, finding purchase with his claws in the fabric of my blouse.

"Whoa," Nick said, watching us situate ourselves.

"I had a cat growing up," I offered. That was true, at least.

Sam rode home like that on my shoulder, like he had done with my mother a million times, and Nick and I talked about music and dinner and were cocky enough to make plans for a few more summer weekends. All the while, I could feel Sam's ears twitching with interest against my hair.

At Nick's, I found myself staring at Sam, who had made himself comfortable on my pillow while Nick showered. Mom knew where I was, which meant that Magda did too. I didn't quite understand, but it felt like my mother's plea for me to come home.

"What does she want from me?" I asked the cat in question, knowing full well that he couldn't answer me. As my mother's familiar, Sam's unspoken language was decipherable only to her, as Mickey's was to Mary.

Sam licked a paw nonchalantly.

"If you're supposed to be a messenger, you're terrible at it," I told Sam. How bad was it at home that Mom was getting involved? *Is my family safe?* I wondered suddenly. Maybe the fallout from Harry's was even worse than Mary had let on.

Dorothy? Do I have to go home?

Yes, mein Liebling. It's time, came the answer.

Tears sprang to my eyes. I wasn't ready to face whatever awaited me at home. I wasn't ready to say goodbye to Nick. I felt myself wanting to reveal more of my true self to him. I wanted more time to figure out exactly how to do that.

Now? I asked again.

Go now, Liebling, before it's too late, Dorothy whispered.

Soon, I promised.

Sam froze midlick and eyed me above his whiskers. "Soon, I swear!" I told him.

Thirty

But I was out of time. In the wee hours of the morning, from somewhere in the depths of the dream river, Dorothy whispered urgently, *Wake up, mein Liebling. Hurry.*

I felt Magda nearby, drawing me into the ice floe, begging, *Chunsch, Lisbett, chunsch. Wachst auf.* I had never heard Magda like that before. Weak. Tired. Pleading. The shock of it woke me thrashing in the sheets in Nick's bed. He snored on gently next to me, oblivious.

Sitting upright in bed, I felt the ice floe rush in all at once. I closed my eyes and cast out for my grandmother's steadfast amethyst-purple energy. As I soared above the river of energy between Minneapolis and home, over so many energies resting peacefully at that hour, my inner eye saw my mother's ruby red and Mary's warm, golden yellow nearby.

My heart dropped into my stomach. Magda's energy was just a whisper of purple clinging to the house on Lake Street. Magda Watry was dying.

I panicked, thinking I had gotten it wrong, not trusting my abilities so far from home. There had to be an explanation for it. Mary hadn't said anything about Magda being sick—but it could've been sudden. Maybe Mom had sensed something Mary didn't when she sent Sam. I wouldn't know until I got home.

I felt ill. Magda was dying, and there I was in some strange man's bed. *Disgusting.* I felt bile rise in my throat. I rushed to the grimy first-floor powder room and vomited a stream of acid in violent heaves that left me gasping.

You are disgusting and Magda is dying, I told myself.

I slumped to the bathroom floor. The last few weeks didn't matter. Magda casting on me, Solstice, the fire, running away—none of it mattered. I just had to get home. I had to see Magda.

When I opened my eyes, Sam was watching me patiently from the doorway of the powder room. He blinked once, twice, three times.

Oh, I thought faintly, holding back fresh tears. *This is what you came to tell me. You knew. This is why Magda didn't come for me herself. She couldn't.*

Time to go home, I told the reflection in the mirror after rinsing my mouth and face.

I crept around in the dark with Sam at my heels, dreading Nick waking up and having to explain myself. I cast a light sleeping charm over his sweet, limp form under the twisted sheets. With Magda on her deathbed, it didn't matter if I used magic. Nothing mattered but getting home. I had to talk to Magda before . . . I couldn't bring myself to finish the thought.

I dressed in a stolen T-shirt from Nick's closet. *Something to remember him by,* I told myself. He wouldn't mind. I hated myself for doing it, but I also took two tens—enough to get home—from Nick's wallet. I gazed one last time on Nick's sleeping form and turned to go.

I paged through the phone book in the kitchen and called a taxi. I loitered, debating if I should write Nick a note, but I ultimately thought it would be better if I departed from his life as quickly as I had come. He might think he had dreamed me. I could never give him what he needed, never let him truly know me. My heart was bound, promised elsewhere, not my own to give, and it was time to make good on that promise.

I replaced the phone book and stepped into the predawn Minneapolis stillness with Sam in my arms to wait for the taxi that would take us to the Greyhound station and the bus that would carry us home.

*   *   *

I waited until six AM to call from the bus station. The bus west to Kandiyohi County didn't leave until nine.

Mary picked up after one ring, expecting me.

"It's me," I said.

"I know," she said. "Magda had a stroke. They're taking her to the clinic in Crichton. You need to come home."

"I know," I said. "I'm coming."

"I know."

"I have Sam," I said.

"We figured," she said.

I didn't know what else to say, what else Mary needed me to say. She was clearly mad at me for leaving, for dumping everything on her. I would have to address that, but it would have to wait until I got home and made things right with Magda.

"I'll see you soon," I said, and hung up quickly before Mary's fury had a chance to spark again.

*   *   *

In the quiet of the bus among the other drowsy passengers on the road to St. Agnes, I tried to sleep, to prepare myself for what lay ahead. I closed my eyes, and sheer exhaustion took me away.

But I kept jerking awake, realizing I was dreaming of Magda. In my dreams, she turned into a raven and flew away, always out of reach. I couldn't talk to her, my anxiety about our reunion, about making it in time, pouring into my dreams. Magda always said to me, "There's no use crying over spilt milk," and I knew, deep down, that I couldn't change the fact that I had defied her. I couldn't change that we had fought, that she was furious with me. I had been angry with her too. I still was. All I could do was show up and hope for the best.

I closed my eyes to sleep again. *There's no use crying over spilt milk. What's done is done. Rest,* I told myself. *This may be your last chance.*

The next time I closed my eyes, though, I saw Magda's beautiful amethyst light coming toward me in the spirit world. She was still half raven but looked at me through her own eyes, reaching a wing tip toward me across the dream river.

The next moment her spirit slipped away, sucked from the raven form as pure energy passing in front of me in the dream river, half in our world, half in the next. I surged forward through the ice floe, flailing wildly toward her, but her beautiful purple light blinked and went out.

Magda was gone.

In the ice floe, I saw my family nearby. Mom sighed and swept her mother's eyes closed. Mary hovered, waiting to be called to be useful, casting over and over for Magda, her fingers working in midair as if pulling yarn from a skein, as if she could pull Magda back from the edge.

I awoke with a gasp. I would learn later that Mary too had doubled over with shock when Magda's amethyst light blinked out and evaporated into the whirlpool of white light between the worlds of the living and the dead. A few fellow passengers roused from their dozing and shot me curious looks. I buried my face in a perplexed Sam's neck to muffle my anguish as hot tears streaked down my cheeks.

I tried to cast out the ice floe for her again and again but was unable to access it. *Magda's gone,* I knew then, with absolute certainty. When her heart was no longer bound to the cedar chest, our power went with it—our magic was untethered, unprotected, exactly what Magda had feared. I recalled with a shiver what Nick had said about his dad, gone from earth. I doubted myself for a moment, but I knew deep down that what I saw was real. It registered faintly that my abilities, that itching in my fingers, had been as strong as ever every time I dared to cast, even so far from Magda's cedar chest.

The shock of Magda being gone—*How can she be gone?*—and the fact that my grandmother, my teacher, my guide was gone—*dead?*—I could barely think the word—knocked the breath out of me.

The weight of Magda's absence settled around me like a fog. I was too late. I should have left the minute Sam showed up. I could've made it in time. The grief and shock and guilt washed over me in waves. I would never see Magda again in this life. We would never reconcile. She would never pat the floor next to her for us to go through notes from the cedar chest again. And I would never hear her side of the story, what she thought happened on Solstice, what exactly had happened between Magda and my mother.

I couldn't change what I had done. I couldn't change that I hadn't been there for Magda at the end, even if she didn't need me—I was sure that Magda would find her way into the light on her own, unlike the very young or the ill, who were sometimes afraid to go. Magda had ferried many other lives there; she knew the way.

Feeling gutted, I alternated sleeping and crying as I hurtled toward home and the dark clouds gathering there. I was too late, by mere minutes. I would carry the guilt of not being there with Magda for the rest of my life.

*   *   *

I called again from the bus station. The stolen bike was long gone from where I had stashed it. I was relieved to hear Mary's voice.

"She's gone," Mary said tearfully. "We just got home from Crichton."

"I know. I felt it."

"I wish . . . I wish you had been here," Mary said.

I sighed. I didn't know how to respond. I wished that too, and it cut me to the core.

"Can you come get me?" I asked finally.

She hesitated. "Can't you call John? There's so much to do here . . . and now without Magda . . ." Her voice was flat, ambiguous.

"Can't you borrow the station wagon? It won't take long," I begged. I thought briefly of asking for Dad to come, but I wavered, remembering Dad with his head in his hands on that sidewalk in Minneapolis. I wasn't ready to see him.

"Mom needs me. It was a long night . . ." Mary trailed off. I wasn't ready to face my mother either.

I sighed and rubbed my brow in frustration. "Okay," I said. "I'll figure it out. Tell Mom I'll be there soon. And . . . I'm sorry."

I hung up and stared at the pay phone on the hook. Annie crossed my mind, but at that hour, her mother and her car would be in Paynesville at her mom's latest job. I was terrified of how John would react, however justified, but I knew it was time to confront that thorn. I needed him for the moment.

I dropped my actual last dime in the pay phone and asked the operator for the Weseloh residence.

Mrs. Weseloh answered. "We haven't seen you around here since Solstice, Elisabeth," she said with an edge in her voice when I asked for John.

"Yeah, it's been busy," I mumbled. There was no way the entire town didn't know about my disappearing act. John might have kept mum about it at home, but Mrs. Weseloh certainly knew.

"Sure," she said. "I guess I'll go hunt down John in the yard. You hold tight." Deeply ingrained manners won out over whatever ill feelings Mrs. Weseloh was harboring.

"Hi," John said after a long pause. His voice was devoid of emotion.

"John," I said. "I know you must be mad right now, and with good reason, but I need you. Magda died this morning. I'm at the bus station, and I . . . I need a ride. Mary won't come. She's even madder than you . . ."

John hesitated long enough that I thought he wasn't going to come.

"Okay," he said with a sigh. "I'm coming. And I'm sorry about Magda."

*   *   *

When I climbed into the cab of the El Camino, it felt like a year had passed. The radio was off, the silence oppressive. Sam played dumb and made himself comfortable in a sunbeam on the dashboard.

John gaped at Sam, perplexed.

"Don't ask," I said with a sigh.

"What the hell, Elisabeth?" John said quietly, without putting the truck into gear.

"I'm sorry," I said automatically, prepared for it to be my new refrain.

When I couldn't make more words come out, John sighed heavily and pulled onto the main drag of St. Agnes toward home.

I gazed into my lap as John drove slowly, responsibly. The bright, cloudless afternoon was a shocking contrast to the gloom that hung between us.

"I had to get out of here," I said finally. "I know that's not a good excuse. I just needed to make a point. I didn't mean for Solstice to get so out of hand, but Magda . . ." I trailed off. Anything else I could've said sounded trivial to my own ears. It felt wrong to blame the dead.

I couldn't be silent and accept it like my mother, I couldn't say.

John jumped in. "You burned down Harry's. You left. Without a word to your family or Mary or anyone. What if something happened to you? What would I have done then?"

His voice trembled with an icy rage that made him barely recognizable. He was like a snake coiled to strike, and I was scared. I had pushed John Weseloh too far.

"John," I said, urging him to make eye contact. "I'm sorry. For leaving you, for Harry's. I'm so sorry."

"You made me look like a fool," he said, refusing to look at me as he squeezed the steering wheel with both hands.

I looked away, staring out at the heat-scorched farmlands. *What happened to this place? How did things get so bad?* Minutes ticked by in deafening silence as John pulled off the highway into Friedrich.

"I needed to get away for a while," I said filling the dead air. I hadn't known what would happen after Solstice. "I needed some time away from Magda, and now she's gone. I can't believe I wasn't here with her." That was the truth, at least.

John sighed. "Well, that's what you get for taking off."

"I know," I said, a sob rising in my throat.

"Hey," he said, watching me anxiously out of the corner of his eye. "Sorry. I . . . I just love you so much, Elisabeth. I don't know what I'd do without you."

John pulled over on the side of Rose Street, kitty-corner from the VFW. He reached over to take my hand, and it took every ounce of strength in me not to flinch as I remembered Nick's touch just hours prior. Nick would be awake and wondering where I had gone, another name on the long list of people I'd hurt.

"Don't you ever do something like this again," John said, squeezing my hand in his. "If we're going to be together now, it's going to be different. There will be rules."

I was too stunned to say anything, too afraid of the wild look in John's eyes. *Does he mean to just take me back?* He pulled me across the bench toward him and bent to kiss me. I wanted to dodge his mouth, but his big hands, strong from years of hauling feed and muscling machinery through clay-packed earth, gripped my arms on either side. I shut my eyes tight and let him assault my mouth with his, hoping it would be over soon. I had to get home.

"John," I said quietly when he drew his mouth away from mine, leaving saliva around my lips and chin. "I have to go."

"I've given up so much for you, you know?" John said, ignoring me. He gripped me tighter, mashing my breasts against his chest, his big arms around my frame. "I've given up everything to be with you, and then you run off and disrespect me like that? I won't stand for it."

John shook me suddenly by the shoulders so hard my teeth rattled. From the corner of my eye, I saw Sam with his hackles raised, growling from his perch on the dash.

"Do you hear me?" he screamed as I saw stars. "You may be a Watry, but I'm a man too. I won't be disrespected!"

I tried to nod as tears streamed down my face, but I was afraid to move, to push John over the edge. I didn't know what he would do next.

"You're not going anywhere," John said, eerily calm once more. He pulled me against his chest, digging his chin into the top of my head. "No, you're not going anywhere," he repeated to himself, whispering into my hair.

"Okay, I'm sorry," I croaked to make it stop. "I'm sorry, John, I'm sorry."

In the back of my mind, I knew it was my fault. I had always wanted to get a rise out of John, and I'd finally pushed him too far. I'd felt so guilty for saddling John to a Watry woman's half-heart, so guilty that he had no future of his own. But when his shiny prize disappeared suddenly, it had been too much for him to take. I had thought John worshiped me, but it turned out that he wanted to possess me.

In that moment, I knew I would never tell John the truth about what I'd done, where I had been those couple of weeks, and I would absolutely never tell him about Nick. It would break John if he found out, and God only knew what he was capable of. Nick would be my private shame.

I was afraid to move, afraid to breathe.

"Never again, Elisabeth," John said coolly, and pushed me roughly away from him. I didn't recognize the look in his eyes as I slid back across the bench. Sam stepped down into my lap, putting his fourteen pounds between me and John. He didn't take his eyes off John, glaring in that way that only a cat can.

I turned away to see a figure watching us from the front steps of the VFW. Even from a hundred yards away, my father's tall, thin silhouette was unmistakable. Ashamed, I dropped my eyes and pretended I hadn't seen him as John drove off, oblivious.

It was shocking how easy it was to let John hold my hand again on the seat between us, pretending nothing had happened. *There goes the Watry-Ridder girl and that Weseloh boy, together again like always.*

Thirty-One

I could've sworn my eyes were playing tricks on me when John turned into the driveway. The house was leaning like a drunk staggering sideways out of Radgard's.

"What the hell happened here?" I said under my breath, unable to tear my eyes away from the bald patches where singles had peeled away from the roof.

John ignored my comment. "I'm glad you're home," he said, too sweetly. The change in him from minutes before was chilling.

I gave the best smile I could muster for him. "I'll call you," I said, quickly gathering my things, tossing Sam over my shoulder, and opening the door.

Across Lake Street, the late-afternoon sun reflected fiercely off the waves, shining like polished silver. I thought absently that it was the most beautiful place in the world, then I walked like a stranger through the front door that nobody ever used. I could hear quiet voices coming from the kitchen and steeled myself for the coming storm.

I was surprised to see Cousin Mildred sitting at the kitchen table with Mary and Mom, all three with their heads hung low, staring into untouched coffee cups. The conversation stopped cold when I hesitated in the doorway. Only Mildred looked up, openly giving me a curious once-over, the prodigal daughter returned, tail between her legs. I knew the whole town would hear at bridge that week about my bedraggled appearance and the bags under my eyes, surely to be taken as a sign of my guilt and deceit. Dazed, I wondered if John had left marks on my arms, but I refused to look and draw attention there. Sam wriggled out of my arms and went immediately to swirl around Mom's ankles, purring. Mom didn't look up.

"Where is she?" I asked, stepping into the room.

Mary finally lifted her head to meet my eyes. "Meijer's came to get her from the clinic, then we came home," she said. "You can go see her over there today, or it'll be at the wake on Friday."

Cousin Mildred pushed back from the table with her eyes glued to me. She heaved herself part by part to standing. With a nod to my mother, who didn't so much as glance up, Mildred said, "I'll be going, then. You let us know what we can do for you, Helene."

Cousin Mildred didn't move, though.

"Helene," she said again, more forcefully, waiting until my mother looked up. "She meant the world to me too," Mildred said, her voice shaking.

Mildred wiped her eyes quickly, patted Mary on the arm, threw one last skeptical glance in my direction, and trundled out the kitchen's side door.

I cautiously took Mildred's vacated seat, feeling like an intruder interrupting my own family's grief for the woman that I loved more than anyone on earth. I was unsettled by feeling such equal anger and suspicion toward a woman who could no longer speak for herself, compounded by the shock and anger I felt toward John, and myself. *I deserve this.*

"I'm sorry," I said without prelude.

"We'll talk later," Mom said after a stretch of silence. "There is too much that needs to be done. We were resting a moment now, but we'll see Father Kevin first thing in the morning."

"What . . . what can I do?" I asked.

Mom lifted her head and gave me the same skeptical once-over. She had the air of a woman too tired, or too busy, to be angry.

"You can start by making supper," Mom said. She wandered into the next room with Sam at her heels, leaving me stunned at the table with Mary.

"That's new," I whispered.

Mary glared at me. "Welcome home, I guess," she said. I wondered for the umpteenth time what exactly she knew.

"Mare," I said, reaching for her as she stood to follow Mom. "I *am* sorry."

Mary looked up with a smirk that surprised me, pursing her lips before responding. "It's a little late for that. Magda spent the last month cleaning up after your mess. She did a pretty impressive charm on Harry's, in fact," she said, pride flashing across her face before quickly disappearing. "But your disaster wore her out. She gave everything she had to clean up after you."

I nearly choked. Was it my fault that Magda was gone?

"I gotta go," Mary said without explanation. "Now that you're back, you can deal with this." She gestured vaguely around the kitchen, shoving her chair back with a screech.

I let her go, too tired to bother with more apologies. Mary didn't want to hear it anyway. I opened the fridge and started the soothingly familiar motions of browning meat for hot dish.

*   *   *

My father appeared in the kitchen just before supper. I could've sworn my stoic Dutch father's eyes watered as he gazed upon me.

"Elisabeth," Dad said, crossing the room in two strides of his long, thin legs.

"Dad, I—" I started. He cut me off with a wave of his hand.

"I'm glad you're safe," he said, gathering me in his arms for a long embrace.

"I didn't mean to, on Solstice—"

"I know," Dad said. "But that's between you and your mother and sister."

I wanted to say something about Minneapolis, about John, but it was too fresh, too shameful. It felt like a punishment of my own making, my just desserts for what I had done. And my father was of a different generation, a different honor code, one in which what happened between men and women was not discussed.

Dad released me, wiping his eyes. Neither of us would say anything more on the matter that day.

*   *   *

That night, I biked into town. I had to see the remains of Harry's with my own eyes. But even I wasn't prepared for what greeted me there. When I saw the burnt-out husk of the lake's famous supper club, a place of joy and weddings and birthdays and anniversaries, I sank to the sidewalk and wept for what I had done. Even if Magda had cast on me first, it was my fire charm that had gotten so out of control. It would take me years to pay back my debt to Harry, but I'd never be able to earn back his trust.

*   *   *

Mary was out late that night with Tim. That was another new development. I was in bed by the time she got home. She announced herself by turning the lights on, not bothering to be quiet as she got ready for bed.

"Hi, then," I said, sitting up. I rubbed my eyes. "How's Tim?"

"Fine."

"All right then," I said, taken aback. It seemed Mary was going to shut me out for a while longer.

She shot me a look. "Are we doing this now?" she asked.

"Doing what? I already said I'm sorry, Mare. What else do you need me to say?" But I knew it wasn't enough, not yet.

She spat the questions at me rapid-fire while bustling around the room and changing with her back to me.

"Where have you been?"

"The Cities . . . but you know that already."

"What were you doing?"

I sighed. "I needed some time to think."

"Is that all you're going to say?"

"Mary," I tried, my voice serious. "You don't know how bad it was for me."

"So tell me!" she cried, slamming down onto her bed next to me. "Talk to me! You had the words living and breathing inside you, and you left, and you can't even say why."

"And it hurt me too to do that. I cut myself off from magic, and it was terrible, like I was missing a part of myself. And you don't know what Magda did," I countered.

"It doesn't matter what she did. You know the rules of magic as well as anyone, and you still let anger and resentment blow up your magic like that. You should've known better."

Everything she said was true, and I was suddenly so tired. I didn't know if anything I could say would be enough for Magda, for Harry's, for everything. I gave up and retreated into my covers.

Mary said into the air heavy between us, "I'm not stupid, Lisbett. I know what this has cost you. I know things." She jabbed her sternum with an index finger for emphasis.

"Do you?" I asked, as Mary turned out the light.

Did Mary know I had given my heart? Or rather, had it taken? Did she really know? Even as mad and bratty as she was acting, I wanted to protect her. As horrified as I was by the idea of losing my heart to preserve the family's magic, after keeping Nick at arm's length, I knew I couldn't subject Mary to the same fate. I was determined to give her a shot at happiness, even if I couldn't have it for myself. But her attitude was making it hard for me to want to spare her.

* * *

I didn't get a chance to talk to my mother until after lunchtime the next day, after Father Kevin left. Mary announced she was heading to the beach. I suspected she wanted to be comforted and spend time with Tim. I suspected she wanted a break from me too. I, for one, didn't mind her going, as I was exhausted from trying to find the words to defend myself.

I hesitated in front of the attic door. As I stood there with my hand hovering, about to knock, I recalled Mary's visions of Dorothy, standing in that exact spot, her hand pressed against the wooden door at the top of the stairs. The image came to me like I had seen it with my own two eyes, or dreamt it.

Are you with me, Dorothy? I asked.

But she hadn't answered me since the morning Magda passed, since we were cut off from the ice floe.

I knocked softly, then pushed the door open without waiting for a response. Mom sat on the edge of the bed. She was about to put her shoes on or take her stockings off but hadn't decided which, her hands slouching ineffectively toward her feet.

"I . . . I wanted to see if there's anything else I can do? The church is all set, the VFW . . . Cousin Mildred will direct the ladies about the food . . ." I trailed off. I didn't want to talk about the logistics, but I needed to stay busy. Anything to keep my mind off Magda and John and Nick.

"Mm-hmm." Mom made that sound that I often did myself, sounding like her old self. But then she said, "Thank you, Elisabeth."

Is she not mad at me?

My mother looked at me where I faltered in the doorway, as if she hadn't seen me clearly for a very long time.

"I know you were mad," Mom said finally. "But you need to be careful. This town can forgive a lot, but we don't need to test them."

So that was it. She expected me to step right back into Magda's place, and I found myself nodding and accepting it. Magic was a part of me, for better or worse, and I couldn't deny it. And I had to admit, I had missed it dearly after weeks of being cut off from my abilities.

I longed to sit beside her on the bed, for her to rub my back, like she had only ever done for Mary, and tell me it would be okay. My mother met my gaze, stopping me in my tracks.

She continued, "You needed to do whatever you were going to do, and that's fine. I understand. Everything I ever did was to protect you and Mary, but now Mother's gone, and you should know some things. About our family. About Magda. There was a lot to your grandmother that you didn't see. She wasn't exactly the saint everyone thought she was."

My mother's voice was calm and clear, and I barely recognized the woman before me. But finding her voice after so long must have been taxing. She looked away and turned to lie down.

"Mom, on Solstice, it was Magda," I said urgently. "I mean, yes, I wanted to annoy her, to stir things up, but she cast on me first. She—"

"I know, honey," she said, sounding tired.

"You knew?" I asked with relief. Had my mother felt the ice floe all along? Had she felt Magda cast on me? And she hadn't done anything about it?

"I didn't break this family," Mom said firmly as she pulled the covers up to her chin. "You didn't break this family, Elisabeth. My mother did that. Now leave me alone. I need to rest."

Too stunned to argue, I turned out the lights, closed the door, and let her be.

Thirty-Two

When I returned from the lake the next morning, the sight of the house keening perilously stopped me in my tracks. I knew I was cut off from the ice floe; I'd found something akin to TV static when I tried to access it. I wasn't positive what it meant, but I had to try, before the horrible evening of the wake would be spent talking to neighbors and busybodies about Magda and Harry's and Mr. Raymond.

Still dripping in my bathing suit, I closed my eyes and felt for the ice floe. I knew it had to be there, but I couldn't access it the same way. But lots of other practitioners used magic—there had to be another way. Without the cedar chest to supply me with new words, I closed my eyes and tried a familiar protection spell.

Fiir und Wasser, Äther und Eërde.

Nothing moved.

Äther und Eërde, Fiir und Wasser.

Nothing.

I tried another approach, concentrating on the ground beneath my feet, the wind on my skin, feeling the elements so I could make use of them. Nothing. I laid my palm flat against the side of the house, feeling for a hint of anything, any of the living, moving energy that I *knew* was there.

Nothing.

Desperate, I retrieved Mary from the kitchen, thinking we could do it together, magnifying each other. But we had to start with something simpler.

"Help me form some clouds? Please?" I tried to ask nicely.

"Okay," Mary said with an eye roll.

But she followed me outside and gave me her hand. We drew the fingers of our free hands together in tandem, similar to how we would conjure water charms, willing any moisture in the air to amass. I held a picture of a big white fluffy cloud like from a painting in my mind's eye. I said the words out loud, and Mary repeated: *Chunsch Wulche, Wulche chunsch.* But the seconds droned on, and the heavy air hung stagnant around us.

"Why isn't it working?" Mary asked, her eyes closed tightly in concentration.

"One more time," I said, squeezing Mary's hand in my own, my desperation increasing.

What now, Magda? Dorothy? Anyone?

I saw Magda's cedar chest, already bound to half of my heart. Even with Mary's power to supplement my own, without a full guardian bound to our power source, we were cut off from our abilities. I silently begged for Magda's cedar chest to open, for all the secrets of the universe and the ice floe to be restored. In my mind's eye, I reached toward the cedar chest but was rebuffed with a physical jolt like an electric shock. The other side had closed off and would stay that way until we finished the binding spell, somehow without the ice floe to guide us.

"Damn it!" Mary swore out loud, surprising me as she threw down my hand.

I watched as she lifted her arms to attempt for herself what I had failed, and then my little sister, who had been steely faced since my return, began to beat at the house with a steady incantation of every charm she could think of. Her words hung in the still morning air, useless, pretty words, but the house didn't budge.

The tip of her tongue poked between her teeth in concentration as Mary shot off round after round of charms, the veins on her neck standing out with the effort. Her arms strained forward, threatening to pull away from her shoulder sockets as she threw everything she had at the house, which sat unmoved. The other side remained firmly closed to Mary.

Frustrated to the point of tears, Mary dropped her arms in a huff. But she held her head high, defiant, as the tears rolled down her cheeks.

"What if we lose it forever?" she asked through her tears.

"I won't let that happen," I said. "It's my responsibility to fix this."

"Oh yeah? What are *you* going to do? Run away again? Burn the house down?" Her eye roll was brutal.

"Your attitude isn't going to help us either," I spat back at her. "Anger won't help you reconnect. Anger won't bring Magda back."

She wheeled around on me. "You're one to give advice, Elisabeth Watry-Ridder. Look what your anger did to us," she hissed.

My own name hit me like a curse squarely in the chest. She was right. I reached for her hand, a plea for her to understand, but she snatched it away and stomped back into the house. I watched her go, tossed another lazy charm at the house myself—equally ineffective—and followed her.

"I will fix this," I said out loud, a promise to Mary, to the house, to the universe.

* * *

I wanted to hide during the wake. I wasn't ready to see people. I could barely look at Magda. But John took my arm and steered me through the crowd gathered at Meijer's Funeral Home.

It was all I could do to smile weakly as our neighbors eyed me warily. But a few of the men, mostly farmers, surprised me: not only did they not avoid my gaze, but they were brave enough to say,

"Glad to see you home, Elisabeth," or, "Condolences to your family, Miz Watry." John smiled too broadly at that, clapping backs too heartily, and I wondered how bad the drought was. How desperate were the men in town if they were ready to welcome me back after what I had done to Harry's?

I was relieved when Annie and her mother got there. Annie pulled me into a tight embrace.

"I'm glad you're home," she whispered.

She raised her eyebrows at me. I had been too tired to return her calls since I'd gotten back. "But we need to talk," she said, her tone turning serious.

I nodded, and she grabbed my hand, pulling me away from John to the restroom. I felt John's eyes on us.

"I was so mad at you," Annie blurted the moment the door closed behind us. "I mean, I couldn't believe what happened on Solstice. That was really something else. And to think, I could've been working at Harry's. That is, if Harry would've let me try my hand at serving. Lucky for you I ended up at the Sports Shop, or I would've really been mad at you. But then I saw you looking like a ghost in there and decided you were having a rough enough day already."

"I know, I'm sorry," I said automatically.

"That was pretty stupid, what you did," she said.

"I know," I said with a sigh.

"You're lucky you didn't kill someone," she said. "People are . . . talking. No one wanted to be the first to go back to see Magda, but then they went when they realized they still need water charms. You're lucky. I think the church ladies are the most scandalized, but they'll come around when they need something."

"Really?"

"And where have you been, huh? Your dad's been pretty worried."

I thought, unwillingly, of Nick and his beautiful dimple and the confident, grown-up way he had about him, immediately followed by another wave of shame splitting me open.

Annie must have seen it, as she rushed to ask, "So, what are you going to do now?"

"What, now?" I asked, gesturing at my black dress. "I'm pretty much back in the same boat as before, only now I know what's out there." *A man who makes me feel like I have a working heart.*

The ladies' room door opened then, saving me from explaining further. "I should get back out there. We'll talk more soon, I promise."

We would leave it at that, for the time being.

Thirty-Three

Saturday was even harder than I'd imagined it would be. The procession to church was made unbearable by a dry, crackling heat. As the mid-July sun rose above us, the day was too bright, scalding at eleven AM, in flagrant contrast to the darkness I felt inside. *Isn't it supposed to be rainy and miserable for funerals?* The sun felt like a slap in the face, a reminder of the heat wave that had tortured the county in my absence.

As sweat dripped down my back under my stiff black dress, my discomfort felt like a deserved punishment. And there was no hope of influencing the weather until we reconnected to the ice floe. I walked silently beside Mary, whose dark hair hung loose in a curtain across her face, braids forgone that morning in carelessness or grief. Our parents walked on ahead, oblivious to the tension still sparking between us, as the procession picked up congregants in Magda's last parade, until almost the whole town was making their way up to the church on the hill to pay their respects to Mrs. Magda Watry-Dornen. Even though Magda had dropped Grandpa Earl's Dornen surname when he passed, it seemed right to include it on the printed programs when she was about to lay beside him in the family plot for eternity.

As my father and his brothers and a King cousin shouldered Magda's casket to the front of the church and Father Kevin welcomed us and started the funeral mass, the facts sat starkly in front of me: Magda's cedar chest required a full guardian, and my half-bound heart wasn't going to cut it. With Magda's heart released from the cedar chest, we risked losing our magic for good.

I barely registered the first minutes of mass as I sat with my head hung low between Mary and our father in our regular front pew, mere feet from the plain red cedar casket Magda had requested. After Grandpa Earl's funeral, Magda had written specific instructions for her own, down to the hymns. It was infuriating—she had left us written instructions for even the luncheon menu, but there were no instructions for the binding spell. She had been planning to do that herself at the equinox, but she had simply run out of time. Magda Watry had been caught by surprise. By me and my reckless insubordination, I remembered.

I paid more attention when Mary stood to give the readings. Despite the grief she had been giving me since my homecoming, she looked surprisingly calm and read in an unwavering voice. Magda had strangely chosen 1 Corinthians for the second reading, typically saved for weddings. As Mary finished the last lines, "Love does not delight in evil but rejoices with the truth," it was all I could do to make myself mumble the appropriate "Thanks be to God" in response. *Magda had a strange relationship to the truth*, I thought.

I was lost in my own thoughts, plagued by guilt, as Mary slid back into the pew next to me and the cantor started the Celtic Alleluia. Was I allowed to grieve if it was my fault Magda was gone? My guilt was compounded by the confirmation from my mother: Magda was not who I'd thought she was. How was I supposed to grieve for my dead grandmother when I didn't really know her? Then I felt terrible for having such ill thoughts about my formerly untouchable grandmother, my hero who could no longer defend herself—especially if I was to blame.

Mary, intuitive even in her anger, picked up my hand and gave a hard squeeze. For the millionth time in my life, I felt like Mary knew more than she possibly could have. I should've stopped

doubting her, but old habits die hard. It was hard to see her as anything other than the dark-haired little girl who knew all the squir-
rels and birds and rabbits in the area by name. I was relieved at the
temporary truce, moved by Mary's sudden kindness, and hopeful
that we would be able to move past it all.

Father Kevin had started his homily and was enumerating all of
Sister Magda's good deeds and her lifelong service to the Church. I
nearly burst out laughing at his description of Magda as a "defender
of the faith," and Mary dug her nails into my palm to keep me from
giggling. Mom leaned across Dad and fixed me and Mary with a
look—*This family has a reputation to uphold*—and we both straightened up.

I was shocked to find myself racked by ugly, uncontrollable sobs
when Father Kevin gave the final blessing, the organ started to play
the Salve Regina, and Magda's casket was borne out of the church
on choruses of "Hail, Holy Queen." As I stood with my family to
follow the pallbearers, I couldn't contain myself. I tried to stop,
acutely aware of the mess I must've looked in front of the town and
many folks who hadn't seen me since that awful Solstice night, but
I couldn't. I was torn between the immense guilt and suspicion I
felt toward Magda and the overwhelming knowledge that they were
taking her away to put her in the ground and I would never see her
again on this earth.

*   *   *

John found me off to the side in the churchyard after mass. Without
a word, he kissed my cheek and hooked his arm through mine, and
I let him.

"Thank you," John said to the well-wishers for both of us, shaking
hands like he was already a spokesman for the Watry family, like he
had already reclaimed his prize. It felt strangely like any Sunday in
Friedrich, except we were all baking like ants in the sun in our black.

As the crowd began to make their way over to the VFW and the
family to the cemetery behind the church, my father approached us.

"John," he growled. My father extended a hand, and John noticeably winced as they shook hands. I wondered exactly how much my father had seen the other day.

Shriveling under my father's gaze, John dropped my arm. I spotted Annie out of the corner of my eye and waved her over.

"We'll see you there," I lied, exhaling gratefully as Dad gripped John's shoulder and steered him toward the cemetery.

"How is John not madder at you?" Annie asked, watching them go walk away.

"There is something wrong with that boy," I said, the words slipping out before I could censor myself. It was the closest I had ever come to telling Annie the truth about me and John.

I motioned for her to follow with a jerk of my head and drifted toward the side of the white clapboard church, out of view of prying eyes, and collapsed in the grass. I tried to speak, to explain myself, but only a raspy squeak came out before the tears streamed down my face again.

"Okay," Annie said. "Okay, then." She slid down the side of the building to sit beside me, and I leaned my head into her shoulder. "Do you want to go out to the cemetery?"

"I can't," I squeaked, the tears coming faster. *I can't watch them put her in the ground*, I thought. Annie wrapped her arms around me, and she didn't say anything else for a long time. She didn't have to. We sat on the side of the church like that until everyone had made their way to the VFW.

The luncheon was in full swing by the time we made our appearance, skulking in the service entrance. I felt like I had been stamped with the scarlet letter, a pariah, but I picked up my face the best I could, straightened my back, and with the help of a nip of rum from Annie's purse, started working the room to say hello to all of Magda's mourners like the good Watry-Ridder girl I was. We had a reputation to uphold.

Thirty-Four

Everything felt different in the light of day. I awoke early the next morning, easily reverting to old patterns after aimless weeks of sleeping late, and lay under my covers listening for the regular sounds of the house. But everything was changed: I didn't hear Mom down in the kitchen or footsteps from upstairs. It made me deeply uncomfortable that all the Watry-Ridder women were hiding in bed as morning broke over the lake.

I was completely drained of emotion after the funeral, but some primal instinct drove me to the lake to ground myself before unraveling Magda's web of secrets, before I figured out what exactly to do about the ice floe and the binding. The water was a shock to my system. All the strange energy and resentment I had picked up since Solstice came pouring out the minute I dove into the chilly morning waves.

Mom and Mary were still dallying upstairs when I returned in my towel. I felt stronger, calmer, for the exertion. Alone in the kitchen, I made coffee—which itself was surreal, as I was never the first one up to make coffee. That had always been Magda's or my mother's job.

With a comfortingly familiar mug secured in my hands, I found myself drawn to Magda's room, pulled by some gravitational force.

I was surprised that it looked so normal, untouched in the days since she had passed. Someone, my mother probably, had made the bed with tight corners, and everything was put away in its proper place, as if Magda might rush back into the room at any moment from bridge at Harry's or Cousin Mildred's to claim some forgotten artifact.

I was unsure what I was looking for exactly—*what didn't she tell me? What did Magda Watry take with her to the grave?* I opened her closet and pressed my nose to a sweater, feeling at the same time like an interloper and like I was the only person in the world who deserved to touch her things. It smelled like sage and fire and something subtler, earthier. It smelled like Magda. I dropped the sleeve, then rifled through for the black silk robe with the intricate beadwork. I slipped it over my shoulders, feeling immediately protected and at home, and slid the closet door closed.

I turned slowly, and there it was, taunting me from the foot of Magda's bed—the cedar chest. Magda's stupid magic box, the source of my power and my pain. I had been delaying the inevitable until after the funeral. It was time to face my destiny, the mystery of our family's cedar chest. I had tried to outrun it, but I had to accept my fate as the head of the family now that Magda was gone. She was gone too soon, and that would be my burden to bear.

But before I could open the chest and tear it apart, Mary's voice stopped me cold.

"What are you doing?" she asked in open accusation.

"I . . . I need a charm," I stuttered lamely, turning to meet her eyes as she leaned casually against the doorframe.

I subconsciously mirrored her body language, leaning back against the edge of Magda's high sleigh bed. Mary eyed me skeptically from the doorway, one eyebrow raised.

"Fine," I said. "I need the binding spell."

Mary's face remained unchanged, showing not an ounce of surprise or curiosity. *What does Mary know about the binding spell anyway?*

"Couldn't you use a summoning charm?" she said.

I sighed, failing to suppress an eye roll. "Come on, think about it. If we can't use a charm to fix the house right now, how am I supposed to use a summoning charm? How are we supposed to do anything when nothing's working?"

"Okay, okay. There has to be another way," Mary said firmly. Her stare was so fierce that I had to look away.

"It has to be here," I said, ignoring her. I waved a hand vaguely toward the cedar chest. "Magda was going to finish binding my heart this equinox. How would she do it without the words?" I asked aloud, even as I knew the answer. The guardian didn't need instructions. But if I was cut off from the ice floe, I couldn't access the cedar chest's power to provide me the words. The anxiety that had been building inside started to pour out, the words coming faster and faster. "We can't need magic to protect the magic; that doesn't make any sense. We need to reconnect to the ice floe. Nothing will work until we're back at full strength."

Mary stormed across the room, and for a minute I thought she might hit me. "Listen to me. Do you even want this?" she said, grabbing me by the shoulders.

My breathing was fast and shallow in my chest, unbearably loud to my own ears. *Do I even want this?*

I threw up my hands, defeated. "There's no other option. I won't be responsible for this family losing anything else. Generations of magic won't end with me. Besides, I don't know who I am without magic. I tried that."

And Magda will get what she wanted after all.

Mary cut her eyes at me. "You can't do this alone, you know. Aren't you going to ask me what I know, Lisbett?" An edge had crept into her voice.

I hesitated, taken aback by the new tone in Mary's voice. She sounded like me. When I didn't respond right away, she rolled her eyes to the ceiling and turned hard on her heel. I followed her to the kitchen and waited as Mary poured herself a cup of coffee. She faced me, shoulders raised protectively around her ears.

"Mare," I said, filling the silence. I took a deep breath. "Magda bound my heart before I could even talk. She gave my heart away for this family. I am stuck with this. *You* don't have to be."

"Great-Grandma Dorothy told me," Mary said, clearly relishing watching me flounder in surprise.

"When?" I asked.

"I've known for a while," Mary said with a sharp look. "Dorothy has talked to me for a long time, and she drops these little nuggets over time. But I think she talks to Mom more. I think she's *here* for Mom. I've seen her aura following you too. She hasn't been around here much lately, though."

When Dorothy was silent in Minneapolis, she must have been watching Mom or Mary. I shouldn't have been surprised that she guided all of us, but she had felt so special to me in particular.

"Mare," I tried again. "Then you know what Magda did. You know why I had to leave."

Mary's lip quivered. "Not like that. You hurt people and endangered the town. And you left me alone with Magda to clean up after you."

I started to open my mouth but couldn't find the words. She was right, and I was ashamed.

Mary looked around the kitchen thoughtfully. "It wasn't always this way," she said, echoing Dorothy. "It could be shared. Heck, you shared it with Magda for seventeen years!"

"No, no way," I said instantly, waving my hand to cut her off. "You see how terrible this has been for me? I didn't even know I could do . . . what I did on Solstice. It was so out of control. And one of us giving up our heart is enough. This doesn't need to involve you too."

Mary narrowed her eyes at me. "Dorothy said you'd be stubborn."

"Stubborn about what?" Mom said, suddenly in the doorway between the living room and kitchen.

It was jarring to hear so many complete sentences out of my mother's mouth in the same week.

"I need the ice floe to receive the binding spell," I said, watching her, "and I need the binding spell to reconnect to the ice floe."

Mom looked thoughtful. "Maybe."

"What do you mean, maybe?" I asked, incredulous.

She poured herself a cup of coffee and joined us at the table. "Your grandmother should've done this," she said with a sigh, gripping her mug with both hands. "There's a lot of things Mother should've done differently." She grimaced.

"Mary, you may not want to hear it all," Mom continued before either of us could interrupt. "But we will need you, and it's your right to hear this too." She spoke slowly, holding Mary's gaze.

"I'm staying," Mary said firmly. "I'm as in this as you are," she said with a pointed look to me.

Mom pressed her lips together in a tight line. "You both know by now that my mother was a complicated woman. She made the choices she thought were best for her family because of choices that were made before her time."

Mom had that familiar, far-off look in her eyes that I'd seen my entire childhood. I worried that she would retreat back into herself; that it was too much for her, that we would lose her again.

But then she kept talking. "We need to call Dorothy," Mom said. "It's best you hear it from her. And without the ice floe, we'll have to do it the old-fashioned way, with a séance and a witch in each of the compass points, which means we'll need Cousin Mildred."

Astonishment broke through Mary's defiant pout. She leaned forward across the table, jaw agape, as did I, both of us hanging on our mother's every word.

"Girls, come now," she said with a pointed look at each of us. "I know you know this. Fire feeds on earth and wind. Wind feeds water, and so on. It's not just a silly saying. It's a formula. With a little pressure and a proper coven . . ."

"Now?" Mary asked.

Mom shrugged. "Mother has been gone for almost a week now. The house is falling apart. And here we are. If we're going to act, now is as good a time as ever." She glanced at the clock above the sink. "If we hurry, we can catch Mildred before she heads off to Sunday supper at the lodge."

"So I was right," Mary said, turning to me, triumphant. "You can't do this alone. You will need me."

"We'll see," I said.

Mom straightened up and her gaze swept over me, her eyes lighting on my swimsuit underneath Magda's beaded robe. "Elisabeth, go put some real clothes on. Mary, fetch eight of Dorothy's silver spoons from the china hutch."

Mary went without another word. I climbed the back stairs slowly, taking my time to gather my thoughts. I dressed in denim and a plain blouse but slipped Magda's black silk robe over my shoulders again. I couldn't explain it, but I wanted Magda close to me.

When I returned to the kitchen, Mom was counting candles. Armed with thirteen new red tapers, eight silver spoons, a lemon peel, a scrap of cloth, and a box of salt, we headed for Cousin Mildred's.

Thirty-Five

Cousin Mildred's house was a small white rambler in the center of town with neatly painted black trim. The Andersens' home next door was nearly identical except for the dazzling pink-studded rosebushes under Mildred's windows, her pride and joy since her "good-for-nothing sons" had dared to up and leave for jobs in Nebraska and Texas.

"That woman next door," Cousin Mildred had once stage-whispered to Magda, "would never have the patience for roses. Roses take a certain temperament."

As we approached, I wondered what Mildred knew of her dear cousin Magda, now that the memory charm would be wearing off. I also wondered absently who their fourth was for bridge now that Magda was gone. Any doubts of the family likeness were immediately erased when Cousin Mildred suddenly opened the door, Mom's hand hovering over the doorbell before she had a chance to ring.

"Well, then," Mildred said through the screen door, taking in me and Mary before her eyes settled on Mom. "I figured you'd be coming along sooner or later. Hello, Helene. Hello, girls. I suppose you'll be wanting to come in, then."

Mildred stepped back into the house with the door ajar, waiting for us to follow. Mom shrugged at me and Mary over her shoulder.

When we were all seated around Mildred's dining room table, coffee served in her good china and thin sandwiches distributed—suspiciously precut into triangles with a swipe of margarine and one sliver of ham each, an indication that she had been expecting us—Cousin Mildred cleared her throat indelicately.

"When Magda passed," she started loudly, "it was like I came out of a deep fog. I keep remembering little doodads I haven't thought about in fifty-odd years. It has taken me all week to think that I've remembered all that I'm going to remember."

Mom and I exchanged a look above our coffee cups. I'd wondered how long Cousin Mildred had been under Magda's enchantments, and if they were only memory charms like we gave Father Kevin or Magda's own special varietal for her cousin. And who else had Magda charmed over the years?

Mildred didn't stop for a reaction, clearly relishing being the center of attention. "I knew Magda didn't tell me everything, but I could never remember what I wanted to ask her. Now I feel something I haven't truly felt since I was a little girl. My grandmother Margalit, sisters with Magda's grandmother Clara, wasn't around to teach us, so I never really knew what to call it, and when I moved back to Friedrich as a young woman, I never understood why my mother didn't want me to live here. But I felt so blessed to reconnect with my dear cousin Magda, someone who could explain what I had felt for all those years . . . but then it all got very foggy."

Mildred looked as if she were talking to her empty house, saying out loud all the things she thought she had forgotten. My mother, for her part, said nothing, only nodded, and Mary and I followed her lead. It was strange to be taking cues from my mother after her silence for the better part of my life.

When Cousin Mildred rambled to a close, my mother leaned forward in her chair. "Mildred," Mom said. "See, those things you felt as a little girl, that is why we're here. You, like us, have inherited an old power. We need your help now to channel it. You can be an essential part of this. We need you—for a séance."

"Well," Mildred said in a huff, turning her head to my mother again. "I suppose this is about you, then," she said with a pointed look to me. "Yes, Magda once used me for one of these, I think."

I only nodded, afraid to set Cousin Mildred off, but I desperately wanted confirmation from my mother: *Is it true? Did this old biddy help Magda before? How much magic was in those old claws?*

Mary surprised me by reaching across the table for Mildred's hand.

"We are not responsible for the sins of our mothers," Mary said, her dark curls falling loose across her face. "We won't make any excuses for those who came before us. We can only make it right now. But only with your help."

Cousin Mildred harrumphed but didn't pull away. "Now, I practiced charms with Magda a few times," she said, "but she was so bossy and kept me under close instruction. I can't say for sure what I know and don't know—it's all so foggy—but yes, I suppose I could be of service."

The septuagenarian broke into a shockingly wide grin, exposing a full set of her own teeth, albeit yellowed with age.

"We can't do it without you," Mary egged her on.

"Yes," Mildred said confidently. "I'm glad you came to me. I have been waiting my whole life for someone to ask me to do something, and now here you are, begging me for help, and I'm the only person in the world that can do it. Isn't that wonderful."

She smiled to herself like the Cheshire cat.

"It is, because we're going to call Dorothy now and clarify some things," Mom said matter-of-factly. She motioned toward me and our bag of supplies. "Do you have a smallish mirror we could take off the wall, Cousin? And another chair?"

We watched as Mom carefully laid Dorothy's spoons to mark the meridians between the cardinal directions, forming a star within a circle of the new red candles. Mildred returned with a gold-framed mirror as Mom pulled a fifth chair to the table. She took the mirror from Mildred and set it on the fifth chair, then placed the cloth and lemon peel in the center of the table and opened her hand to let a fistful of salt cascade down on the lemon peel.

I watched, fascinated. I had never seen Mom navigate a magic ritual before.

"Mom," I marveled. "I didn't know you could do this."

The training was clearly there, despite my mother's deliberate choice not to practice magic. Whatever had long simmered between Magda and my mother had been enough to keep my mother away from her abilities, from the calling of all the women in our family. I was awed to see how easily it came back to her.

She smiled. "It's been a while, but until seventeen years ago, I did everything you do. I . . . well, you'll understand, I hope. But I spent thirty years doing this too."

"That's where you come in," Cousin Mildred said, pointing a crooked finger at me. *God, what did Magda tell her during their coffee chats? What did Mildred forget over the years?*

My mother motioned for us to sit in the chairs now carefully rearranged in the four points of the compass rose. She reached for my hand and Mildred's on the other side. I looked at my mother with new eyes and took her hand firmly in my own, her palm up, mine down.

"Good," Mom said as I reached for Mary on the other side, my palm up, hers down.

Mary and Mildred completed the sturdy square of Watry women. The fifth chair sat just outside the reach of our arms.

"Together," Mom said. She held Mary's gaze firmly for a moment then looked into my own eyes, a reassurance, a promise. "Follow along, Cousin. You'll get it," she said, squeezing our hands.

Mom started the Alemannic incantation out loud. *"Mir süeche unsre Großmuedere. Mir süeche unsre Ähne. Chunsch Dorothy Watry, Dorothy Watry chunsch."*

Mary jumped in confidently, and I followed. Mildred listened for a few rounds, then added her voice to the chorus.

Chunsch Dorothy Watry, Dorothy Watry chunsch. We call upon our grandmothers. We call upon Dorothy Watry.

Mom and Mary pulsed their intention steadily while I fought to keep my mind from wandering, to keep the anxiety from creeping in. *What if it doesn't work? What if Dorothy can't help us?* But soon enough I was carried away, mesmerized by the words.

Mir süeche unsre Großmuedere. Mir süeche unsre Ähne.

Our voices became one, and time stood still.

I see you, Dorothy, I know you.

The room exploded with light.

* * *

I blinked hard, and there was Great-Grandma Dorothy in the fifth chair where the mirror had been, as if she had dropped in for kaffeeklatsch. Mary and Mildred sat blinking in the astoundingly bright light; it was Cousin Mildred's dining room but not, a place in between, suspended in time and energy and light between Dorothy's timeless realm and our own.

Dorothy, whom I hadn't heard from since Magda had passed, since my connection to the other side had been disturbed, smiled a warm, knowing smile at each of us in turn. Her eyes lingered on my mother. Tears leapt to Mom's eyes, but she smiled back, basking in her grandmother's radiance. Dorothy filled us all with a warm light; I innately knew that the others felt as happy and safe and warm as I did.

"Oh my," Mildred said in wonder when Dorothy's gaze lighted on her.

"So," Dorothy said, folding her hands on the table in front of her. "Here we are, meine Lieblinge."

"Is Mother here, Dorothy?" Mom asked urgently, with a sliver of apprehension.

"I felt it when she crossed," Dorothy said, her voice high and clear, pulsing light at us.

I felt wrapped in her embrace, warmed to the core.

"But my daughter is still wandering," Dorothy continued. "It may take time for her to settle, for her spirit to seek its new mooring. She is adjusting to the loss of physical form. It took me a while, too, for my bits and pieces to reform from where they were scattered like stars in the sky. She will find her way eventually, but we can speak openly now. She is not here to listen. What do you want to discuss, meine Lieblinge?"

In the circle of light, my mother gave me a knowing look. When I hesitated, momentarily forgetting what we had originally come for, Mom urged, "Go on, Elisabeth."

"Magda left us without the full binding spell," I said in a rush. "My heart is half-bound, and we have no way to complete it. I don't understand how, but I know it's mine to finish."

Dorothy fixed me with a stern look.

"My darling, I will always be here to guide you. But why do you think I led you away in the first place? I think it is high time you knew the full story of what my daughter did, but you must first hear what my mother, Clara, did. Then maybe you will understand."

I glanced at my mother, but she betrayed nothing, her gaze steady on Dorothy.

"My mother did something awful," Dorothy started.

Maybe we come from a long line of terrible people, I thought.

Dorothy shot me a look. "None of that now," she said. "We all try the best for our families, but women like my mother had a different way of going about it. And after I crossed over, I had to watch my daughter make the same mistake."

The room stood still, bathed in that warm, white light. My awareness of my own breath faded away; there was nothing but the sound of Dorothy's voice.

"When I was a very little girl, my mother and father and I shared the house with my mother's sister, my aunt Margalit and her husband, all of us under one roof. It was chaotic, but it worked. My mother, your great-great-grandma Clara, shared the business with Margalit, working side by side as they had since they were girls, raised to do everything together as one, four hands of the same heart."

Mary shot me a knowing look at that. I pretended not to see, keeping my focus on Dorothy.

"I was old enough to wonder why Aunt Margalit didn't have any children, and I know now that she had been trying for years," Dorothy continued. "There are some things that our abilities cannot alter. And I think my mother was getting used to the idea of making me the sole guardian. Soon she was set on it, one way or another.

"So you can imagine how shocked my mother was when Aunt Margalit had a pregnancy that took, and how surprised we all were to learn that Margalit, at age thirty-seven after a decade of trying, was carrying twins."

Mildred made a knowing sound at that, and I realized faintly that one of those twins would've been Mildred's mother.

Dorothy continued, "Two little girl cousins for me to share the family business with. But my mother wasn't prepared for that. She could not imagine a world where the guardianship was diluted further, from two sisters to three cousins. She wasn't about to let my shiny new cousins take away what she was determined to give to me alone."

"Like Mother," Mom emphasized.

"But that's not how it works," Mary interrupted. "Air feeds fire. Our abilities can magnify each other."

Dorothy looked from Mary to me, lips pursed hard. "Jealousy does strange things to people," she said, her gaze settling on Mary.

I blinked hard. My little sister knew that lesson firsthand.

Dorothy continued, "When my cousins Lottë and Katherine were one year old, starting to toddle around after Margalit, who was full to the brim with the joy of motherhood at long last, my mother did something awful. She acted out of jealousy and out of fear.

"I was playing outside one day—it was early fall, and I was calling straggling monarch butterflies to the yard—when I heard a terrible noise. It sounded like a lightning bolt splitting the house in two. I ran inside to find my mother in Margalit's bedroom standing over the cedar chest. Her chest was heaving, and I saw . . . Aunt Margalit in a heap on the floor, like a pile of laundry, cursed by her own sister."

"My poor grandmother," Cousin Mildred whispered, clearly pained.

I felt as if I were floating above myself, like Dorothy was talking about someone else's family. But then again, considering my fight with Magda . . .

"I don't remember much else except the sound of the twins crying and crying. I will never forget the sound of their terrible wailing and how very, very quiet Margalit was. My mother turned toward me then, and I was scared. But she scooped me up and took me upstairs to bed and told me it was all a bad dream. I believed her for a long time.

"Uncle Ned took Margalit and the twins away and raised them in St. Agnes, without magic. Without their family. Without their birthright. Margalit was never the same again. My mother told me that it would all be mine and mine alone, and I believed her. I carried the cedar chest by myself, letting Mother fully bind my own heart when I was eighteen. I was afraid of what she had done, how she cursed her own sister's heart, but I never knew if my memories were real. I was never brave enough in my life to confront my mother.

"But then I saw the same dark root of fear in my own daughter. I wondered if the burden might be shared again, but Magda had other ideas. I saw firsthand how Margalit was struck down when she was separated from our natural-born gifts, and I was scared to do anything that might disrupt our power. I bound my daughter's heart alongside my own when she was eighteen, as became our custom. Without turning to cousins, by then I didn't have another choice."

Dorothy became quiet. The light dimmed a bit in the room; I felt a cool breeze whirl around the table, and I saw Mary shiver as she felt it too.

"We don't have much time," Mom said. She watched Dorothy closely.

"Then you better get talking, Helene," Dorothy said with a nod.

My mother sighed deeply and looked directly into my eyes, tearing up. "I'm sorry, I can't," she whispered, sounding like her old shadow self.

Whatever it was, it had been buried in my mother for a long time. Anger flared up in me suddenly. *Tell me*, I urged her silently.

"Go on," Dorothy said firmly.

My mother shook her head. "How can I?"

Dorothy reached an ethereal hand to Mom. "We'll show them, then. I'll help you."

I felt my mother squeeze my hand, and the room fell away entirely.

Thirty-Six

I heard my mother's voice in my ear, but I no longer saw the confines of Cousin Mildred's dining room or Dorothy's spirit form. As my mother spoke, narrating for us, it dawned on me slowly: Dorothy was somehow showing us Mom's memories.

"It was the summer after I turned thirty," my mother's voice said in my ear.

Even as I felt the chair solid beneath me, I was simultaneously back outside our house looking in. It materialized before me as if in a dream, but it wasn't exactly the house I knew. Magda had not yet painted the door plum, and my father had not yet tamed Grandpa Earl's unruly hostas along the garage.

The hunched shape of a young woman peered over something fascinating in the side yard, where my father would later build the fire pit. The yard exploded with the muted pinks and yellows of the June lady's slippers and prairie roses. The woman was soft around the edges, the fine lines not yet settled into a permanently furrowed brow. Her hair cascaded loose to her waist, streaks of darker tawny and honey tones in the sea of blonde. I knew that it was my mother, but it was like looking at a fun house mirror image of myself, right down to the muscular calves.

I was vaguely aware of my own thoughts beneath the surface—
how am I seeing this?—but they came to me from very far away,
filtered through two decades of my mother's memories.

"Just watch, Elisabeth," said my mother's voice.

Young Helene stood, the object of her close examination in
her arms: she scooped up a giggling, bright-eyed, chunky-legged
toddler with a shock of blinding white-blonde chick's fluff for
hair. I recognized myself in miniature, the telltale heart-shaped
face and sturdy shoulders. When Helene turned, her stunningly
round belly in profile under a plain blue linen dress foretold
Mary's impending arrival. *Another daughter,* my young mother
thought, *in September under a harvest moon.* I felt my mother's
hope in every fiber of my being as she shared the memory of
anticipation growing inside her. Underneath, I sensed my mother's fear.

This is the part Mary isn't going to want to hear, I realized.

We were transported inside now, into a room lit by a single
white porcelain lamp on the table next to an antique hand-me-
down rocking chair. Young Helene rocked her limp toddler, passed
out like a tiny drunk with heavy limbs and an open mouth. Helene
tenderly laid her firstborn daughter in the crib, turned out the light,
and left the door cracked. She hesitated in the doorway, listening
one last time for her daughter's steady breath, a sigh, the sounds of
the nursery settling into sleep.

Young Helene's attention wandered to the sunny yellow light
within her, as unique to Mary as her fingerprints. I felt the gentle
glow coming from within me, and it disturbed me to feel my own
body's empathic response to my mother's memory. Mary's energy
wasn't yet bright, dazzling like the emerald green radiating with
every breath from my toddler self, but that ball of warm yellow
energy, no larger than an apple at the time, was already a soothing
presence to Helene. Helene ran her fingers over her belly subconsciously, smiling as she thought, *She's already reading me.*

. "Helene."

Young Helene startled as Magda's voice cut through the dim hallway. She turned slowly to face her mother, trundling around like a horse in a stall.

"Solstice is in two days. This has gone on for long enough," Magda said quietly, plainly, gesturing to the swell of Helene's stomach.

Helene glanced nervously to the cracked door behind her, then stepped urgently toward Magda.

"I have told you over and over, Mother. I'm not going to do it. It's unthinkable," Helene hissed, her stare formidable.

"I have given you too much free rein," Magda said with a shake of her head. "I let you run around wild, and who knows what you would've done if I hadn't put Jacob Ridder in your path. You have always known that this responsibility would be yours alone, and that you would pass it along to a daughter. To a single daughter," she emphasized.

Helene's hands flew instinctively to her belly as she enfolded herself and the light within her in the circle of her arms.

"It's too late," Helene said, unsure of herself.

Magda smiled that tight, close-lipped smile I knew all too well. "It's never too late," she said calmly.

I recalled involuntarily the pennyroyal I had given Mrs. Andersen, suddenly understanding what Magda intended.

"You just try," young Helene said through gritted teeth.

Magda reached a hand toward Helene's arm; her daughter flinched away.

Magda said quietly, firmly, "We cannot let the guardianship be split. Look how that ended last time."

"This baby is six months along. You will not take her from me," Helene said, biting each syllable.

The scene changed again, and I instantly felt the energy of another Solstice. Toddler Elisabeth played in the corner of the kitchen while Helene with Mary in her belly drew on a primordial magic as old as life itself, serving Friedrich with a smile pasted on her face.

It was suddenly night, and the powerful Solstice moonlight—
an auspicious sign, I thought automatically—poured through the
windows of the house on Lake Street. Magda had begrudgingly
gone to bed. Young Helene smiled to herself, knowing that her
mother must've mistakenly thought it was safe to leave her irate,
determined daughter alone under that Solstice moon.

We watched as Mom bound her whole heart to Mary. All love
for Jacob Ridder, love for Helene's toddler daughter, was wiped out
in a flash of brilliant white light that I recognized instantaneously
with a shudder.

"What are you doing?" Magda's voice said from the darkness
beyond the circle of white light.

"It's already done," young Helene said. She was smiling, triumphant, and filled with a light that would bind her to Mary forever.

My mother's heart was for Mary, and Mary alone, from that
moment on. Mary, in turn, was protected in a layer of Mom's own
ruby-red energy, an impenetrable defense of the strongest magic.
Magda would never be able to touch her, born or unborn.

"Oh, Helene," Magda said from the darkness. Her voice was
sad, trembling. "You don't know what you have done. I only want
what is best for this family," Magda said.

"So do I," Helene said defiantly.

*   *   *

"Mary, honey, I would have done anything to protect you," Mom
said, breaking the spell. Her voice caught in her throat.

The room disappeared, and we were once again in the warm,
mystical alcove of the in-between place with Great-Grandma
Dorothy.

"But in protecting Mary, I lost you, Elisabeth, in the bargain,"
Mom said, her voice barely above a whisper. Tears rolled down her
cheeks like glass.

"I lost you to Mother, Elisabeth. But I knew you'd be okay." Her
face broke open with pride underneath the tears. "Your light was

so bright, I knew you'd be okay. Even as I had to give you away to Mother."

Take her, then. She's yours.

My mother's words from the dream world echoed freshly in my ears. My entire life, I had thought my mother had no interest in me. I had belonged to Magda whether I liked it or not. I'd thought my mother was weak or, at worst, cruel. I thought she had passively fallen into that silent, zombie state over time; I'd never imagined that my mother would have been exacting enough to choose it for herself.

I was speechless.

Mom said urgently, "Elisabeth, I need you to understand. I couldn't do anything to poison you against Magda in her life, and Mother was right, in a way. There had to be someone to carry on when I bound my heart to Mary and refused the cedar chest. I am so sorry, honey. I gave you up to Magda because I couldn't let her take Mary. My only purpose in this world has been to protect you girls."

This was the secret my mother had buried beneath her silence. I had that feeling again like I was floating outside myself, the vague thought coming from far away that Cousin Mildred had hit on a treasure trove of gossip.

Dorothy addressed Mildred as soon as I'd had the thought.

"You are part of this now, too, dear cousin—an important part," she emphasized, appealing to Mildred's sense of self-importance. "You are sworn to protect this family's secrets now. Or else— Elisabeth will charm you for the rest of your days."

Mildred harrumphed again but acquiesced. "I don't know why you all seem to think I can't keep a secret."

Mom's gaze locked on Mary, who, like me, was unable to find the words, stunned into silence. Her face had gone pale beneath her vibrant summer tan.

"After that, Mother did things differently," Mom said, turning back to me. "It was easier for me to say nothing at all, to stay out of the way, than to risk harm to either of you girls. Besides, she was different with you, Elisabeth. I knew you'd be okay, despite Mother being more determined than ever to preserve the sole guardian, one pure line to protect the magic."

I squeezed my eyes shut. I was quickly losing faith in anything Magda had ever done.

My daughter lost her way long ago.

Mom exchanged a knowing look with Dorothy.

Dorothy made a small noise. "I suppose I had something to do with that. She was obsessed with the Clara story. I told Magda her grandmother's version of events, ignoring what I had seen my mother do with my own eyes. I meant it as a cautionary tale, but my bullheaded daughter took it another way. I tried to subdue the same darkness in Magda that I had seen as a little girl in my own mother, a self-reliance turned to obsession. But Magda did things her own way, especially after I crossed over."

Mary spoke suddenly. "That's why Great-Grandma Dorothy protected you, Mom. She couldn't stop Magda from . . . from . . . trying to get rid of me." Her voice was barely above a whisper. "You couldn't stop Magda from the other side, Dorothy, but you protect us how you can."

Dorothy nodded. "Always. I didn't do enough to change my daughter's path during my life, but I'll be damned if I can't protect her daughter and granddaughters in my afterlife."

The fire in her voice reminded me ironically of Magda.

Mom nodded. "When you were almost two, Elisabeth, after Mary was born, Magda made you her own. She bound your heart on the fall equinox, seventeen years ago, to make sure you would always be hers and couldn't go rogue like me. She's held a tight grip on your future ever since. Until you stood up to her on Solstice."

The white light in the room dimmed further, and a persistent buzzing, like a chorus of bees, filled my ears.

"Dorothy," Mom pressed. "We don't have much time. Elisabeth needs the binding spell. Without Mother here to do it . . ."

"You'll be fine," Dorothy said. "Give me your hand, mein Liebling," she said to me sweetly.

But the distance between Dorothy's ethereal form and my earthly one suddenly seemed enormous.

"I . . . I can't," I stuttered, straining toward her across time, space, energy.

I no longer heard Dorothy's voice but felt it pulsing at me, pure energy. The room between the spirit world and ours began to collapse.

Your mother and sister have led you here. Take my hand, Elisabeth.

I had felt only a fluttering of connection to the spirit world since Magda had crossed to the other side. It was like feeling in a dark room for the light switch. I knew it was there—it had to be—but I couldn't find it. Where the onionskin-thin veil had once divided the realms, an impenetrable steel curtain closed the spirit world off to me.

I can't.

The candles on the table reappeared before me, and my eyes bore into the red wax, concentrating.

It's not working, it's not working, it's not working. I can't do it.

But as surely as my own thoughts played on a loop, I heard a tiny voice beneath my own doubt from somewhere deeper. From the nothingness where the ice floe should have been, a pinprick of white light illuminated in the back of my vision field from somewhere behind my right ear, so small that, at first, I doubted its presence. But it glowed steadily, small and warm, and brighter by one long second after another as the murmur grew stronger in my ear— *Fiir und Wasser, Wasser und Fiir.*

I saw from my peripheral vision that Mary's lips were unmoving beside me, but her voice became clearer in my mind, my sister breaking through the energy field first when the channels of light were darkest.

Mary's voice grew with the pinprick of light, which spread from the right side of my vision field across to the left. Mary reached across to Mom, a thread of light skating between them. I felt more than saw a hesitant bridge of light from my mother. My mother reached for me, and I felt her voice joining Mary's. Even Cousin Mildred's voice joined in. We were rebuilding our connection to the ice floe fiber by fiber, light by light.

Fiir und Wasser, Wasser und Fiir.

I felt nothing but my pulse in my throat. Fear seized me, and I spiraled. *What if I never see the spirit world again?* I felt sweat pooling under my arms, soaking the delicate silk of Magda's robe, my breath short in my chest.

Through my panic and the buzzing growing louder, I heard Dorothy as if from far away. *Take my hand, Elisabeth. We are here for you.*

The buzzing grew louder in my ears; the room grew hazy. I heard Dorothy's voice growing closer but light as birdsong.

Take my hand.

Light pulsed at me from all sides. I reached for Dorothy, and I felt a pinprick of light open in my chest. The curtain began to lift between the worlds as I reached out a hand in the spirit realm, and as surely as I held Mary's hand on my right and Mom's on my left, I felt Dorothy's thin, elegant fingers—so similar to Magda's—grasp my forearm, and lightning jolted through me.

My heart split open, the invisible river of pure rainbow energy swept me away, and the room went dark.

Thirty-Seven

My forearm burned where Great-Grandma Dorothy had gripped it.

The haze cleared from the room, revealing once again the disconcertingly bright sky outside Mildred's front window. I rubbed my eyes, dazed, blinking at Great-Grandma Dorothy's chair and the mirror there once again. As the room came slowly back into focus, Mary gasped. My forearm burned white hot as Cousin Mildred began to jabber on around us.

"Well! Wasn't that something? I haven't seen Cousin Dorothy since, well, since she passed, of course . . ."

An angry pink welt rose across my forearm, Dorothy's handprint marking me. Tiny white lines grew out of the scalded pink flesh and arranged themselves into shapes and letters, small, cramped handwriting, spreading across the flat underside of my forearm toward my wrist and Mary's hand gripping my own.

"Lisbett, the words," Mary whispered, awestruck.

Mom dropped my hand and leaned across the table to inspect it closer. "How efficient. I remember the ceremony, but the words, those I had from Magda . . . You see, Mother destroyed any scrap of variance in the spell after I bound my heart to you, Mary." She started to turn to Mary, but I stopped her.

"Wait, but you remember the ritual?" I asked.

"You needed to understand, Lisbett, before we go down this road. You needed to know why it has fallen to you. Why Mary . . ." Mom's eyes watered again as she turned back to Mary.

I realized Mary had yet to say a word since our communication with Dorothy had ended. She was unnaturally pale.

At that, Mom tapped both hands lightly on the table. "Girls, let's leave Mildred to it. We have some things to think over ourselves. Cousin, thank you for lending us your power today. You helped us reach Dorothy. You helped us get back this inkling of light from the other side. And thank you, Dorothy"—she raised her voice and her eyes to the ceiling—"for your constant guidance, for giving us a path forward."

Mom hustled us from the room. I thought Mary might be sick when we made it out the front door into the beautiful afternoon sunshine, but she stayed upright and shuffled steadily toward home.

I studied my arm as we walked. It throbbed less already, the words becoming part of me, already subsiding to the faint white of scar tissue. The words, a shadow of the words Magda had chanted over me in the cedar chest as a child, looked similar to the Alemannic I was familiar with but were yet unfamiliar.

"Südbadisch," Mom said flatly, seeing what was written there when I held my arm out to her. "It predates our Alemannic grandmothers. Mother didn't teach me much."

"Why didn't Magda teach it to me?" I asked, puzzling over the script.

My mother's look was deadpan. "I assumed she wanted to wait until now, until she finished your binding this fall. She would've taught you then, when it was too late to back out. But she . . ."

"She ran out of time," Mary finished. A bit of color was coming back into her face.

"This is what you want?" Mom asked me.

I thought of the overwhelming, itchy feeling in my hands when I had tried to suppress my magic, and the desperate way the our neighbors looked at me during Magda's funeral. The farms were turning to dust. They needed us. They would look the other way about Harry's when their livelihood was on the line.

I nodded dumbly. "I have to do this," I managed through the shock settling over me. "It's my birthright, and it's time for me to accept it."

I felt a zing from Dorothy again. *What?* I asked her silently, before realizing that I could feel her again.

"Wait!" I cried. "Dorothy, can you hear me?"

Yes, Liebling. I'm here.

I grinned. "Mare, we're back," I said, gripping Mary's arm in joy.

She smiled weakly. "Thank God," Mary said. She held out a hand to levitate the bag of spoons and half-burnt candles over my shoulder. It rose a few inches, then slumped back against my side.

I groaned and tried it for myself, but the bag wouldn't go higher than a few inches.

"Ugh," Mary groaned. "I guess we're still at half strength."

"What now?" I asked Mom.

"I guess it's time for the binding," she replied.

"Won't we need to wait for the equinox?" Mary asked.

"Girls, did Magda ever teach you about the Lion's Gate?"

Mary shook her head.

"On August eighth every year, Sirius, a sister star to our sun, begins to rise," Mom continued. "It's not the equinox, but it could be another powerful portal for us to try, if we can't wait that long."

I contemplated the unfamiliar words across my arm. "I think we have to try. Our magic is in peril every day that we remain at half strength like this."

"A sister star, huh?" Mary asked.

I felt her eyes on me but kept my gaze on the sidewalk beneath my feet. As far as I was concerned, there was nothing to do but wait for August to come.

* * *

Back home, I climbed the back stairs wordlessly to our room, where, despite the early evening daylight outside my window, I crawled under the covers, fully dressed, to sleep away the pressure of the day.

I fell into a deep dreamless sleep, but I awoke to darkness later when I heard Mary come in.

"Dad was asking about you," Mary said, flipping on the light callously.

I groaned. I had barely spoken to my father since returning home.

"I guess I'll catch up with him tomorrow . . . ," I said as I sat up in bed blinking, unsure of the day and hour. It came back to me slowly. *Still Sunday, the day after we put Magda in the ground*, I thought.

"He's worried about you," Mary continued. She undressed with her back to me. "So am I."

"You are? What about you?" I asked. *Magda tried to . . . get rid of you . . .* I couldn't make myself say it out loud.

"Mm," Mary mumbled. She surprised me. All the ire she'd spat at me before seemed to have evaporated with Great-Grandma Dorothy's spirit. *Or Mary has bigger things on her mind*, I thought.

"Mare," I said, daring her to look at me. "Do you think I killed Magda?"

That stopped her short. Mary turned and met my eyes before looking away.

"Oh," she said. Mary sat down on her bed, distracted. "No. No, I didn't mean that. I was just . . . But no, I didn't mean it. It was her time."

"I didn't wear her out?" I asked anxiously, voicing the fear that had been in my heart since I'd walked in the door.

"It wasn't your fault," she said finally as she turned off the light. "I know she cast on you first. I know what she put you through."

I squeezed my eyes shut against the dark, making myself take a beat before responding. "So you wanted to make me feel bad, then? You knew, and you were just guilting me?"

She climbed into her bed beside me. "It was so hard without you," Mary said quietly. "The town was eerily quiet for a week after Solstice. I didn't know if anyone would ever trust us again. If Tim would talk to me. Magda was so mad, raving, practically. But then people started to trickle in. Magda was too distracted, so I took care of some of them, and it felt good. But I wish you had been here."

"Listen," I said, cutting her off as much for my sake as hers. "I'm home now, and I promise I'll take care of everything. We need to get through the binding, then everything will be back to normal. It will go on like it always has and always will, and nothing will ever change in this house or town ever again."

I almost believed myself as I said it.

Mary's sigh cut through the dark as she adjusted her covers. "That's what I'm worried about," she said, exasperated. "You don't want that. And you don't need to do it alone."

I brushed her off. "After what Mom showed us? I'm surprised you want anything to do with Magda and this place anymore. Why should I let you throw your heart away for this stupid family?" I asked. The words turned to acid in my mouth. "Seriously, I don't want you to give up your future too. I meant what I said. Two Watry-Ridder women giving up their hearts is more than enough."

I thought of my mother, her heart bound to her unborn child, giving up her birthright for her daughters. I thought of John—*You're not going anywhere, Elisabeth*—and knew he'd never be satisfied with what I had left to offer him. The idea of subjecting Mary to that same fate, a fate that Magda had tried to extinguish her from, was too much.

"Didn't you hear a single word Great-Grandma Dorothy said?" Mary asked in frustration. "It used to be shared. Between sisters. Who each had their own families and their own loves, and it *worked*. How on God's green earth do you think it's been working shared between you and Magda?"

"That's different," I said reflexively. "That was out of necessity. Magda didn't want it shared anyway; she did it to spite Mom."

"Why do you keep defending her?" Mary snapped.

"I'm sure Magda had her reasons," I said reflexively. I was dizzy with trying to reconcile the damning portrait of my grandmother that had emerged in death with the one I had known in life.

Mary sighed, pulled her quilt up to her chin, and turned on her side away from me. "Fine," she mumbled to the wall. "Be like her, be like Clara. See where that gets you. But let me tell you right now. They were wrong. *You* are wrong."

I listened to Mary's furious breathing deepen into the evenness of sleep, leaving me to contemplate an unflattering version of myself: *Am I just like them? Am I like every other power-hungry, stubborn person in this family?*

I wasn't ready to admit it to myself, but the idea of sharing the guardianship annoyed me. I'd grown up the expected heiress, the special one, and Mary was just my little sister—who Magda hadn't wanted to exist. I couldn't admit that I liked it that way, being the shiny Watry-Ridder girl. It was all I had ever known, and after straying for a while, I had missed it.

*　*　*

By the time I came downstairs in the morning, Dad was long gone to the mill offices, business as usual. I found it unfair that the men went about their business while we Watry-Ridder women were scrambling to hold ours together by the seams. Mary sat fuming at the kitchen table behind a box of Life cereal for cover. I blew past her and out to the lake without a word.

The water, already warm in the late morning, drew the fire from me. My arms, loose and weak after weeks of not swimming, cut through the water sluggishly as I thought to myself, *We are at an impasse.* Mary wanted to help, and I wanted to protect her from it, and keep my special status. But as I pushed myself up onto the wooden dock, I thought, *Why does Mary want to help me anyway, after I left her with my mess?* Even as I asked myself that question, I already knew the answer: because we were sisters, and Mary would forgive me my sins. Maybe she already had.

*   *   *

Mom threw a wild rice hot dish from a well-wisher in the oven that evening, and the familiar nutty aroma piqued my appetite in a way that I hadn't felt in days. Dad got home, his timing impeccable as ever, as Mom pulled the casserole from the oven. It felt strange, but also nice, to gather around the table the four of us, and tuck into generous heaps of steaming hot dish. But Magda's empty chair was a stark reminder of her absence.

"Mr. Pedersen was asking after you girls in town today," Dad enunciated slowly, his tone overly casual. He didn't look at any of us in particular as he focused on assembling the next perfect bite.

"He wondered when you might be ready to see clients, after the respectable amount of time, of course. It's none of my business, and I didn't say one way or another, but if there's any timeline you want me to spread around town, I'd be happy to do it," Dad said to his plate.

"Tell folks that we'll be ready after the Lion's Gate," I said impulsively.

"And when's that again?" he asked.

"August eighth," Mary and I said together.

"All right then," Dad said, then changed the subject. "Mary, how's Tim? I had a nice chat with his parents at Magda's. They seem like nice folks."

*   *   *

After supper, I followed Dad to the living room as Mary and Mom tackled the dishes by hand, a task that went faster with the assistance of a few charms, but our connection to the ice floe was so tenuous. We didn't dare use magic on anything without real consequence— like attempting to straighten the house.

Dad settled into his favorite armchair and opened the newspaper. I didn't know what I was going to say until it came out of my mouth.

"Dad?"

My father looked up, and seeing me hovering in the middle of the room expectantly, he refolded the paper and let it fall. As he did, I sat on the edge of the upholstered chair nearest him.

"Elisabeth?" Dad said, matching my tone. He eyed me curiously.

"I need to ask you something. What is it like being married to Mom? For you, I mean? What is it like for you?"

Dad's face was impassive as he gathered his thoughts. If I'd surprised him with the question, he showed no sign of it.

"Well," my father said slowly. "I love your mother. I always have, since grade school. You know that."

I nodded, waiting for him to get to the good stuff.

"But it hasn't been easy," he said. "I grew up in awe of Helene like everybody else in town. She barely acknowledged me until well into our teens, but I always knew she was special. But I also grew up in awe of Magda, and I knew they were a package deal."

I nodded, grateful for this response. I was painfully aware that I had never dared to speak to my stoic Dutch father about anything so emotional before, and I was surprised that he opened up so easily.

"Has . . ." I had trouble forming the question. "Has Mom loved you enough?" I asked quietly. "Is this life enough for you?"

My father hesitated, chewing on my words. I didn't know what he knew about Mom's heart, about her bond to Mary, but I had to think he knew more about what went on in the Watry house than he let on. I needed to know what it felt like on the receiving end. I perversely needed to know what I was doing to John, if I got what was coming to me.

"I have always loved your mother," Dad repeated. "And I love you girls. The rest doesn't matter much."

I sighed, thinking that nonanswer was as much as I was going to get from my stoic Dutch father.

But my father surprised me. "Is this about John?" he asked.

I could have sworn our abilities had rubbed off on my father. Or that he had seen as much in town as I feared he had.

I nodded, my cheeks flushing hot with shame.

"It's your choice, Lisbett," my father said, choosing his words carefully. "And I won't say much on it—but I will say, it's not easy being the man of this house. I have long thought that John could handle it, but now I'm not so sure. It's harder than it looks to swallow your pride for decades on end. So it's up to you. But know this: if John ever lays another hand on you, I'll kill him."

Thirty-Eight

I couldn't make myself do it that evening. I busied myself instead cleaning every last nook and cranny of Magda's room and laundering all the bedding. I collapsed into her bed, cleansed of her rosewood and earth scent, well after midnight. I was too tired to outrun the doubt and guilt that had been piling up all day, but there it was, waiting for me when I closed my eyes.

I awoke the next morning to a soft, slanting rain outside Magda's window—rain that the county so desperately needed. I knew better than to try to swim in the lake in a rainstorm, despite the apparent absence of thunder or lightning. I lingered as long as I could over a cup of coffee, sitting silently across the table from my mother. It almost felt like before Solstice as Mom absently reached up to stroke Sam, who had gladly reclaimed his spot around her neck like a gray stole with white paws. When Mom left the room, I picked up the phone and dialed the Weselohs'.

"Elisabeth," Mrs. Weseloh said with mild surprise when she answered on the second ring. "John's chorin' in the barn. I'll ask him to call you later?"

"Oh, thank you, Mrs. Weseloh," I mumbled. "Would you mind asking him to come over here when he's done, please?"

I sighed when she hung up. I didn't mean to hurt Mrs. Weseloh too, but she was so entangled in the lives of her boys, especially the last one she had at home. I could hear in the strain in her voice that she would do anything to protect her youngest son from heartbreak. If only she knew what kind of man her son was turning into. Even in our small town, I realized that might very well be the last time Mrs. Weseloh would speak to me.

✱ ✱ ✱

I heard the El Camino pull up around noon, as the sky opened up into a full torrential downpour. I slipped out the side door and waved for John to follow me around back to Dad's shed. My mother was the only one in the house, but I couldn't bear the idea of a single person witnessing the storm about to break. John nodded and jogged through the rain behind me.

The yard was already turning to mud underfoot when I pulled the door to Dad's shed closed behind us. We were both soaked through; my blouse was plastered to my body. If John objected to the locale or found it strange, he didn't show it. His face revealed nothing, waiting for me to show my hand.

"Come here," John said, holding his arms out.

"John," I said. My voice was a period, an ending. I had expected my voice to tremble and was surprised to find only strength there.

John's face fell as I hugged my arms over my chest where I stood inside the doorway. He dropped his arms lamely to his sides, a small sound escaping his lips.

"Oh," he said, watching me as intently as his hunting dog on prey. "What's this, then, Elisabeth?" His voice was sterner than I realized possible.

"We need to talk," I said evenly. "It's over."

John nodded, solemn. He turned, his movements wooden, and motioned with a jerk of his head toward the workbench. I responded automatically, going to lean there beside him, my shoulder pressed lightly against his as we had done a thousand and one times, since our budding friendship in junior high watching Friday night football to the first time John dared to ask me to Sharp's after Solstice. We had sat shyly, obliviously happy, pressed together on one side of the booth across from Annie and who knows who she was dating. It would've been all too easy to lean into him, to pretend nothing had happened, to go on as we always had.

But everything had changed. John was not the same boy he once was, and I was not the same. I was finding a version of myself that was equal parts family responsibility and possibility, and—I hoped—fully, inextricably magic. I searched the small space above us, damp and muggy, looking for the right words. But no words would be right.

John saved me the trouble. "I'm sorry," he said suddenly, a stream of apologies falling from his lips. "It will never happen again," he said. "I didn't mean to. I love you."

As contrite as he was, John had that same caged-animal look in his eyes. I never wanted to see it again.

"John," I said, eyes pointed skyward toward heaven, Dorothy, God, anyone.

His anger ignited as he cut me off quickly. "I knew this was coming. I knew it the minute I called your house and Mary said you were gone. I didn't expect you to come home, to be honest. I thought you were through with Friedrich and through with me." John sneered, the passive farm boy unrecognizable. "I thought you found something better."

My blood ran cold. I couldn't help myself. "I did, John," I said calmly.

A small storm crossed his face, and for a moment I thought he might hit me. *Let him try.* I faced him and stepped back to put as much physical space between us as possible among my father's lumber and broken appliances.

"My family is better," I said, feeling braver by the minute. "My sister is better. I choose Mary," I said, knowing it was the truest

thing I had ever said. My sister and I would be family, the partners
to each other that we Watry women could never have elsewhere.

John's brow darkened as those words hung between us. The normally confident, placid eighteen-year-old boy before me deflated.

"You're like a lightning strike," John said. "Pretty to watch from
a distance, but you'll burn real quick through anyone who gets
close. You'll burn out eventually."

I threw out a hand, and with a few silent words and a twist
of my wrist, begging the ice floe and Dorothy to come through, I
threw the shed door open behind John, letting in a sudden gust of
rain and wind.

"Bye, John," I said. "Go home now."

John sucked his teeth and shook his head, but to my relief,
he went without another word. When I heard him pull out of the
gravel driveway, I collapsed on the floor of my father's shed and
sobbed, the dam finally breaking in me. I sobbed until I was empty,
not caring about the sawdust that clung to my wet skin and hair.

*   *   *

I wandered through town that afternoon without a destination or
a purpose, letting people see I was back. I was defiant in spite of
my clinging hair and smudgy face. *Let them think it was me who
brought the rain.*

Walking through Friedrich again, I sensed I had become
dangerous, especially after the recent horror of Solstice. The girls
gripped their boyfriends a little closer when I passed in front of the
window at Sharp's, which was packed to the gills with teenagers
and moms and kids seeking refuge from the rain. *I still look like
one of you. But now you all know how dangerous I am*, I told them
silently. *How dangerous we are.*

But I knew—beyond Solstice, I had picked up the scent of the
world. I represented the threat of being bigger than Friedrich, bigger than the Watry women of Lake Street. I reeked of the outside
world. I saw how the other girls looked at me as I paused in front of

Sharp's, as if deciding whether to go in for a tuna melt. Annie was right—it would take the women the longest to come around. But when they needed love charms, they'd be back. Until then, they'd watch over a shoulder, a hair flip, a second glance, before their eyes flicked to their boyfriends, saying with their eyes, *You don't belong here. This will never belong to you.*

Keep him, I thought, determined to be as dazzling as any electrical storm Kandiyohi County had ever seen. After years of Magda telling me I needed a man beside me, I finally knew it wasn't worth it if he was going to try to possess me like John.

As I turned back at the end of the block, I shivered in my wet clothes. In the old world, I would have wanted to be snuggled up to John in the El Camino, protected from the rain. In my new world, I passed by Sharp's one more time, daring them all to look away, and headed east along Lake Street toward home.

Thirty-Nine

There was nothing to do except wait for August. I slept a lot, ignoring calls from Annie until she stopped trying. Mary bided her time at the beach or around town with Tim or mindlessly stocking the armoire with herbs and rainwater and what have you. I had a singular focus: not to lose the ice floe before it was time to finish the binding. I cast out obsessively, feeling for the river of light that hugged every fiber of me.

Are you there, Dorothy? I asked a thousand times a day.

Yes, child, she answered dutifully.

One day, an unfamiliar Chevy pulled up in front of the house. I watched out the kitchen window from where I had been refilling my black coffee for the umpteenth time that day. It was about all I could stomach with the nerves that flooded me with the waiting, waiting, waiting. The coffee mug slipped from my fingers, clattering into the sink, when I saw a figure emerge from the driver's side door, unfolding into a leaning stack of a man in a faded flannel shirt.

I staggered out the side door, not bothering to close it, and crossed Dad's meticulously manicured lawn to the driveway.

"You sure are a hard girl to find, Elisabeth," Nick declared loudly, drawing out the syllables of my name like he hadn't tasted them in a while. He stood stock-still at the end of the driveway, waiting for me.

I barely registered the pins and needles of the crushed-rock driveway digging into the naked soles of my feet as I stumbled toward him. I felt my jaw hanging wide open to the world. I stopped a few feet away from him, my arms instinctively crossing over my chest.

"What are you doing here?" I said, barely above a whisper.

"I had to make sure you were okay," Nick said, dropping his swagger. He held my gaze, waiting for a sign, waiting for me to come to him.

Nick looked tired and thinner than when I had left him in July.

When I didn't say anything, he relented. "You left in the middle of the night," Nick said. "I didn't know if you were okay, or hurt, or got jumped walking down the street . . . or if you couldn't stand me anymore."

I softened a little at that, taking a step toward him. I'd left like a thief in the night, and Nick had still worried about me.

"How did you find me?" I asked.

His face cracked into an easy grin at that, that achingly beautiful dimple appearing in his cheek. "The sisters at St. Kate's really go by the book. They wouldn't give me your address, so I stole it. The whole book, in fact, when the penguins weren't looking. Imagine my surprise when I pulled up to the Holbrooke residence and some loud brunette had no idea what I was talking about. Lucky we finally put two and two together, and she pointed me this way."

Thanks for the heads-up, Annie, I thought. I suddenly became very aware of the broad daylight and the inquiring eyes of neighbors driving down Lake Street, ogling the unfamiliar man in front of the Watry-Ridder house.

"Well, you better come inside," I said, with a glance around at the neighboring houses. I motioned with one hand for him to follow me.

"Hey," Nick said, stopping me in my tracks.

I turned back to find Nick's outstretched arms waiting. I tentatively stepped forward into his embrace, and any anxiety about watching eyes melted away. Nick's arms felt like home.

"I'm glad you're safe," he whispered into my hair, arms around my waist.

"Come inside, Nick," I said, stepping back.

"You're the boss," he said.

*   *   *

The house—still crooked, but less so after Mary and I had put everything we had into fortifying charms—was blessedly empty: Mom had gone to Juba's, Dad was at the mill, Mary was God knows where, an otherwise normal weekday except for the sudden appearance of my illicit lover in my family's kitchen that was still clientless. Without a word, I poured Nick a cup of coffee and sat wide-eyed across the table from him. The room felt too small, too warm. There wasn't enough oxygen in the world for Nick to be sitting in the same room as me, or even in the same town.

"I had to make sure you were okay," Nick repeated into his coffee.

"But what are you doing here?" I said with a sigh.

"I tried to call," Nick said. "I tried your number from the sisters, and that loud girl answered and I was scared it was you somehow for a minute, but it wasn't, and I couldn't make myself say anything," he finished with a deep exhale. I thought again how tired he looked.

"Annie," I said with a laugh. "I gave them my friend's number. So you thought you would just show up?" I felt myself starting to scowl at him and attempted to soften my face.

Nick was amused. "And here I thought I was being valiant driving all the way across the state to make sure you were safe. No?"

I shook my head, about to argue with him, but thought better of it. I had left him in the middle of the night, after all. I owed him some explanation.

"My family needed me. My grandmother died, and I . . . I had to get home to take care of things," I said.

Nick stared at me.

"What?" I said defensively. "It's the truth."

"Elisabeth," Nick said quietly, rolling my name around in his mouth in that way of his. "You don't need to lie to me. If you got bad news when you called home, you could have told me that, instead of sneaking away in the middle of the night."

I didn't call home. You're not going to believe this, I thought. *But this is what I wanted, after all—the chance to show Nick all of me, my whole self. What the hell?* I thought.

"You're not going to believe me," I said out loud. "Nick, I need to show you something."

I stood and opened the armoire, then set one of Magda's crystal chalices on the table between us.

I closed my eyes and cast out the ice floe in a tight energy field. The gateway to the other side had cracked open a hair when we communed with Dorothy. I prayed silently that it would be enough. I felt the water molecules in the air shiver under my poised hand, then refuse to budge.

"What are you doing?" Mary said, suddenly over my shoulder. Her calm, clear voice reminded me for all the world of Magda for a split second.

I turned to see Mary in the open doorway between the living room and kitchen, staring down Nick with a mixture of curiosity and blatant amusement across her face. I ignored the question she asked silently with a raise of an eyebrow: *Who's this?*

"What are you doing home from the beach?" I asked reflexively.

"Closed for milfoil today. Nasty stuff. Sheriff has to come to clear it out, since I can't . . ." She gave me a pointed look, then offered a hand to Nick.

"I'm Mary," she said cheerfully, shaking Nick's hand. She was clearly enjoying the situation.

"Nick," he said. "Sisters?"

Mary straightened up beside me to allow the obvious comparison of our features—our matching blue eyes, swimmers' shoulders, and heart-shaped faces.

"Yep," she said, sliding into the chair between Nick and me at the table. She swiveled her gaze from the crystal chalice on the table back to me. "What exactly were you doing?"

"I was about to show Nick what we do here," I said, punctuated by a pleading look to Mary. *Go with it. Please.*

Mary's eyebrows asked me another silent question, but she conceded and grasped my hand on top of the table. Our palms pressed together in unity, despite the strange energy lingering between us.

"Together," Mary said.

I felt it before I moved, the gateway to the other side opening wider, buoyed by Mary's sunny yellow energy, earth and fire. With Mary's hand in my own, I was able to conjure a water charm, calling the water with a downward pinch of my hand and lazy turn of the wrist, for the first time since Magda's death.

Chunsch Wasser, Wasser chunsch.

I opened my eyes to see Nick's mouth open in surprise and the chalice full of clear water drawn from thin air on the table between us. I could see it on his face: he was not scared. Just surprised.

"We're witches, Nick," I said, refusing to shy away from the word. "My mother sent her familiar, the cat, to tell me when my grandmother was dying, and I felt it happen. This is what I had to get back to. This is where I'm supposed to be." I squeezed my sister's hand as I said it, sharing a sideways glance and a smile that neither of us could suppress.

Mary squeezed my hand back once and dropped it. "I'll leave you to it," she said, delighted as she gave Nick one last once-over.

"Whoa," Nick said quietly, after Mary's footsteps had receded to the top of the back stairs. "I knew there was something different about you."

I nodded in acknowledgment. "But it's . . . complicated. My family needs me. I have to straighten things out since my grandmother passed," I said, fighting off that old urge: *He's not family.*

To hell with secrets, I thought, preparing myself to be disappointed. "There's been a disruption in our power," I said, "and I need to fix it. My family is depending on me. This town is depending on me."

My words didn't seem to register. A dreamy smile spread across Nick's face. "I've never met anyone like you," he said.

I pressed his hand gently. "Go home, Nick. I'll call you, I promise, when I get through this with my family."

I won't burn through you too.

"I can't imagine living without you now that I've had you." Nick's smile dropped as he cut his eyes at me. "I'll go, but you bet your ass I'll be back for you, until you turn me into a toad or chase me away."

I rolled my eyes at the ceiling. "I'll be here," I said, standing to show him out.

Nick shook his head and sighed as he stood. "I can't believe I found you, only to be chased away."

Impulsively, I rounded the table and grabbed his shirtfront in both hands. "I said I'll be here," I said firmly, hovering mere inches away from his sly sexy smile. "Give me time, Nick. I'll be right here when I'm ready for you."

If I'm ever ready for you.

He kissed me, more gently than I remembered, then drove away in his borrowed Chevy.

*   *   *

Mary didn't wait to descend with a million questions. She cornered me in Magda's room, where I had been spending many of the long, quiet hours waiting for the Lion's Gate. I retreated there quickly, unable to watch Nick drive away.

"So?" Mary said, climbing into Magda's bed beside me. "Who in the world was that?"

It felt like a normal day, a normal chat between sisters, teasing about boys. I sat with one knee hugged to my chest, gazing out Magda's window at the woods beyond Dad's shed. I didn't answer right away, unsure of which truth to tell. *That's the man I found in Minneapolis when I was cheating on John. That's the man who makes me feel like a person with a whole heart.*

Mary read the silence between us easily. "I don't know who he is," she said, "but I saw something there. He's certainly something, Lisbett. This makes so much sense now."

In spite of the turmoil in my gut, I couldn't stop smiling, my face half-hidden from Mary behind the sheet of my hair. Nick had come looking for me. I wanted to shout it from the rooftops. I could barely let myself consider the possibility—I didn't need a man, but what if I wanted one? What if there was still some tiny chance of me finding happiness, or something like love?

I turned to face Mary, unfolding and refolding myself into a cross-legged position. "It doesn't matter who he is," I said, trying to shake it off. "He's gone, and there are other things I—we—need to take care of." It would take a while for me to break that habit.

Understanding registered on Mary's face as she furrowed her brows at me thoughtfully. I was relieved that she dropped the questioning about Nick so easily. I had been waiting for the sulky teenager to fade after Magda's funeral and for this wise creature to reappear. I was glad to have some inkling of my sister back for the task at hand.

The smile returned to my face unbidden.

Forty

In the end, I was forced to admit I needed my little sister.

"Okay," I said to Mary early the next morning.

I stood in the doorway of our bedroom, which was now Mary's, really. I had claimed Magda's room as my own without argument or protest from anyone, trying to absorb her essence through osmosis. I ventured upstairs only to fish a forgotten shirt from the closet or scavenge for clean underwear.

"Okay, what?" Mary said, peering up at me from under a corner of the quilt pulled up tight around her face.

I realized how early it was, only the faintest signs of light reaching around the edges of the curtains. But I had been up all night thinking about it after Nick's sudden appearance in Friedrich.

"Okay," I said again. I stepped into the room and knelt in front of Mary, my eyes telling her everything, asking her to understand.

I saw her eyes register what was happening.

"Say it," Mary said. "I need you to say it."

I was surprised by how sure she sounded, how grown-up. Her voice sounded more and more like our mother's—now that Mom had reclaimed hers—and less like an echo of Magda's. I supposed we all sounded like Magda to an extent, for better or worse.

"I need you," I said, reaching under the quilt to squeeze her hand. "I can't do this without you. I don't want to. I don't want to be like Magda." The words burned across my forearm like scar tissue caught the light, the silver script shining there. "I need you to do this with me. I need you to let me keep my heart, what I have left. I thought I was protecting you from losing your heart too. But I get it now—you're letting me keep half of mine. You're offering me the chance at something I thought was impossible."

Mary was giving me the chance to be my full self—fully magical, and open to the possibility of love with what remained of my heart. Nick had shown me that possibility, and Mary was giving me the chance to make it real. I had to take it.

I felt Dorothy light up like a pinball machine on the other side. *So this is what you wanted, then?* I asked her silently with a smile.

"I know," Mary said, her own sly smile blooming. "I knew you'd come to your senses eventually."

As always, Mary was three steps ahead of me.

She narrowed her eyes at me. "So this is because of Nick?"

I shook my head and squeezed her hand again. "No, Mary. No," I said with emphasis. "This is because of you. You were born to this, like I was. You're stronger than me too, in a way. Whatever happens with Tim, I see now that you haven't needed me to protect you. You can choose for yourself. We were meant to carry this together, like Dorothy said it used to be."

I don't want to be the version of myself that is afraid to ask for help.

Her glare lightened. "Good," Mary said, satisfied. "We have a chance to do things differently, to do it our way. The way it should've been all along."

It was high time I accepted that my little sister was the balance I needed. Mary pushed me to be a better version of myself, the version I wanted to become. I had been told my destiny from early on, but Mary was giving me a chance to change it, to be different from

Magda or Clara or even my mother. Mary was choosing her future for herself and giving me mine back in the same fell swoop.

Mary rolled her eyes to the ceiling. "You should still call him. There's something there."

I rolled my eyes right back at her and stood up. "Later, Mare. We have things to do first."

*   *   *

"You're sure about this, honey?" Mom asked over her shoulder from where she stood in front of the stove on the morning of the Lion's Gate. She was nervous in a way I had never seen her, bustling between cabinets, opening and closing doors, fussing over breakfast.

"I'm sure," Mary said.

Mary, for her part, was watching the breakfast preparations with a cool and unburdened gaze. Mickey, Mary's white-chinned shadow, purred furiously in her lap, unaware of the monumental day ahead. Mary nodded as she trailed a finger over the curve of his whiskered jaw.

I stood rinsing blueberries in a colander in the sink. My mind wandered, and I let the water batter the fruit longer than necessary. It felt like a holiday, like the Fourth of July, all of us with nowhere to be except preparing a too-large meal that no one was hungry for. But instead it was the morning of a full moon, Thursday of the Lion's Gate. While the town went about their business as usual, our family was preparing for a seismic shift.

Mom ran out of gas suddenly, freezing in front of Mary at the table. The spatula in Mom's hand jutted out at an awkward angle as she stood with her hands on her hips. "What about that nice boy Tim?" Mom asked, the hesitation clear in her voice.

Mary's eyes darted from me to Mom, betraying only the slightest hint of fear. "It's okay, I swear. Tim is like Dad. He's in it for the long haul."

Tim is like Dad. Those words cut me. *I thought John was like Dad too, and see where that got me.* But a small part of me knew Mary wasn't like me. As she approached her seventeenth birthday, Mary was stronger, wanted less, needed less. She would accept the curse of the Watry women staunchly, like Dorothy had, accept that she would never be able to love fully, her first devotion being to the family. And in so doing, Mary was giving me the incredible gift of keeping half of my heart open. She was giving me a chance at love.

"Thank you," I said to Mary with tears in my eyes, overcome with gratitude.

Mary understood immediately, nodding once casually as Mom took in the scene.

"This has to be shared between sisters, like it used to be," Mary said. "Women bound by sibling ties are closer than any other, even mother-daughter. No one's powers more closely mimic each other's than sisters'."

Mary watched Mom to gauge her reaction, knowing as well as I did that Mom had never had the chance we would. Whatever burden Magda had intended for Mom was meant for her alone, and Mom had blown that future wide open by choosing a completely different path for herself. She'd chosen Mary, and Mary, by her own free will, had chosen me.

"Well, okay then," Mom said quietly, turning back to the range.

Her voice was shaky, but the look I glimpsed on my mother's face before she turned away was one of pure pride.

*   *   *

The spell was ancient, the words passed down for generations.

The full moon lit Magda's room as bright as day, light pouring in the windows at the back of the house. Mom and I dragged the cedar chest, Magda's old cache of secrets and ancient magic, from the foot of the bed to the center of the room. We prepared with measured movements to dampen the sound of silver spoons clacking together and the whisper of salt on the naked wooden floor. No one dared break the reverie.

If Mary was nervous, she showed only the slightest hint of it, her lips pressed together in a tight line, looking for all the world like our grandmother.

Cousin Mildred made herself useful by placing thirteen new candles in a precise circle around the cedar chest, stooping at an angle that made me cringe, given her age. She had arrived just before midnight and proudly presented the bag of homemade tapers, hand dipped for the occasion.

"Who knew that the talented baker was also a candlestick maker?" I whispered to Mary.

Mary barked in unexpected laughter but stifled it quickly, flicking her eyes up the ceiling. *Lisbett, please,* she pulsed at me.

Her serious demeanor, split with sudden laughter, reminded me of so many nights of whiskey-fueled philosophical conversation with Nick and the guys. What a world away that was.

"Ready?" I asked.

"Ready," Mary said, nodding. My sister, my balance, stepped into the cedar chest.

I nodded back once, then laid my hands on my sister's chest above her heart—*from dark, light.*

I nodded to Cousin Mildred and my mother on either side of Mary.

Past and present.

I closed my eyes and reached for the ice floe, that beautiful, familiar source of magic and energy.

Für und Wasser.

The words of the binding spell flew from my mouth for the first time. Mom and Mildred joined in, our voices blending into one— one family, one coven—magnified by the sister star rising high in the night sky.

Mary opened her heart to the light of the cedar chest, to the mysteries of generations of magic—and then we truly began.

Epilogue

Six weeks later, on the morning of the autumnal equinox—when day and night, light and dark, are in perfect harmony—Mary and I were in the kitchen showing Cousin Mildred how to wrap herbs and twigs and other elements into beacons. Unsurprisingly, Mary was a more patient teacher than I.

Little by little, we had been teaching Mildred what Mary and I had been taught as children. She came over a few times a week, and it delighted me to see the septuagenarian take to creating water charms and other fundamentals. She asked for hexes once in a while, but we tried to gently guide her to more practical applications of her still-nascent magic.

As clients began to return to our kitchen after the Lion's Gate, Mom mostly left us to it, but when Cousin Mildred came around, Mom assumed her mother's role as Kaffeeklatscherin, gossiping with her second cousin once removed. Mildred took her new role in the family very seriously and became another set of eyes and ears around town for us, taking the temperature of our neighbors and their comfort level with the local witches.

In an attempt to make up for what had happened on Solstice, we were doing an open house of sorts on the equinox. In the pre-ceding weeks, when we were sure that our powers were at full strength, as Mary became more and more comfortable with the full secrets of the cedar chest at her fingertips, Dad had spread the word around town: everyone was invited. We would see clients in the afternoon, and then around an enormous—but controlled—bonfire in the evening, our clients would light their own bespoke beacons to draw our full power behind their intentions for the coming season.

It was my attempt to humble myself before our neighbors, to make good in a more public way. I had visited with Harry and Mr. Raymond individually after the binding spell. Both were apprehensive to see me, especially Mr. Raymond. But Harry seemed open to letting me make it up to him. We brainstormed a list of 101 ways I could help him rebuild from the gutted shell of the old supper club. We would start with a tithing, taking more cash payments where possible for the foreseeable future to funnel any additional funds into the rebuilding.

With Mildred and Mary steadily cranking out beacons and Mom restocking the armoire with the herbs and crystals and candles and other supplies we would need, I wandered outside to check on the day's other projects.

*   *   *

As the equinox approached, the date that was originally going to bind my heart to our magic for good, Mary was feeling more and more comfortable with her new abilities, learning how the mysteries of the cedar chest worked, delighting in the limitlessness of her new skills. She pushed herself to take on the more challenging clients who were returning in numbers that were almost what they were before Solstice, and I was content to take on energy readings and love charms and whatever else came my way. After my hiatus, practicing in any way felt good. It felt good to be of service.

It had also taken Mary a few weeks to get used to the feeling of a half-heart. I didn't know what to tell her, since it was all I had known. I didn't know anything to compare the feeling to, the sense of loss she was feeling. Mom was more helpful there, remembering the sudden transition when she bound her whole heart to Mary.

"It was like a curtain fell," Mom told us one morning over coffee while we waited for clients in August. She searched for the words, something that still gave her trouble. "One day my heart was full of love for your father and my daughter and my father Earl and even Mother, despite our rift. And the next, well, I still cared for your father and Elisabeth, of course, but it was different. The depth was gone. It was like when you walk into a room and forget what you came for. I knew I was supposed to be feeling *something*, but it was just gone."

Mary nodded. "It's different for me. I still have half my heart. It's like there's a crack of light from the doorway, but I can't figure out how to open it further."

"You mean for Tim?" I asked.

Mary blushed furiously. "Yeah. I *want* to feel something more, but I don't know if I can."

"That's how it feels for me. With John . . ." I sighed. That was still painful, like pressing on a bruise. "I knew I was supposed to love him more, like he said he loved me. But I just couldn't. I couldn't figure out how to make myself feel more."

"What about Nick?" Mary asked.

I glanced at Mom, who was suddenly very busy stirring her coffee. I didn't know what she knew yet about Nick. Mary would mention him in passing every so often, and Mom would studiously feign ignorance, letting me keep it to myself until I was ready. We were still rebuilding our relationship, and after so many years of her chosen silence, Mom wouldn't pry. She would let me come to her. It was frustrating, but I knew it would take time.

"Nick . . . was different. I don't quite know how to describe it, but I knew I *wanted* to feel more." When I thought of Nick, I thought of wanting, and choice, and desire. Maybe it wasn't love, or whatever would be possible with a half-heart, but it was different than the weight of obligation I felt when I thought of John.

Mary smiled. "I know what you mean," she said.

It was strange—we were unused to speaking so openly with each other. We'd had our ups and downs, but since Magda's passing, the house on Lake Street had felt more open and filled with light than I had ever known it. In a house where we could invariably read one another and know exactly what the others were thinking, I felt like I could finally breathe when I said all the thoughts out loud that I would have buried before Solstice.

"Have you called him yet?" Mary asked.

I shook my head, blushing. At that, Mary left me alone, and we fell silent, a triad of Watry women contemplating our coffee.

*   *   *

Outside, my father, Grandpa Ridder, and Uncle Dan were scrutinizing the house. Mary and I had worked hard in the weeks after the Lion's Gate to put Magda's fortifying charms back into place, but with Magda gone, my father was ready to take on a larger role in the upkeep of the house. He was ready to gut the place and redo all the haphazard additions that had been slapped on over the years. With the excuse of the equinox open house, Dad had asked his brother and father to come and draw plans with him. They might be millers by trade, but the Ridder men were also meticulous planners and opinionated tinkers. Grandma Ridder opted to stay home, though.

I joined the Ridder men on their inspection of the exterior, shadowing them as they measured and jotted down notes. I was making mental notes myself of what could be charmed in the meantime and what needed to be fully torn apart, when that same borrowed Chevy pulled up in front of the house.

I was astonished. It had been nearly two months since I had seen Nick. I had thought about calling him at least once a week, but as Mary and I were focused on restoring what had been broken, rebuilding, and helping the county rebound from drought and fire and fear, it felt like too much. My heart swelled in relief and joy when I saw how good he looked—healthy, well rested, and sharply dressed in clean brown corduroys and a red sweater. He looked like life had generally turned in his favor, and that instantly made me happy to see him looking well.

I resisted the urge to cast and read him. With my abilities restored, I had been using magic with abandon, even for little things like toasting bread, which Magda would have vehemently disapproved of. But I controlled myself in that moment. I would learn, in time, how things had been going for Nick, if he wanted to tell me.

I strode forward to greet him as he walked up the driveway, before my father or grandfather or uncle could ask questions. They paused their conversation to watch, curious. It was all I could do to stop myself from running into Nick's arms. I wasn't able to love him fully, but I certainly missed him.

"Hi," I said, stopping an arm's length away. I wrapped my arms around myself, partially against the September chill, partially to prevent myself from reaching for Nick, an automatic instinct, even after months of being apart.

"Hi yourself," Nick said, the dimple popping in his cheek. The sun reflected off the lake behind him, the shore lined with the first hint of leaves changing colors.

"What are you doing here?" I asked. It wasn't an accusation.

Nick smiled. "I know you said you'd tell me when you're ready, but I hoped . . . and Mary said—"

"You've been talking to Mary?"

I shot a look back at the house. There was a slight movement, the curtains swaying in the window above the kitchen sink. I cast out for Mary and immediately found her sunny yellow energy hovering in the kitchen. *What did you do?* I pulsed at her.

You're welcome, she pulsed back.

I rolled my eyes, but I wasn't mad.

"She might have called me. Is that okay?" Nick asked. He looked down at me through his long eyelashes, speaking gently, like I was a deer or some other easily spookable woodland creature.

I nodded. "Yes," I practically whispered, my voice catching with emotion.

Nick dropped his gaze, bashful. "So," he said after a beat, "I was thinking about pitching the band to play weddings and things out here at the new country club."

At that, I tilted my head and raised my eyebrows playfully. "Okay, Mary must have given you that idea."

He laughed. "Maybe. Would that be all right with you? If I was here more often?"

"That would be lovely."

Nick grinned and I returned it, my cheeks already aching from smiling. With the equinox sun on my face and ignoring my family in close proximity, I reached for Nick's hand.

"Come on," I said, tugging him toward the house. "Would you like to see a bit of our work? We're having our neighbors over for a special event this evening."

"I may have heard something about that," Nick said with a chuckle.

Thanks, Mare, I pulsed at my sister—my partner, my other half—who was definitely watching us from the kitchen. Nick's hand was strong and solid and warm, and I felt the wonderful feeling— and knew that Mary would feel it too—of possibility blossoming in my heart.

Acknowledgments

Years ago, I started writing a very different book, but in the wake of the loss of my beloved grandfather Robert DeWerd, to whom this book is dedicated, an earlier attempt at writing my family's experience with the American Dream evolved into something more firmly rooted in fiction—and much more magical. While *What We Sacrifice for Magic* is no longer strictly based on my own family, there are echoes of my family in the Watry-Ridder family (Tater-Tot hot dish, for one) and elements of my Minnesotan upbringing in this book that I can't wait for readers to encounter. I am grateful to the too-many-to-name sources that helped me make Elisabeth's 1968 Minnesota ring as true as my own.

This book wouldn't be what it is without the early reads and support from my dear friends, publishing colleagues, and writer-friends: Michelle Archer, Donna Freitas, Laura Peraza, Natalie Riera, Sophie Vershbow, and my VIM ladies: Katie Tull, Emma Caruso, and Kara Cesare. And I could not have gotten through revisions and querying and everything after without the ever-constant support of my writing group: Erin Cox and Jenn Proffitt.

I feel so lucky to have found the best partner, cheerleader, and editor in my agent, Kat McKean, and for the support of all of Morhaim Literary.

Acknowledgments

I owe a huge thank-you to the team at Alcove Press and Crooked Lane Books, especially my editor Holly Ingraham and cover designer Amanda Shaffer, for turning my words into the finished product you now hold in your hands. Thanks to Mikaela Bender, Mia Bertrand, Dulce Botello, Rachel Keith, Rebecca Nelson, Thaisheemarie Fantauzzi Pérez, and the rest of the team for their meticulous work.

To my many other friends and colleagues from Minnesota, GW, NYU, ADPi, Random House, S&S, HMH, HarperCollins, and elsewhere, and to the authors that I've worked with over the years that inspired me to start writing: there are too many of you to name individually, but trust that I am appreciative of every one of you and owe you a coffee or a drink at an apt time in the future in gratitude for your support and enthusiasm for this book. And a huge thanks to the future of agency team for always holding it down and being the best book marketers in publishing.

Finally, to my family, particularly my parents, Thomas and Katherine, and Ryan and Lauren: thank you so much for your love and support. I love you. Mom, I don't have a boyfriend, as of the time of writing, but I have a book!